The Soulless

by

Jonas Saul

&

Rania Stone

PUBLISHED BY:

Imagine Press Inc.
Ebook ISBN: 978-1-927404-75-1
Paperback ISBN: 978-1-927404-92-8
Hardcover ISBN: 978-1-998047-13-0

The Soulless

Chapter One

CERN, SWITZERLAND
Large Hadron Collider Particle Accelerator
Early evening, eight hours before the explosion, April 2022.

"I'm telling you, Mr. Nicholson," Gerard Rohner said. "You must listen to me. Something's wrong here. A lot of people could die. We're talking an entire country, dead." Gerard tapped the top of Nicholson's desk with his knuckles. "We need more time. I need to run more tests to be sure."

Nicholson shook his head, staring at the papers on his desk. "Rohner, we've gone over it repeatedly." He glanced up to meet Gerard's gaze. "Every safety measure is in place. The test runs came back error-free."

Gerard did the sort of nod that was meant to be facetious

—he disagreed with his superior—his face a scrunched mask of unease.

"According to the preliminary tests," Gerard said, enunciating each word carefully, "the magnets won't contain that sort of burst of energy as previously thought. This alone should bring tomorrow morning's experiment to a halt. No further tests should be done today until we re-examine the capacity of the batteries."

He shuffled the papers in front of him on Nicholson's desk, then slid them across to his superior, a slight tremble in his hands. He knew his job well as a physicist and safety technician, but fear was foreign. He was accustomed to stressing from morning until night—anxiety, too—but not fear. Not often, anyway. Until now.

Nicholson stared at him, then took the papers and held them as if they were some random report and not proof that the entire building might be a pile of rubble in the morning— or worse. He lowered his glasses until they were suspended on the tip of his crooked nose. Then he removed the glasses and set them on his vast wooden desk disparagingly. The silence between them thickened, but Gerard wasn't prepared to say a word.

After a deep breath, Nicholson eased back in his chair and wiped the sweat from his brow. "Thank you, Gerard. I'm sure you wasted a lot of time preparing these reports, but you should know there's nothing my physicists *haven't* checked. You're also quite aware that security is a primary goal for the success of this experiment. Many lives depend on it, perhaps all of humanity. I will forward your concerns to my superiors, our benefactors." He glanced away and focused on his computer. "Thank you for your time."

Was he being dismissed? But the particle accelerator may explode in tomorrow's experiment. He was the one who discovered the flaw. How come he was being dismissed?

Gerard shook his head to clear it. He needed to try again before leaving Nicholson's office. It was a grave matter that *benefactors* wouldn't understand. Why would he say that particular word anyway? Science had to come first, then money. What would all the money in the world matter if everyone was dead because the particle accelerator created a series of black holes on Earth?

"Please," Gerard whispered. "Just look at the data I've gathered. If, as you say, your concern is safety, you *must* take another look at the study." Telling his superior what he *must* do or not do could lead to trouble, but so could an explosion. "According to my latest checks, our facility won't survive tomorrow's experiment. Something will happen. The *if* has been taken out of the question. Those documents prove I'm correct. It's now a matter of who will approve such a reckless action."

He'd pushed further than ever before. This verged on insubordination. His limits had been reached. The next level was screaming. What else could he do?

His hands were damp, and his breathing was too fast. Some of his co-workers made fun of him when one of his anxiety attacks came on, and now he was on the verge of another. Human emotions weakened him. He'd worked on suppressing them over the years but causing untold chaos on Earth like nothing ever seen before concerned him enough to *feel* again.

Mr. Nicholson continued to stare at his computer screen —looking at nothing, typing nothing. After a moment, when Gerard finished his final tirade, Nicholson tilted his head to look at Gerard.

"Are you a conspiracy theorist? One who thinks that the powerful crash of subatomic particles in the collider's tunnels will create a microscopic black hole?" Nicholson shrugged and angled his body to face Gerard. "What, you think we'll make a mistake and get the Earth sucked into it, like a meeting of matter and anti-matter where both are destroyed?"

Gerard shook his head violently, sweat beading on his scalp. "No, sir. What I'm trying to avert is the atom smasher." He paused to catch his breath. "You haven't read my reports, have you? Nothing I prepared for this meeting has been reviewed." Gerard had to take another breath. His heart was racing, and it wouldn't slow down. "There's something else wrong, sir. We were the first to make anti-atoms artificially, and doing this test tomorrow will potentially destroy the entire complex with far-reaching consequences."

Nicholson pushed back his chair and stood, his hands resting on his hips, bent slightly at the waist to stare down at Gerard. "It can't explode. Even with the particle speed, it can't explode. The worst-case scenario will be a few fuses blown. The magnets will manage any dispelled energy, I assure you." He pushed up to his full height. "In fact, a large team of physicists should be enough to assure you. I *assure* you, we know what we're doing."

He stepped around his desk and moved to the door, resting against the frame. "The Large Hadron Collider took over a decade to build, costing nearly five billion dollars. We have over twenty member states involved with this project and over two thousand regular employees, with over ten thousand transient scientists coming and going all year." He paused to glance down at his feet. After a moment, he looked up. "Mr. Rohner, as the only physicist expressing any concern, what makes you so sure tomorrow's experiment will go awry?" Nicholson shook his head and opened the door. "As much as I appreciate your interest, *I'm* convinced everything will be fine. Although to calm you down, I'm willing to look at your findings, regardless. Thank you." Then Nicholson gestured with his hands for Gerard to leave.

Gerard rose on shaky legs and walked to the door.

"Sir, if I may—"

Nicholson raised a hand in Gerard's face. "Enough for now." Those three words were delivered in a firm tone. The meeting was over. There was nothing more to say.

Gerard closed his mouth, heat rising to his cheeks. He left Nicholson's office and went back to look at the protocols for the last time. He couldn't figure out how everyone in the building was in danger, and no one seemed to care. Half of the world's particle physics community worked on Cern's experiments. The energy gathered there was the greatest in the world. So how could he have been the only one to make the correlations, and all those bright minds above him hadn't? What if they overlooked the data, saw the issue, and labeled it a statistical error? On the other hand, what if *he* misread the data, and everything would be okay?

Worry took over his body, making him gasp and struggle to breathe. The best thing to do was get some rest to clear his mind. He'd been awake for over twenty hours, and the mental and physical demands had been enormous.

Downstairs, he headed to the staff room to change clothes and felt the eyes of others once again fixed on him. As if being chased, he ran into his car to go home.

He'd secured a house near Cern in Bourdigny to avoid sleeping on the premises with his colleagues. Moving to this lovely village full of dreams and expectations was a different reality from where he lived. He preferred to be on the Swiss-French border to visit both countries on a whim.

Once he parked the car in the garage and entered his lonely house with heavy steps, he moved to the sofa—it was closer than his bed and much softer.

He set the clock to wake him in six hours. That was the amount of time he had before returning to work and monitoring the experiment.

At least with him on site, he may be able to avert the dangers they all faced.

How? He had no idea. But with the will to make things right, the how will reveal itself.

He could no longer bear to think before falling into a deep sleep.

Chapter Two

In Lausanne, Same Time

"Do you have an extra cigarette?" Cassandra Christen asked.

The man waiting at the bus stop turned and looked at her from top to bottom. She had a backpack, and her clothes looked old and dirty. She knew what he saw by the judgment in his eyes, but she didn't care.

"Yes." He surprised her by slipping a hand in his pocket and then withdrawing it with a pack of smokes clutched in his fingers. He removed a lighter from his breast pocket, handed her a single smoke, then lit it.

"Thank you for saving me." A small smile played across her lips as she took her first puffs.

"What is such a beautiful girl doing down here in this neighborhood?"

"Same thing a boy does—survive." Her tone was more severe than she wanted, so she puffed on the cigarette to seem distracted, hoping it would dispel the tension.

The bus approached, and the young man glanced her way again.

"I have to leave. Do you have a phone? Would you be willing to give me the number?"

Cassandra had that impact on men. Even living on the streets, she took regular showers at the community center and donned makeup whenever possible. Living without paying rent didn't mean she needed to be dirty or act like the stereotypical vagrant.

But she wasn't a hooker, either.

"I don't have a phone," she said as the bus stopped in front of the man.

"Will I see you again? I can bring more cigarettes."

"I'm always around here." She smiled at him as the young man got on the bus.

The door closed, and she felt his eyes on her as she walked away from the bus stop.

She needed a safe place to sleep. A year of living on the street had come and gone. She slept wherever she found a spot on park benches, covered grassy areas, and even abandoned vehicles. It didn't bother her so much in the summer, but it wasn't easy in the winter.

She'd been known to light a fire, but it was so cold she couldn't get warm enough, especially when it was raining. Often, she would go to shopping malls to hide from the rain. Many would think there wasn't much of a homeless problem in such a rich country. But with such a high cost of living, the homeless amounted to several hundred thousand people, and all of them had to find a way to eat, sleep, and live.

She had no money for food, either. She always relied on the kindness of others. But no one had a job for her. Out here, she could take on a job as a stripper, an escort, and several other things that disgusted her, but she didn't want to live that way. She wanted her freedom and independence, which meant independence from money, too.

She strode toward the Parc de Milan with slow, lazy steps while puffing on her cigarette slowly, hoping to find the bar that played good music at this late hour.

Thirty minutes later, she found a bench out front, took a seat, and waited for the early evening crowd to gather.

Another night on the street.

Another night of freedom.

Chapter Three

GERARD WOKE ABRUPTLY, HIS shirt soaked through. He'd been sweating in his sleep again. His heart danced in his chest as he gazed around his small apartment. The morning sun hadn't come up yet, the rays not pushing through his curtains.

But something was wrong. Something terrible would happen. He shook his head and sat up, rubbing his face, everything rushing back into his mind, going through mental analysis.

After a deep exhale to calm his heart, he went to the bathroom to pour water on his face.

The reflection in the mirror was a warning. The dark circles under his eyes spoke of stress and exhaustion. Graying hair gave him a salt-and-pepper look, reminding him of his mortality. He wasn't in his thirties anymore, and all his fifty-two years were showing.

He jumped in the shower to wake up, got out, straightened his wet hair, then left his apartment without coffee. He had to get onsite, recheck the system, and observe the experiment so that when things went wrong—which he was still convinced would happen—he could be there to help.

He drove back to the Cern complex, his foot heavy on the pedal, his stomach heavier.

Even while sleeping, his mind had processed the data. Perhaps he'd been misled—not that the experiment would work out, and he was wrong—no, his mistake was in estimating when the whole thing would explode.

That might come sooner than previously expected.

If he were right and hoped he wasn't, the overheating would have already begun. He should have turned off the system yesterday if he had the balls to do it, but he didn't. His father had told him that repeatedly. Gerard was known for not making tough decisions, hence a life of panic attacks.

The sounds of sirens were the first thing he heard as he neared the complex.

He had been right. And there was no joy in knowing that.

Were the safety protocols activated correctly? Why didn't anyone call to notify him? Could they all be dead?

Level one and two staff would have been evacuated from the building. While everyone knew the evacuation rules in the face of a dire threat like this, did they panic and all try to leave simultaneously? That would cause a human traffic jam.

It seemed as if the safety memos were rules for young children that everyone paid little attention to.

He came around the last corner, and the complex filled his windshield. He gasped, leaning forward in his seat.

"No, no," he stammered, shaking his head.

There was no gaining access by car. Multiple vehicles piled up near the entrance, stopping employees from leaving, so many had decided to leave on foot, abandoning their vehicles.

Gerard had to do the same, only he was heading *inside* the complex. He parked as close as possible, exited his car, leaving the door open, and ran toward the facility.

"Let me through," he shouted at several rows of people stampeding toward him. "I have to try to fix it."

His voice fell flat with the din of panic around him. Twice, he was bumped into and almost lost his footing. Once, he got struck by a fellow scientist in a white lab coat, spinning him in a full circle on the spot and only staying upright because he grabbed the hood of a car beside him.

"Fuck," he bellowed at no one in particular, then faced the building and made a beeline for an open side door.

When he reached the entrance, feelings of heroism coursed through him. He could do this. He could shut it down and end the potential crisis while everyone else ran in the opposite direction.

Men like Nicholson would abandon the sinking ship. Is that because he finally understood the ramifications of his reckless actions?

There was no magic red button to press to cancel the operation. It took a series of procedures that had to be done in order, and it had nothing to do with panic and risk.

Could Gerard do it, though? Was he up to the task when everyone else had given up?

If he failed at stopping the particle accelerator from

destroying itself and everyone else in this city, this country, and perhaps the entire world, then no one would ever know.

They'd all be dead.

Running along the second floor of the abandoned complex, Gerard saw a flash of light, felt an enormous impact, and then became nothing but a vapor—which disintegrated.

Chapter Four

ZERO HOUR

Switzerland shook from an enormous explosion.

The shock wave dissolved everything in its path for dozens of kilometers. Thousands of people were vaporized in seconds. No one understood what had happened, as there'd been no time to process it. They didn't feel anything, either, which was a blessing.

No funeral arrangements would be made. No bodies would be discovered.

It was utter destruction.

Black ash rose from the Earth near the explosion's epicenter, forming a mushroom cloud that filled the atmosphere and spread quickly like the ash from massive volcanos.

Simultaneously, seismic activity occurred in multiple places within a thousand-mile radius of the blast.

Speaking of end times, street preachers everywhere radiated with validation as they prophesied the end of the Earth.

Chapter Five

LAUSANNE, SWITZERLAND
Moments After the Explosion

Cassandra opened her eyes.

Something like a shock wave had shoved her several meters off the park bench. Unsure of where she was or what was going on, she stayed low for a moment to clear her aching head. What hit her so hard? Was there an earthquake, a car accident, or an explosion?

She rubbed her scalp with her eyes still closed. There was wetness there. Blood?

The bar that hosted a live band, happy and singing moments before, was now silent. Other than someone moaning in pain, she heard nothing at all. Not even a vehicle was passing by.

A scary thought came to her. Did a rogue country or terrorist drop some sort of nuclear weapon?

She opened her eyes and blinked in the minimal light, then asserted her balance and got to her feet. She had to locate her backpack. It was dark with the streetlights out. She always carried a flashlight as life on the streets could be unpredictable, and she often slept in the shadows. A flashlight could mean the difference between life and death.

But this darkness was different. And the moaning had turned to screaming, coming from several directions and making her heart beat faster. What was happening? Why were they screaming if they survived whatever the hell it was that attacked them?

But *where* was safe? Were they at war?

Still trying to get her bearings, she glanced up at the black sky. There were no stars, no moon, no trace of light— only the darkness and the screams.

People moaned nearby. This had to be an equal opportunity bomb, striking everyone down without discrimination.

Unable to see well in the almost absolute darkness and still without her backpack, she decided to find a spot to sit and wait. Someone would come to rescue them, right? The military, the armed forces, or even the local fire department would show up. Wouldn't they?

She closed her eyes, hugged her knees, rested her back against a nearby building's wall, and emptied her mind of all thoughts. She attempted to shut out all that had happened, to shut out the voices of people screaming.

She yelled at them, hoping they'd stop, but nothing

worked. Minutes clicked by, and still nothing but moans, grunts, and screaming in the darkness surrounded her.

She covered her ears with her hands.

Light flashed across her closed eyelids. She opened them as someone approached with a flashlight in hand.

Several voices cried out at once as the flashlight moved among them, but the flashlight holder didn't stop.

"Here, here," someone said.

"Please, whoever you are, don't leave," a woman bellowed.

"I'm afraid of the dark." A child's voice.

"I need a doctor. Someone, please!" a man shouted.

"Where is my mom?" a little girl asked.

But that flashlight picked up speed and meandered through the carnage of injured people. The person probably hadn't expected to get so much attention. But if he had the only light source in this absolute and sudden darkness, why wouldn't he?

Then the flashlight clicked off, and darkness surrounded them all.

Cassandra pushed up to her feet and listened. Hearing seemed to be the only sense that was still useful.

Did something happen to the person with the light?

"Where did the light go?" someone asked.

"Who was holding it?" Another voice.

"Now what?"

Anxiety seeped in and overwhelmed her. She couldn't stand so much inaction, not being able to do anything. But it was dark—too dark.

Using her hands to guide her and taking slow steps, she

moved toward where the flashlight had last been on. Her equilibrium was off as she stumbled several times for no reason other than losing her balance.

What if she stepped on someone? Or worse, someone dead and lying in a pool of blood?

She stopped moving, repulsed by the idea.

Then the light clicked on a meter to her left, then off abruptly again.

Whispers rose from the people close by.

"Cassandra?" a man called her name.

Puzzled, it took her a moment to recognize the voice.

"Leo?" she whispered, her heart racing. "Could it be you?"

"Where are you?" he asked.

Multiple female voices responded.

"Here."

"Come to me."

"Over here."

"Be careful," Cassandra called to him, but he didn't answer. Did he fall? Did they get to him? "Leo? Where are you? Please talk. You're scaring me."

"Shut up," the voice of an older man said.

Someone or something passed close to her, and she shivered.

"Finally," Leo whispered in her ear. "I found you."

At that moment, she felt safe. She wasn't alone anymore now as they embraced in the darkness. She touched his face and caressed his cheeks, hair, and broad shoulders to ensure it was him.

"Did you come back for me?" She hugged him hard

again, wanting to feel every inch of his body on her. She had missed him so much, and now he was here. "How did you know I was going to be here?"

Leo touched her lips with his fingers to silence her, then kissed her gently.

"I had just arrived in the square when whatever happened, happened. I'd seen you on the bench. I was already coming toward you. It would be a surprise, but something hit me, and I fell backward." He squeezed her arms gently. "When I opened my eyes, I couldn't see anything. I stumbled into the bar. Their emergency lighting was enough to navigate the interior. This flashlight was behind their counter."

"I missed you so much," Cassandra whispered in his ear. "Take me out of here. We have to leave."

The panic and the screams around them hadn't stopped. The agonizing yelling had worsened while they spoke to one another in each other's arms.

"It can't be like this everywhere," Leo said.

"Do you know what happened?"

"Should I turn on the flashlight?"

"I wouldn't. Someone might want to fight over it. Let's just leave this area."

"Cassandra, without the light, we won't get far. We'll find a corner to nestle into, somewhere to sleep for a few hours until the sun rises. The shouting will calm down. They'll grow tired, weary." He hugged her tight. "Close your eyes and escape. Do you remember how we chased the trains that night? Then we rolled on the grass?"

As he eased her to the side of a building at the corner of a street, she imagined herself somewhere else, carefree and happy.

They lowered to a sitting position, then he lay her down, her head on his lap, and she calmed as Leo stroked her hair to put her to sleep. Like a wounded animal in Leo's arms, she waited for the morning, afraid that they would have to face whatever happened when the sun rose.

At least she wouldn't have to face it alone now.

About a year ago, she'd met Leo at the Place de la Palud under the famous clock. As she looked up to see the show, he bumped into her accidentally. It was love at first sight, even though her parents had been fighting that night. They were bickering about letting her go to a friend's party, which they didn't let her go to anyway.

They'd been oppressive and overprotective to the point of suffocation. She loved them but also couldn't stand them.

Sadly, her parents were killed in a car accident a few days later. She was left alone for a while until the bank confiscated her house—there was no one to pay the mortgage. Leo couldn't help financially but was always there when she needed him.

Separated countless times, they ended up having an independent and open relationship, but Cassandra believed in their bond and that nothing could break it. He was a friend, lover, sometimes roommate, and her confessor.

She had recently sent him a message that she had nowhere to stay and was hanging out in the square at night with the homeless.

And now she was in his arms, protected.

Thoughts of Leo warmed her insides, and she rested on

his lap in the darkness, her eyes closed to the chaos of the aftermath of whatever happened around them.

Leo, her watchful guard, didn't close his eyes until the morning.

Chapter Six

SAUDI ARABIA, NEAR MECCA
One Week Before the Explosion

Mujtaba Khan stared at the sky as the first signs of light tinted the morning sky. This was a momentous day for him—he'd never left his country before.

A tourist bus idled to his left. It would take him east of Jerusalem to where he had never set foot and was ashamed of not doing so. He should have already visited a place so sacred as a Muslim.

Before Mujtaba offered his ticket and stepped onto the bus, he glanced around once more. A living-in-the-moment feeling overcame him. This was it; he was really going to do it.

He ascended the few steps and then checked his ticket's

seat number. It was at the back. That wouldn't work as he wanted to be near the front to listen better to the guide, so he plopped down in the first available seat.

Once settled, he stared out the window until the bus got underway. Contact with anyone wasn't something he desired —especially not a Christian. A steady focus was required. His only wish was to complete his goal—the tasks set out before him.

The tour guide took up the microphone and cleared her throat over the speakers.

"Good morning, everyone. Welcome to this day trip. Today, according to the Muslim faith, we'll be visiting the Nabi Musa, the tomb of Moses, in the desert of Judea. Many faithful who wanted to visit and worship at Mecca used this route over the centuries. When they reached the tomb, it was a marker to signal that there was one more day to go and that they were headed in the right direction. From there, pilgrims could see Mount Nebo, where the actual tomb is located according to the Hebrew Bible."

The tour guide was too chipper for this early in the morning as several of the passengers were still yawning, having to wake so early to make the bus departure time.

The driver got underway, easing the bus out onto the dusty road.

"In 1269, a temple was built in the medieval period, and they decided to build guesthouses and inns. Many confused it with the sacred mountain and the tomb itself. In 1820, the Ottomans renovated the church and established a festival for celebrations during the Christian Easter period. This event brought almost fifteen thousand Muslims who spent seven days celebrating before returning to Jerusalem ..."

Mujtaba tuned her out and stared at the desert passing by his window, wondering what Allah had in store for him.

Upon leaving, he didn't speak to anyone in his village—and this wasn't the first time. As an introvert, he didn't like people in general, and he socialized only when necessary, as the Qur'an had taught him.

His brothers had followed the trade path, with shops in their village. These things weren't for him. It was like he had nothing to do with his family, but he had a different mission to carry out, one of a religious nature.

So he ran to the desert once, where he searched for answers. Who was he? Why was he born? How could he better serve Allah? This search for his mission in life resulted in no answers.

And so he continued, going as far as an old Ottoman castle before a traveler found him and took him back to the village. His family had been disappointed and angry with him.

He'd said to his father, "And if you should count the favors of Allah, you could not enumerate them. Indeed, Allah is forgiving and merciful. I urge you to follow his example."

This didn't go well, but his faith was more robust than the family bond.

Recently, he didn't know where to start his new mission. But when he learned that the Kaaba would open for maintenance in Mecca, he felt deep in his soul that he had to be there. If he missed this window, he would miss the opportunity to search for it—as per the visions he'd been having.

The Ark of the Covenant needed to be located, and he was the man who would find it.

Allah told him so.

Yes, it was daring of him, unheard of, but what if it *was* there? In a hiding place where no one had thought to look? He would never know if he didn't try, and it was time.

The Kaaba has been a location of worship since ancient times. In any case, no one could spend much time inside the Kaaba. Only a select few ever gained admittance. The others prayed outside.

Now, on the bus to Jeddah, then to Mecca, he had said goodbye to his village without saying anything to anyone about his mission—which was one of a personal nature. He wasn't in the mood to explain or discuss it. The journey was only two and a half hours, but the waiting seemed like a century. His stomach was already knotted, and he was grasping it imperceptibly while lost in thought.

Before entering the center of Mecca, everyone went through a security check. One man carrying false papers with the objective of mocking Allah was stopped and detained. The unbelievers had no purpose in Mecca. It was forbidden.

When Mujtaba got off the bus, the crowd was endless. As far as the eye could see, there were pilgrims.

He'd never considered entering the Kaaba, a room with marble floors, inscriptions, and columns, while lacking any windows. Apparently, the faithful could even enter with their shoes on, but he wanted access during the cleaning.

Not knowing where to start, he found a policeman and asked when the cleaning would begin.

"It's scheduled between the morning prayers," the officer

told him.

He would wait. Patience was always rewarded.

After some time, the morning sun had crested the hills in the distance and was already so hot it felt like it was piercing his skin with embers. He heard the imam begin the common prayer. A crowd gathered, and some of them stared at him because he wasn't inside with the others.

After ten minutes of prayer, there was a prolonged honking.

The time had come.

A procession of cars pulled up, with dozens of police officers clearing the road. The keyholder exited with the guests, and the police formed a circle around them, holding hands.

Meanwhile, a contingent of police officers had gone ahead and formed another circle around the Kaaba.

The number of pilgrims in the area was immense, and only a coordinated police force could keep everything in order—he hoped.

The spectacle was stunning to watch, but it left him feeling defeated. He could not accomplish what he had set out to do.

Heart racing, he realized that his mission had failed before it even got underway. He had to find a solution to his dilemma and get inside the heavily guarded Kaaba.

He recalled meeting an older imam who had come to his village to visit a relative years ago. They had long discussions late into the night about the meaning of life, and the imam had invited him to Mecca to continue their conversations. This spurred him on, knowing he could drop the imam's name if needed.

Would that help him? Only time would tell, and Allah was on his side.

Pushing his way through the gathered crowd, he moved to the other side of the Kaaba's entrance. Once he overtook the faithful, he climbed to an upper level. Below, he saw the police in a circle with the guests wearing their official white caps accompanying the keyholder. It was hard to distinguish anyone from anyone else, with everyone wearing white.

Mujtaba got into position near the access and waited, watching everyone intensely, eyes narrowed.

Then he saw the man who had visited his village.

Allah was merciful. Allah was great.

Without losing another moment, he approached him.

"Peace be with you, Shaykh," he said.

"Peace be with you," the imam responded with a calm, serene look. "What can I do for you, my dear friend? Do you need guidance?"

"You may remember me. I'm Mujtaba. We met in my village at Amir's dinner and spoke for many hours."

The imam studied his face momentarily, seeing him for the first time, then nodded. "Ahh, I do remember you now. I'm glad to see you here. How did you come to such an area?" The imam frowned. "This is not the time for Hajj."

"I need your help in entering the Kaaba. I have an essential mission, and I must get inside."

The imam eyed him suspiciously now, his head tilted to the side. "What kind of mission do you have?"

"It's in the hands of Allah alone."

"You know, my child, that this can't happen." The imam

shook his head, squinting in the sun. "No one has invited you. Imagine all the believers of Allah coming in whenever they wanted. The order is spoiled. My apologies lest I offend thee, but you aren't important enough to get in."

"Perhaps that is the case in your eyes." Mujtaba stood taller. "But in the eyes of Allah, I am unique, I am important enough, and I am on his mission. So, help me, my brother."

Shaykh stared at Mujtaba with a penetrating look, a puzzled expression on his face.

Mujtaba's response was in accordance with the word of Allah, who was great and powerful, and perhaps Shaykh didn't want to upset him because he nodded after a moment.

"Come with me. I promise nothing." He gestured for Mujtaba to follow him.

Excited with the prospect that someone would help him, he hurried down the stairs behind Shaykh and approached the police cordon that guarded the Kaaba.

The door had already been opened, and the first believers were entering. Shaykh moved close to one of the officers with more decorations on his uniform than the others and whispered something to him.

The policeman stepped away, walked to the keyholder, and whispered something to him. The keyholder glanced at Mujtaba and signaled him to come forward.

Mujtaba almost ran at the man, his nerves rattled, his stomach clenching. At any moment, one of these men could end his mission and draw the wrath of Allah, but so far, they hadn't.

When he got to the keyholder, he kissed his hand.

The keyholder said nothing in response to the gesture of

respect. He just pointed at an access door, showing Mujtaba how to get inside the Kaaba.

Without hesitation, Mujtaba entered the Kaaba while whispering prayers to Allah. They handed him a cloth dampened with Zamzam water, scented with roses.

To gain entry, he was expected to clean.

Then he understood what the imam had done.

He'd told them that Mujtaba was one of the cleaners and was lost, unclear where to go or what to do. Under the guise of working on the interior of the Kaaba, he was given access and authorized to be inside.

That worked better than he expected.

Several cleaners were working on the marble floor and the walls. Others were wiping another section of the interior with a dry cloth. As Mujtaba began to wipe a wall, he searched for a ledge, something that suggested another crypt, but his search was in vain.

Praying to Allah, he continued his covert search. If what he was looking for was there, he would indeed find it.

Shortly after, disappointed that the cleaning had ended without success, he exited with the others and thanked the keyholder for the tremendous honor he bestowed upon him.

Then, according to the ritual, he walked the circle of the Kaaba seven times—the center of the Earth—while praying, then left the area dejected.

His mission would not end so quickly, though. He wasn't naïve to think so.

Once another ticket was bought, a train ticket this time, he boarded the train bound for Jerusalem, about a thousand miles away, hoping for better luck.

Chapter Seven

Nabi Musa, Jerusalem
The Night Before The Explosion

Mujtaba stayed at the stone-built inn of Nabi Musa, which looked like a fortress in the desert in the middle of nowhere. Some pilgrims lived there like monks, which fascinated him.

After resting for an afternoon nap, he ate dinner in the inn's restaurant and then made his way to the Tomb of Moses.

When he arrived, he first prayed and worshiped at the foot of the tomb.

His anxiety was pervasive, so he waited until the area emptied, then returned to the tomb and searched it. There were many fabrics with inscriptions on the top that he couldn't read. Since the area was only lit by candles, it wasn't easy to see where things could be secreted.

Where would the Ark of the Covenant be hidden? How big was it?

Allah sent him to locate it, but how faithful could he be if he failed at every turn?

There was nothing left but to open the tomb to search inside. He wouldn't defile it, but he had to look, at least.

What if Allah sent him to the correct location this time? If the solution to all the world's problems were in there, would opening the tomb be considered right or wrong? Allah was a prophet. Who would dispute what he said if that was the case?

Mujtaba uncovered the tomb with one fluid motion, then fell upon it to see where it opened. Perhaps it had been sealed permanently because nothing moved when he pried on the edges.

Praying for forgiveness to the prophet Moses, whose peaceful rest he was about to disturb, Mujtaba pushed the upper frame with all his strength.

Something cracked, then budged upward.

He almost fell inside when it popped open because he was leaning too far. A cloth covered with inscriptions was spread out over nearly two and a half meters, with another transparent fabric draped over the rest of the area.

He yanked them out and tossed them on the floor to his right.

Under the material, he found a few relics but nothing else. As he tried to lower the case, it slipped from his hand with more force than he intended, making a loud bang. The noise immediately brought several late-night pilgrims to the access area of the tomb.

When they saw Mujtaba holding the lid with the cloths of the tomb on the floor, they shouted and stumbled forward to grab him. He was forcibly dragged out into the courtyard.

Shoved to the ground, he covered his head as they kicked him just outside the building. Their utterings accused him of being an infidel who came to cause harm to Islam. They shouted how it was a great sin to desecrate such a sacred tomb.

One man kicked him in the back and yelled that he deserved to die.

Mujtaba shouted between blows, "I didn't want to hurt anyone or disrespect the Prophet." He grunted after another well-landed kick struck his lower back. "I am a messenger of Allah. I'm on a search, a great need for all humanity. We are in danger. Allow me to regain my feet, explain myself, and save you all."

They didn't listen to him. Nobody cared about his words. The ancient holy tomb had been desecrated, and he was the one who committed the crime.

They left him on the ground after becoming exhausted from the violence.

The man who had professed that he deserved death whispered in his ear that if he returned to the holy tomb, he would be killed on the street.

Alone, bleeding, and in pain, Mujtaba rolled into a ball and waited for the pain to subside enough to get to his feet and stumble back to his room at the inn.

After some time, sleep took him, and he woke to the feeling of being shaken.

The vibration of an earthquake moved the ground upon which he slept.

The streets were empty, and the sky had begun to brighten with the early morning sun. Sore, covered in bruises and blood, he got to his knees and prayed to Allah.

Then, a strange wind extinguished the few candles still lit outside the monuments, and absolute darkness reigned.

And he prayed and prayed.

Chapter Eight

Lausanne, Switzerland
The Morning After The Explosion

Cassandra opened her eyes, but she couldn't see or focus clearly. She rubbed at her eyes in a panic.

"Cassandra," a man said. "Wake up."

"Leo?" she whispered.

"I thought I lost you," Leo said. "I just woke up and couldn't find you." He pulled her into a hug. "But you were right beside me."

Her eyesight improved enough for her to see him looking at her. She glanced up at the sky and was startled. She had never seen anything like it. A cloud of dust and ashes floated high in the air, restricting much light from passing through.

She held his hand and got to her feet. A sharp pain shot

through her head, and she rubbed her temples, her eyes closed.

"Are you okay?" Leo asked. "Here, let me see." He touched her gently, examining her.

"I'm fine," Cassandra said.

She opened her eyes again and looked around them. The sun had risen but was as dark as a day with thick cloud cover.

More than half of the people smiling and singing in the square last night were hurt. The windows of the buildings were broken out. The unlucky ones walking on the sidewalks had been cut down from the rubble that dropped off buildings. Blood was everywhere, marking the tragedy like a stain. People who could stand on their own two feet stood silent, staring at the landscape of terror, at each other, at the black mass in the sky.

The thick dust seemed to gradually lower toward the ground like it had a mind of its own. Hovering, then lowering, like a swarm of millions of tiny insects.

"What happened?" she mumbled, holding Leo's hand. "And what the hell is that black shit? Let's go somewhere, find *some*one, see if we can get an update." She glanced over at the front of the bar. "But first, I want my backpack."

Less than ten minutes later, they found her backpack with everything intact. Then they meandered through the chaos and found back alleys to traverse, searching for a policeman, a reporter, anyone who could tell them what happened.

In the center of town, they accessed the main road. There, as expected, were more ruins. Cars had stopped where their owners had been injured. They now blocked most of the area for vehicular traffic. Bodies were scattered haphazardly everywhere, some moaning in pain, many not moving at all.

The best option was to leave on foot. When would the city have electric power again? Did they still have clean water? Staying in Lausanne was dangerous, so they kept moving.

They stopped to catch their breath in front of a traditional house with large plants lining the front walkway an hour later. The burgundy shutters were damaged, and cracks could be seen in the walls.

An elderly man wearing dark sunglasses sat in a wheelchair at the front door under a broken lamp. He held what looked like an old radio in his lap as he called out to a woman over and over.

"Elise? Elise? Where are you? Please come home, Elise."

Not wanting to startle him, Cassandra motioned to Leo to wait, then slowly moved toward the old man, unsure if he saw her through his dark glasses.

"Sir?" she said softly. "My name is Cassandra. Can we help you in any way? Do you want help to get down the stairs? Is there someone we can call for you?"

"Elise? Elise? Where are you?" he repeated.

"Sir, I'm not Elise. I'm Cassandra. Can we borrow your radio for a minute? Does it work?"

"Elise? Elise? Where are you?"

That was getting maddening.

"He can't hear you," Leo said from behind her.

"As I've gathered."

The Elise he beckoned for was probably out of the house when everything happened, and now he was alone and scared, so he shouted out for her in despair.

When Cassandra got close enough, she tried to take his hand.

He screamed and pulled away from her.

Cassandra moved back a few steps, and then Leo stepped around her and quickly snatched the radio from the man's grasp.

The older man shouted for them to leave him alone.

"I got it. Let's go." Leo moved away from the house.

"And what, just leave this old man alone? Shouldn't we wait for his Elise to show up?"

"Are you crazy? I'm not waiting here all day while he shouts like a lunatic."

The older man continued to wail but at a lower volume now.

"Calm down," she said soothingly, then remembered he couldn't hear her. "I'm near you, and you're safe. Everything'll be fine." Cassandra took his hand and tried to calm him down that way.

The man didn't jump back this time. "Finally, Elise, you have come," he said.

Cassandra glanced back at Leo.

"I was afraid I lost you," the man said, his sobs calming, his chest hitching less.

Leo played with the radio, swinging the needle from right to left, searching for a station, but found no success.

"Do you even know how that works?" she mumbled beside him. "How long do you think its batteries will last?"

He ignored her as he played with the dials. When he found a voice, he adjusted the squelch. The first station he found spewed religion through the static.

"Christians, it is time to repent." The voice could be discerned quickly enough. "The sky has turned red, which is something we can't overlook. It's the sign of the Antichrist. He's here among us. Doomsday is here. Pray for your soul, the souls of your loved ones, and your neighbors, and ask for purification. None of us will survive without it. The black dust will envelop us all and lead nonbelievers and sinners to Satan. The explosion at Cern was purely the work of the Devil. Man invited him and welcomed him when he wanted to know where life came from, looking for the God Particle. Now the Devil sucks and spits his ashes. Repent, repent."

Cassandra stared at Leo, then smacked his shoulder lightly. "Come on, change it. I don't want to hear such nonsense. Try to find something normal?"

"Elise?" the old man said. "Didn't I tell you? I knew they would come, and I couldn't prevent it. It was too late. I didn't have enough time …" The older man appeared agitated as he began to cry.

Cassandra caressed his back affectionately, sorry he was in this situation. Something red was on his cheeks, and when she bent to get a closer look, she saw that it was his tears—they'd turned the color of blood.

She shivered, the feeling coursing up her spine. She had to do something, but what?

"I'm going inside this man's house."

Leo fixated on the radio, then gave her a curt nod.

She stepped away from the old man and entered through his front door.

Once inside the front foyer, she found the living room on her right and the kitchen down a short hallway. A napkin rested by a salt and pepper shaker on the kitchen table, the remnants of a dinner for two still on the table. He certainly wasn't alone last night. She took the napkin from the table and returned to wipe the old man's eyes.

When she removed his glasses, she jumped back, horrified to find he had no eyes.

She stumbled several more steps backward.

It looked like his eyes had been gouged out with a spoon, leaving two matching red craters on his face.

After a deep breath, she approached him again. Hands trembling, she wiped his face. There had to be a logical explanation for his condition. Doctors weren't butchers. No one would do this to another human being.

Leo hadn't looked up. He just continued the search for something on the radio.

He found a channel where a voice broke in. "... And electricity hasn't been restored yet. Telephones are still down. We can inform you that a large explosion came from the Cern complex, where the Large Hadron Collider is located. According to preliminary reports, all houses within a massive radius of the explosion's epicenter were destroyed. We don't have confirmation on the staff and residents of Cern. It's impossible to estimate the number of dead and injured at this early stage, as many are trapped in rubble throughout the area. The material damage is incalculable. The country is in a state of emergency, even though this tragedy has not been officially announced yet. What worries us is the black dust hovering in the morning sky. No one knows where it came from or when it'll disappear. Get out in the open and don't approach the ruins of buildings. Stay tuned for more news.

Help is on the way. May God be with us."

"Now what?" Cassandra asked. "What are we going to do?"

Leo's eyes found her as he turned off the radio. "What can we do? Certainly, help is on its way, right?"

"We need supplies. Water and food, several other essentials. Who knows how long it'll be before help gets here." Cassandra felt despair choking her.

"I have money with me," Leo reassured her.

"What do you mean? Money will be completely useless right now. What are you going to buy with it? From where?"

"Let's go then. We can't sit around doing nothing."

"What about him?" Cassandra asked, looking at the old man.

"Leave him," Leo replied, his tone cold.

"What if Elise is dead or hurt? He'll die alone. We can't just leave him."

"Of course, we can." Leo set the radio down and stepped away. "He'll be a weight on our shoulders, and I'm not carrying him."

"Leo, that's not right."

He turned back to look at her. "Okay, we'll leave him behind for now, and later, once we have some supplies, we can come back and check on him."

"But Leo, he may have food. He may have all the supplies we need." Cassandra stepped back inside the house without seeing if Leo would join her.

She opened all the cupboards and drawers in the kitchen, then the refrigerator. They were empty. Maybe Elise had gone shopping, and that was why she was gone.

"Come on out of there," Leo called to her from the front door. "It can be dangerous. The house may fall on your head. The explosion damaged it, and there's no reason to risk your life in this old man's house."

She took one last look at the wooden floors, antiques, and heavy velvet curtains, then stepped outside.

"Leo, I'm sorry. I'm not leaving unless we take him with us. He's helpless, and now I feel responsible for him."

"Cassandra, are you crazy?" Leo's face contorted into disbelief. "I bet he needs a ton of medication. The responsibility you're taking on is bigger than you're aware."

She shrugged, defiant to the end. "I'm going back in to check the bathrooms for meds."

Cassandra stared at Leo with a piercing gaze for a moment longer, then re-entered the house.

She carefully climbed the stairs to her left, breathing in the dust within the damaged house.

It wouldn't last long in its current state. The place would be labeled condemned as soon as the authorities assessed it.

She went straight to the bathroom on the second level, hoping to find what she was looking for.

Inside a medicine cabinet, she located over a dozen bottles with Vincent Etter on them. They were ordered alphabetically along the shelf. All the common diseases and ailments she knew were there—cholesterol issues, uric acid, hypertension, etc.

But next to them, some other medications scared her. Antipsychotics and antidepressants. She grabbed one and read the words mania, schizoaffective psychosis, and anxiety disorder.

She huffed out a breath. All these meds and nothing for his eyes. How was that possible?

She took them all, stuffed them in her pockets, and headed back down the stairs before the ceiling caved in on her head.

"His name is Vincent," she told Leo. "He has no real illness other than the common problems of old age. Let's go now." She grabbed the handles of the wheelchair, and Leo took the bottom. Together, they eased it down the stairs.

"Elise, please no," the old man said. "I'm afraid to go out. They'll find me and kill me when they do."

"Don't worry, everything will be fine," Cassandra said calmly as she gently touched his shoulder.

They pushed the wheelchair to the pavement, and the three of them continued on the same road without a single protest from Leo about taking Vincent.

"Where are we going now?" Leo asked, looking at Vincent.

"I have no idea." She shrugged, thinking about it. "How about we leave him at a hospital if we see one? Maybe Clinique Cecil. It's private, though. Let's leave him there, and they'll find his Elise eventually." She leaned sideways to look at him. "You're right, though. We don't know what we'll face next, and we can't have him with us. I just couldn't leave him behind all alone in that house."

Several people had stopped on the other side of the road as they looked skyward. Cassandra followed their gaze and saw that the sky was still filled with some sort of ash, hiding the sun. The black dust seemed to have lowered even more and now rested several meters above the roofs of the houses.

There was as much light getting through as any overcast day, but she shuddered what it would be like when night fell.

After walking through town, she could see the magnitude of the disaster. Houses were severely damaged, and several people were trapped in them, screaming for help. In some cases, passersby helped. In other cases, they didn't.

It was all a matter of fate, which seemed so cruel.

Strolling with the wheelchair through the panic and anarchy became more complicated than she had imagined. The streets were debris-filled, and people were afraid to enter their homes.

"Elise, they will come for us," Vincent said from his wheelchair. "They've already arrived, just as we said."

Cassandra didn't pay much attention to his words. The spectacle before her was like watching a Hollywood destruction movie on a cinema screen.

While lost in her thoughts, observing the devastation, a small earthquake shook the ground—an aftershock.

Many people dropped to the ground, terrified they'd be injured or killed. No one knew how severe it would be.

Leo wrapped his arms around Cassandra and covered her with his body as they stood there behind the wheelchair.

The earthquake lasted several seconds. Then, it calmed to a soft rumble and stopped. Leo released her and stepped back.

Cassandra held tight to the wheelchair. Without saying a word, she pushed the wheelchair and got moving again. Up ahead, the roads were so jammed and blocked they had to change their plan. They'd never get to the hospital that way.

So they turned toward the train station, but things only

got worse.

At the time of the explosion, a passing train derailed and collided with the platform. Rescue crews hadn't arrived yet, and the smell of burned flesh mixed with smoke was nauseating.

There were so many dead people; she couldn't fathom it. A few had survived, but they moaned in pain, caught under the weight of steel beams or the side of a train car.

"Let's take the tunnel crossing under the station to the other side," Cassandra said. "Otherwise, we'll have to do a whole circle with the wheelchair."

Leo nodded. "Wait here. I'll go see if we can get through first." He ran down the stairs and disappeared into the gloom below.

Cassandra turned to Vincent. "Tell me about Elise," she said close to his ear, hoping he could hear her.

"I was waiting for her, but she didn't come."

Surprised he caught her words, she leaned close again and said, "Is she your daughter?"

"No."

"Your wife?"

"No."

"How is she related to you?"

"Elise, where are you, Elise?" Vincent disappeared again into his darkness as if he hadn't heard her questions, leaving Cassandra with no idea how she could locate his Elise.

"Do you know where she might be?" She tried once more, but Vincent was lost.

She had caught a small window of clarity that had lasted seconds. Even his facial expression was empty again.

"Elise, we have to hide, get away. Before it gets dark, they will chase us when the night comes. I see them coming, Elise. Let's go now to hide, please."

Not knowing what to do or how to communicate with him, Cassandra held his hands and caressed him gently on the back. She felt sorry for him, his despair, his loneliness.

How long could she be expected to handle a man in such distress?

And where the hell was Leo?

What was taking him so long?

Chapter Nine

**Nabi Musa, One Hour From Jerusalem
The Morning After The Explosion**

In his haste to get back to Jerusalem, Mujtaba had been able to steal a car after the owner had left it running on the side of the road. Well, the owner hadn't just left it running. He'd passed out and was on the ground beside the open door of his car, the vehicle in park, the keys in the ignition.

It was an opportunity that presented itself to Mujtaba, and he had to take it. Allah always found ways to further his aims, and Mujtaba was a loyal servant. When he needed to get to Jerusalem, Allah set it up so it could be so.

And now, on Route 1 en route to Jerusalem, he periodically peered up at the black dust hovering in the air above him. It blocked out most of the sun's light, making him press the gas harder. Jerusalem was close, and he needed to get there before something terrible happened—like that dust descending upon the land and overtaking him.

He hadn't seen anything like it. After the earthquake, he took the opportunity to slip away from the others. He had discarded his bloody clothes in the wilderness, retrieved his backpack, and found the car that a regular worshiper of Nabi Musa probably used. Stealing a car was a new experience— an exhilarating one—but Allah was with him.

As soon as he arrived in Jerusalem, he would abandon it undamaged. Eventually, the owner would be located, and the most he would've stolen would've been the gas in the tank.

He could have initiated his search directly from the holy sites, but that might have proven too dangerous. He never wanted to go against what was allowed—his faith prevented such actions. But if he had to, he'd do what was needed to fulfill his destiny. The one set out by Allah himself.

Important religious sites were always guarded and crowded. But for Mujtaba, there was no choice in the matter now. He had been called to duty, and upon completing his duty, the current calamity facing mankind would cease.

How would this happen?

He had no idea. It was his visions that told him he was the chosen one. So, onward, he would go until the how revealed itself.

He crossed the desert, passing the small villages before Jerusalem. Driving carefully to avoid missing signs, he passed outside the Mount of Olives to his left. The desire to drive in and stand among the 150,000 tombs and the places where the prophet Jesus walked overwhelmed him, but there was no time for such pleasures.

He continued driving and saw the signs for the Garden of Gethsemane, where the prophet was betrayed at the foot of the Mount of Olives.

Minutes later, after steering around dozens of vehicles scattered haphazardly throughout the roadway, he made it to the Jaffe Gate entrance to the old city of Jerusalem. He seemed to recall up to seven entrances, four of them being more popular. The busiest was the Jaffe Gate ingress, next to the Tower of David Museum.

But now, the car was no longer an asset. The car had become a liability in such a small, tight area.

In addition to that, the police presence increased once inside the old walls, which signaled that it was time to park the stolen vehicle.

He turned into the parking lot, where the empty tour buses were parked on his left. After searching the car, he couldn't find a cloth or napkin, so he popped the trunk, found one in a spare bag of tire-changing tools, then wiped the steering wheel and the gear shift.

According to the movies he'd seen from America, leaving behind fingerprints could implicate him later in the crime of stealing a car—something he didn't want to have to explain.

Once the car was wiped clean, he shouldered his backpack, left the keys in the ignition just as he'd found it, then strolled toward the city entrance. Although exhausted, he kept up his pace while trying not to think about his overall mission to avoid the heightened anxiety. Even though it was still morning and there were damages to some of the buildings from the recent earthquake, many people flooded the area from the gate to the square.

Police were stationed under the gate to stem the flow of the devout. It appeared to Mujtaba that there were simply too many religious people searching for answers and prayers to keep the pious crowd from entering.

Mujtaba needed inside posthaste. His mission was far superior to the faithful prayer the rest sought after.

He reached an emergency exit on the side and found a way to pass under the bars. Once inside the old city of Jerusalem, he walked with speed and soon saw the Western Square, which ended at the Western Wall farther ahead. It was known as the Wall of Tears, about which he had heard so much. Hundreds of Jews who didn't have access to the Temple Mount—it belonged to the Muslim community for the most part, even though it's revered as a holy site by Judaism, Christianity, and Islam alike—prayed in front of it. They hoped that their prayers would be better heard because it was the holiest place in the world, thus their desire to be as close as possible to it.

According to the Jewish faith, the Temple Mount is the holiest site in Judaism, where God's divine presence is manifested more than in any other place.

For Mujtaba's purpose, it's also where it's believed that King Solomon built the first mount in the tenth century B.C. to house the Ark of the Covenant.

Mujtaba knew why the area was swarming with people at the moment—the black dust hovering above everyone. It terrified anyone whose eyes fell upon it, and now everyone wanted to seek their God for help.

Mujtaba traversed the narrow roads, meandering around dozens of the faithful, muttering to themselves until he found the entrance to the Temple Mount. It was a hectic location, with hundreds of Jews wanting access, but a line of police wasn't allowing entrance at the moment.

However, he could pass through without being disturbed since he was a Muslim. He showed his ID, received a nod and a hand gesture to enter, then walked by the crowd with his head bowed as they booed.

Before him rose one of the holiest places in Islam. His body felt like an electrical current transmitted through him as he laid eyes upon it for the first time. His legs trembled with emotion as he climbed the stairs one by one. With each step he climbed, he felt closer to Allah. The stairs were so wide they could fit at least twenty people ascending simultaneously, side by side.

He reached the square and looked at the Dome of the Rock. A majestic octagonal building with a gold-plated dome filled with thousands of ceramic tiles and mosaics. A masterpiece of Islamic art in the style of the rotunda. A sacred place for so many religions, which belonged to Islam.

The foundation stone the temple was built on is believed to be the site where Abraham attempted to sacrifice his son and where God's divine presence has manifested itself more than any other toward the Jews.

The site's Islamic significance derives from the night journey of Muhammad and the origins of the creation of the world. It's believed that the Prophet Muhammad began his night journey from the rock in the center of the structure.

Christians consider it sacred because the temple played a

decisive role in the life of Jesus, but the Romans destroyed it in seventy C.E. In its place, they built a temple of Zeus.

Then, it fell into the hands of the Persians and then to the Muslims, who ordered the construction of the dome. It was and still is sacred to the Muslims because they believe Muhammad ascended to Heaven with the archangel Gabriel to pray with the greatest prophets of Allah: Abraham, Moses, and Jesus. There, he saw Allah on his throne, surrounded by angels. After this prayer, he called the people to believe in him and unite under the Muslim religion, saying the first prayer while facing the Qibla.

Violent clashes between Christians and Muslims followed. Eventually, the Christians succeeded, captured Jerusalem, and built their headquarters next to the dome, which they believed was part of Solomon's Temple. They kept the dome as a symbol, put it on their seals, and used the same architecture for their churches across Europe. As for the Jews, they believe that Abraham went to sacrifice Isaac, and it is, for them, the holiest place on Earth. When they pray, they turn toward the foundation stone.

Standing there now, before such history and so much bloodshed, Mujtaba humbly pondered how to get inside so he could dig in search of the Ark of the Covenant without being shot for his efforts. Should he start in the First Temple, the Temple of Solomon, or where Noah stopped after the flood? Would he find what others have searched for for centuries?

White ihrams—worn to signify they're all the same in front of Allah, whether rich or poor—flooded the area like a human blizzard. They probably thought that they'd be protected from what was coming if they entered the dome, as that black dust hovering over everyone's heads did not offer feelings of tranquility.

The soldiers had laid siege to the dome, likely fearing destruction from the massive crowds. That reduced his odds to literally nothing, perhaps a chance in a million that he'd gain entry without an issue.

So he changed direction and made his way to the Al-Aqsa Mosque, where Muhammad used to pray before Allah told him about the Kaaba. In search of an isolated area, he descended the stairs to El Marwani Mosque, an old mosque otherwise known as Solomon's Stables. This area was empty, even though it was one of the holiest places of Islam.

Surely Allah would help him. He stopped to lean against a wall to catch his breath, doubt seeping into his thoughts.

What next? Where should he go? Couldn't Allah offer more direction—

At that moment, staring across the open expanse of the underground vaulted interior of Solomon's Stables, the answers came to him.

Mujtaba now knew what to do.

Even though none of those searching for prayers were down here, they still had a guard posted outside the door, a weapon strapped to his shoulder. As soon as the guard saw Mujtaba approaching, he gestured for him to leave.

"You must go somewhere else," the man said.

Mujtaba pretended a lack of understanding and continued walking toward him.

The guard's eyes bored a hole through him. The man was of medium build, similar to Mujtaba. They were the same height, dark-haired, and roughly the same body type.

Mujtaba pretended he wanted to talk to him and continued closer, his hands raised near his waist.

The guard seemed to calm down when he saw Mujtaba's smile, lowering his weapon.

When Mujtaba was close enough, he opened his mouth to speak, then drove a fist in the man's throat, placing it neatly under his chin.

The guard stumbled back, bumped into the wall, and grasped at his neck, his eyes bulging as he stared in shock at Mujtaba. The guard attempted to call out, but his mouth spasmed open and closed without a sound as he gathered that breathing was more important than talking or shouting.

He slid down the wall slightly, his hands going for his gun.

Mujtaba latched onto the weapon's barrel and violently lifted it over the man's head, the strap coming loose from the guard's shoulder.

Then he used the butt of the weapon to mash it into the guard's face.

The man's eyes rolled back in his head as he dropped to the rock floor.

Mujtaba dragged him behind a wall, then undressed the guard quickly. In minutes, Mujtaba was fully dressed as a guard, his weapon now strapped over his shoulder.

He used the guard's zip ties on the man's wrists and placed one of his socks in his mouth to gag him. When the man woke up, he couldn't allow him to warn anyone.

Confident in his new uniform, he climbed the stairs, stepped out into the shaded sunshine—that dark cloud hovered even lower now, obscuring most of the light—and moved toward the Temple of the Dome. Strolling along as one of the uniformed guards, no one gave him a second look.

A large crowd had gathered around the temple. He had to push through when he reached them, commanding that they allow him access to move forward.

He quickly counted ten armed guards making up the temple's perimeter, even though his stomach felt sick with anxiety. Sweat had burst out on his forehead. He had to blink away the salty drops as he placed himself—an imposter in uniform—into a questionable position upon the security detail of such a holy site.

Although, it was quite fitting that he was dressed as a guard on his first visit to this holy place. He was one of Allah's most devout followers. Why shouldn't he be guarding, touring, and visiting the sites upon which the Prophet once walked?

Once in position, he turned to face the crowd, standing with the other officers near the entrance.

Then he waited for the right opportunity to slip inside unseen.

He didn't have to wait long as an Arab started fighting with the man beside him over a dispute about a stolen position in line. They argued, and soon, the situation escalated to fisticuffs. Several men on either side jumped in to break it up, which ignited half a dozen people into a brawl. The guards responded, with several leaving their positions to break up the fight.

Mujtaba took advantage of the commotion and stepped backward. He entered the temple as his fellow guards engaged in the fight or stood watching it.

Once he descended the stairs into the holy site and turned to the right, he saw the Foundation Stone. It was fenced off for protection from the many faithful visiting every year.

He moved around the small room, observing the luxurious mosaics on the floor until he approached the railing that blocked access to the Foundation Stone.

There was no way he could dig *under* the rock. That would require heavy machinery and tools. He didn't even have a shovel, and if he did, it would be useless. The noise that any digging created would have the real guards shooting him on sight.

Was the location wrong? Could he have made a mistake? Did he fail Allah in this risky endeavor?

To the right, there was a staircase. He glanced at the entrance—no one had followed him inside yet—so he jogged over to the stairs and descended them two at a time. He entered a cave with a lamp suspended from the roof. It took him several moments to realize he was in the Well of Souls. Legends say that the voices of souls echo while waiting for Judgment Day.

He looked around, but only rocks and more rocks made up the Well of Souls. A small wall built from the natural rock face was in the corner to his right. Worshippers would kneel before this area and pray to their individual deity.

Behind that outcropping would be the only place someone could hide something the size of the Ark of the Covenant down here.

It had to be behind what was called The Mihrab.

He placed his fingers on the edges and attempted to pry it back, but it wouldn't budge. There was a hook embedded in the side of the marble. Perhaps that was used to open it. He needed the tool that worked with the hook to get the Mihrab open and examine what was behind it. That was the only way.

He scanned the room. Two chairs, two fans, and several copies of the Qur'an were stacked in a pile on the other side of the small room.

There was no tool for the hook.

The only option was to return to the floor above and continue his search there.

Halfway up the stairs, he stopped. Voices had made him cease his ascension to listen. After a moment, he eased back down the steps.

Being seen wasn't an option. Being jailed or killed would end the mission Allah had sent him on, serving no purpose other than shame.

If they decided to check down the stairs, he would have to pass himself off as a guard without flaw to avoid consequences. Otherwise, it would be a dirty prison cell for an indeterminate time.

Luckily, the voices above moved away, and he started breathing again. But they would return if he made any substantial noise. He had to wait for the right moment to check the upstairs area for a tool, yet time was running out. His presence would be discovered soon, so he had to work quickly. And the likelihood of that guard he assaulted being discovered soon had to be considered as well.

Moving stealthily, he climbed the stairs slowly to avoid bringing any attention to himself. When he neared the top, he leaned upward to see if anyone occupied the Foundation

Stone area. It was empty now, but he heard guards whispering something close by. They spoke of the people outside—that if they came all at once, the monument would be destroyed, and there would be injuries, perhaps death.

The voices of the faithful out front had started chanting Allah's name.

Mujtaba moved back down the stairs and scanned the cave-like room one more time. The fan sitting above the Mihrab gave him an idea. He grabbed it and broke the back off, disassembling it quickly. Then, he took an iron section and tried to bend it to make it into a hook shape. It was easier than he had initially imagined.

Holding his breath, he dug around the edges of the Mihrab, sweating profusely now. After minutes of chipping away at it, the small outer area separated from the rock wall, but it wasn't enough to peel off the marble-carved façade of the Mihrab.

He needed to see what was behind it. He needed it peeled back enough that he may be able to climb inside.

One last look behind him garnered another idea. He grabbed a heavy book from a pile by one of the chairs and pounded it against the folded iron to make more of a hook. After hitting it several times, he stopped to listen, but no one approached his position.

Armed with a stronger hook now, Mujtaba pried and yanked at the front of the Mihrab and separated it from the rock wall. After another ten minutes of pulling, he'd pried it back far enough to slip in behind it now.

When he peeked inside, he saw nothing back there, to his great disappointment. Just a recessed area like a rock cave.

Irritated, he smacked the wall with his open palm.

It was time to leave.

A piece of chipped stone dropped to his feet, revealing a small hole. Mujtaba eased closer and tried to peer inside but couldn't see anything as it was too dark. He could slip his hand inside the hole, where he applied pressure and widened the hole even more.

Piece by piece, he tore small bits of thin stones away from the hole, making it round enough for his head to fit. Chipping away at it, his shoulders would soon fit. Minutes later, the rock and dust debris piling at his feet, he could crawl through the hole.

Mujtaba grabbed a candle from the place of prayer and sank it into the mud inside the hole. With a light on the inside, he climbed in after it.

From inside the hole, he glanced back out into the room. There was no way he could cover his tracks. If someone entered the Well of Souls, they'd see and investigate the carnage he'd caused. Should he climb back out and fix things? Arrange them to cover his tracks? Or should he just carry on with his search?

Voices approached from somewhere above.

They must have heard him.

That made his decision for him—dilemma solved.

Mujtaba moved away from the hole so the candlelight wouldn't reveal his position, then sat and listened to determine how close the voices were. Ears alert, sitting inside the small cave a meter away from the hole, breathing became a chore as his lungs filled with dust, making him want to cough. He held on as long as he could, clearing his throat quietly.

Finally, the conversations outside the wall ceased. He lifted the candle and aimed down the length of the cave behind the Mihrab.

It was a small tunnel.

This had to be it. The Ark of the Covenant would be at the end of this tunnel, buried in some room that hadn't been explored for centuries.

Hope restored, he crawled deeper along the cave, the candle held high, hoping to find what he sought.

Crawling and slithering like a snake, he soon reached a point where the passageway narrowed. He pushed onward until the rock roof lowered and the floor raised until he ended up in a tight crawlspace with little wiggle room.

He edged onward on his stomach, the hole ahead just wide enough for his shoulders, but then he had to stop.

Gasping for breath, the stone walls around having wedged inward, the candle extended at the end of his arm. He saw how the rock narrowed to something only a mouse could manage.

Mujtaba was stuck. He couldn't crawl farther.

It was over.

He'd reached a dead end.

Chapter Ten

Leo gave one last look at Cassandra and Vincent before descending the stairs into the tunnel that should lead to the other side of the tracks. Below ground was slow-moving due to the darkness. The minor amount of emergency lighting guided him, but chunks of rock obstructed his way.

Leo crept forward, careful with each step. He had to crawl over a large slab of granite that had broken off the sidewall. The spectacle before him caused a shudder to course through his upper body when he rounded a corner.

One of the train cars sat sideways, broken and crunched up like a monster's hand had once held it too tight. A mass of iron and concrete was fused with flesh and blood, which stained the broken window frames of the behemoth: the passengers, all victims of a violent end. Amputated limbs were scattered across the platform. It was as if he was staring at the aftermath of a terrorist bombing.

He moved forward anyway, nudging limbs aside to avoid tripping on a forearm or an elbow. No one moaned, no one screamed. Down here, in the underground railway, only the dead remained. There was nothing he could do for anyone, and the passageway to the other side appeared to be blocked, so he eased back toward the stairs and then stopped.

Something had moved in the shadows near the back of the train car. He caught it in the periphery of his vision, but nothing was moving now.

Drawn by curiosity, he took a few steps toward the area where he'd seen the movement.

From somewhere to his right, a woman said, "Don't go." The voice echoed throughout the underground, making him slow and search for the voice's origin.

He spied a woman lying on her back. He was close enough, with just enough light, to see her chest moving.

Could she still be alive down here?

Without thinking about it further, he ran to her.

"Are you okay?" he asked, staring at her dust-covered face.

On his knees beside her, he inspected the length of her body and saw her legs trapped in a pile of rubble. Blood smeared the area where her legs disappeared.

She breathed rapidly, which meant there was still hope for her.

"Stay with me," he said. "I will see about getting you out of here."

He grabbed at the stones and tossed a few smaller ones aside. When he got to the bigger ones, they wouldn't budge.

He tried again, but the large stone was the size of a twin mattress—it wasn't going anywhere under one man's strength.

The woman coughed up blood and opened her eyes.

"Don't waste your time with me, Leo."

Leo's face scrunched up. He stared at her for a heartbeat. "How do you know my name?"

"You're Leo." She coughed. "Am I right?"

He nodded, and when she didn't respond, he said, "Yes, I'm Leo."

"You have Vincent with you." She croaked out the words. It sounded like a statement, not a question.

"Ma'am, you're creeping me out." He eased back a little. "How could you know all that?"

She coughed again. "Just tell me"—she swallowed—"is Vincent with you?"

So it was a question. "Yes, he is."

"Cassandra, too?"

"Holy shit, man. How do you know all of us?"

She coughed, and blood rolled down the side of her cheek. "Vincent told me."

"But how? He's outside waiting with Cassandra. I'm the only one who came down here."

"You can't help me," she whispered.

Leo dropped back on his butt and stared at the woman. "But *how* do you know our names?"

"Vincent told me you'd come. Now let me tell you what he said. You have to look after Cassandra. I don't know how much time you have." She coughed and spat even more blood. Speaking about time left, Leo felt the woman's time could be measured in minutes. "Tell Vincent Elise will see him again soon. Send him my love …" Her voice faded, and her chest lowered.

Then, it didn't move upward again.

Leo waited for an entire minute before he palmed the woman's eyes closed.

Then he got to his feet and shook the dust from his clothes. After staring at Elise—this was the Elise Vincent had cried about—she still creeped him out by what she said—he turned and headed toward the stairs in a trance.

What the hell just happened?

What did Vincent know, and how could he have told Elise anything about them?

If Vincent actually knew Leo and what he was up to, what if he told Cassandra?

By the time he got to the main level again, he realized he needed to find a way to ditch the man in the wheelchair.

Cassandra could never learn Leo's true intentions for her. Otherwise, she'd run, and he would fail.

He refused to fail even in light of the catastrophe they were facing. That was why he came looking for her last night.

He was a man of his word.

And no withered old man in a wheelchair would undo what he'd taken a year to put together with careful planning.

No man would stand in his way.

Chapter Eleven

"WHERE THE HELL WERE you?" Cassandra shouted at him.

Her patience had grown thin, but when she saw his face, it was obvious by the serious look in his eye that something terrible had happened below ground. "Leo, tell me what happened?"

He stopped in front of her and took her hands without looking at Vincent. "Cassandra, please. We must keep moving."

"But you're different somehow. What happened down there?"

"Where is Elise?" Vincent asked.

Leo snapped his head to glare at the old man.

"Did she die?" Vincent continued. "Did you leave her all alone down there?" Vincent burst into tears, the red streaks rolling down his cheeks.

Leo released Cassandra's hands, moved around the wheelchair, grabbed the handles, and started pushing.

Cassandra watched him, confused. What else could she do if he didn't want to talk? Leo's face had gone expressionless. He seemed unwilling to answer her questions about what changed his demeanor, and Vincent was now hunched over as if grieving for Elise.

What caused Vincent to ask about Elise and inquire as to why Leo didn't help her? Did Vincent think his Elise was underground? Had she taken the train early in the morning when the earthquake hit?

Cassandra marched along behind Leo as they headed down the street without discussing which way they were going.

Weren't they still looking for a hospital?

She shook her head, thinking about how the world had gone crazy and her traveling companions had, too.

She studied Leo from a few steps behind, wondering what could have happened to the man she once knew. She wanted him to stop walking and explain what happened but decided to give him his space for now. How could she know what sort of trauma he faced underground? Maybe he saw something that put him into some sort of shock.

Farther on, they reached an unblocked pathway to the other side of the fenced-off train tracks. Leo headed that way, telling her he still intended to get to the hospital.

Leaving Vincent in the hands of professionals was step one. Finding out what was bothering Leo would come next.

She quickened her pace to catch up as Leo moved faster, roughly manhandling the chair.

"Aren't you going too fast for a man of Vincent's age?" she asked.

Leo didn't acknowledge that she spoke. He just kept on walking, putting distance between them.

"What's the big hurry?" she shouted.

When he didn't look back or say anything, she glanced up and saw the black ash had lowered even more. Maybe they needed to be inside when it got to their level. Or at least be wearing masks to be able to breathe through it.

She fixed her gaze back on Leo. Whenever there was a bump in the road, the wheelchair shook, startling Vincent, his hands going out to the sides for balance. He was in Leo's hands now, and she couldn't do anything about it.

She'd known Leo for a long time. He wouldn't hurt a blind old man in a wheelchair. Would he?

The hospital was several more blocks away, but there was a supermarket before that. Vincent had to eat something to take his medicine—they all needed to eat something as exhaustion was setting into her bones.

She wondered how the man would behave without his antipsychotics.

As they passed the next train station, they saw what was left of it. Those who could have left after the explosion had already done so. Those waiting for the train either died instantly or were left helpless and died shortly after that.

Cassandra wiped at her eyes, and her fingers came away with a film of crushed ashes.

"Leo?" she said as they neared the tracks.

He stopped to look at her this time. His eyes were bloodshot and leaking, and the whites of the sclera faded to a deep crimson.

Leo turned away from her without saying a word, then tried to lift the wheelchair over the rails.

They shouldn't have taken that pathway earlier. Now, they were crossing the tracks to get back to the side they'd started on.

Before Leo stopped to catch his breath, Vincent rocked in his chair, hands clinging to the armrests.

"What's wrong?" Cassandra asked, closing the distance his walking speed had created. She moved closer, placing a hand on his arm. "You're acting as if you're someone else. At least let me help you with that."

Leo remained expressionless, his glazed eyes taking her in.

She leaned down and grabbed the wheelchair to lift it over the rails when he didn't move or say anything, but it was impossible. It was just too heavy for her with Vincent's weight.

How could Vincent help? They didn't know whether he could walk or not, and so far, neither one of them had asked him.

Finally, after taking a few deep breaths, Leo tilted the chair back, and together, they managed to get him over the tracks and onto the opposite platform.

Fortunately, it appeared as if no train had been expected on this side, so no travelers were waiting at the station when the explosion hit earlier that morning.

Leo turned to her. "We need to go to the supermarket first."

Cassandra nodded, thinking about giving Vincent his

medicine. "I agree. We should eat something. Get Vincent a water bottle so he can take his meds."

"Then let's keep moving," Leo said, pushing Vincent ahead.

After getting across the train platform and back out onto the street, the magnitude of the disaster was worse on this side of Lausanne.

Cassandra gawked at the abandoned cars. Some were smashed, with a few sitting canted on their sides, and even a couple were upside down. Smoke rose from the hood of two vehicles. Several buildings in the area had crumbled in the aftermath of the earthquake.

While staring at the devastation, an explosion from a building to their left made Cassandra scream.

This agitated Vincent, and he cried out Elise's name again.

"We need to keep moving," Leo shouted, pushing the wheelchair up the road even faster.

Cassandra ran to catch up as her stomach filled with nerves.

Leo turned onto the road that led to the supermarket. At least if they ate something and drank some water, they'd likely feel better.

But she quickly saw that things wouldn't play out as she suspected.

When the store came into view, people were running in and out of the shattered front doors like angry wasps surging from a broken hive. The once calm and peaceful population had turned into predators—every one of them out for themselves.

Strangers looted the store, clutching their stolen goods close to their chests as they ran, fearing that someone would snatch the items from their hands at any moment.

"Cassandra," Leo said, grabbing her arm and snapping her out of her trance. "Wait for me here with Vincent."

She nodded.

"Can you do that for me?" he asked.

She met his gaze and nodded again. "Of course."

"Good, but do something else, too."

"What's that?" she asked, her gaze wandering over Leo's shoulder to stare at the people climbing through the supermarket's front window.

"Do not listen to a thing this old man says to you."

She looked back into Leo's eyes, then frowned. "What?"

"As evidenced by his antipsychotic meds, he's off his rocker, literally."

She glanced at the top of Vincent's head, then back to Leo. "What could he possibly tell me that would make any sense?" She was genuinely concerned about Leo's warning. What the hell was he worried about?

"Anything he may say will be the ramblings of a lunatic, an insane old man, nothing more."

Cassandra nodded. This was obviously important to Leo. Something about Vincent was bothering him.

"Fine," she muttered. "He's mad. Nothing he may say is to be listened to. Got it."

"Good. I'm serious." He placed both hands on her shoulders. "Wait for me here. Speak to no one. I'll bring us food and drink. Cool?"

She nodded again. "Cool."

He ran off before hearing her final response.

She watched him go, a weird pit in her stomach warning her something was off with Leo.

Vincent sat quietly, his head down, chin against his chest. Would he mind if she took a few of his meds to calm her nerves?

Just last night, she'd been on a park bench with half-closed eyes, listening to wonderful music while a cool breeze caressed her face. But something happened, and she woke in a nightmare, a place of chaos. This world, these people, would never be the same after this—*she* would never be the same after this.

So why did Leo have to be so mysterious? What was he hiding from her about the old man?

Glass shattered somewhere at the front of the supermarket, catching her attention. Three men exited the building through a hole in the side door they'd just kicked out.

Laughing and carrying on like a regular Saturday evening on the town, the men headed toward her and Vincent. They waddled awkwardly as all three were laden down with loot stuffed into pockets and bags filled to the brim suspended from their hands.

She acted as if she didn't notice them, her eyes on the front of the supermarket.

Women could often tune in to men and determine what they would be like from just one look—which could be construed as unfair sometimes, but it is what it is—and these guys were pigs. If they stopped to address her, she'd have to cry for help and hope someone was close enough to hear.

As she feared, the men stared at her as they neared her position behind Vincent's wheelchair.

One of them whistled at her.

Vincent must have felt something was wrong because he lifted his head. "Elise? Elise?"

"I'm here," Cassandra whispered and held his hand.

"What's happening?"

"It's all right." Cassandra glared at the men. "Everything's fine."

"Hey, baby girl," the taller man said, his eyes roaming up and down her body. "Why don't you leave Grandpa for an hour and come have some fun with us."

"I'm waiting for my husband." She averted her gaze to the supermarket, praying they'd keep walking.

"Hey," the guy looked back at his buddies for support, and they nodded at him to continue. He faced her from a meter away. "Leave Grandpa for a bit and come with us." He smirked, his mouth going up sideways. "You ever had three guys at once? If not, you don't know what you're missing, baby."

They moved closer, undressing her with their eyes.

Cassandra edged back behind the wheelchair, that pit in her stomach growing to fear-induced proportions.

Two of them were in their mid-twenties, and the tall speaker of the three was older. All three had the glassy-eyed look of being stoned out of their heads.

"We can feed you, too." He held up his arms. "See, we got shit to last us through this apocalypse."

How was that a negotiation?

She looked the leader in the eyes and held his gaze. "I'm

not going anywhere with you. I'm waiting for my husband. Now get lost—"

"Come on," he pleaded, his head back and tilted sideways. "Leave with us. We have beer for you, too. Since you won't be able to walk straight for a few days when you've had three guys at once, you're welcome to stay the night and go another round tomorrow." He glanced back at his buddies again, then faced her. "See? We're nice guys. Food, beer, and shelter. And a good time for everyone involved." He leaned closer and lowered his voice. "Look, it's the end of the world. Let's fuck our way off this sick planet until we can't see straight. This is a win/win situation for all of us."

Like anything he was saying would make her jump at the chance to be held down and taken by three complete strangers.

"As I said—"

"We want company," he snapped, cutting her off. "You look like you'll do just fine." The man tried to grab her arm but missed when she jerked back. "You think cops are going to come when you scream, bitch? This is the new world order —the great reset bullshit. And if we're all about to die, I'm getting my dick sucked as often as I can by whatever woman I choose. Now, you're coming with us, fuckin' cunt." He lunged at her, dropping one of his grocery bags.

Cassandra jerked back, jostling the wheelchair, when her grip tore off the handle. She searched the front of the grocery store, but there was no sign of Leo.

"Come on now, don't play hard to get. You won't like how rough we can be if you make us *take* what we want. I won't play nice, and I won't be gentle. When you bleed, that'll be your fault, whore."

Cassandra scanned the front of the market's entrance again, ready to yell for Leo, but no one was in sight.

She'd have to handle things on her own.

Which was something she didn't want to have to do.

But this was a new world.

And the man was right. The cops wouldn't be coming anytime soon.

She moved around the wheelchair and planted her feet.

The man was about to become a eunuch.

Chapter Twelve

CHIEF TAJ SHAHIDI WATCHED the crowd amassed in front of the Temple of the Dome entrance. It had grown to an insanely large and chaotic mass of heads and shoulders swaying in time with their chants, their prayers. It didn't bother the chief, though. In fact, this mass of human faithful was his preference. He wanted the chaos to show his men how things should be done to keep order. This would become a demonstration, an exercise for his men to learn from, and he relished the opportunity to teach them something valuable in real-time.

They would respect him for it, and his superiors would give him the promotion he deserved.

"Chief Shahidi." An officer rushed up on his left, wiping sweat from his face. "There seems to be a problem."

Shahidi waited several moments, then turned to the

young officer. "What problem?" He kept his tone firm. The subtext was, *This better be serious*.

"Can you come with me, please?" the officer asked, raising his voice over the crowd's din. "I've been summoned to bring you to the Fountain Stone. We think we have a break-in."

This made Shahidi blink once and turn his body to address the officer. "A break-in? How's that?"

"Sir, someone—" The officer looked around, then edged closer. "Someone broke through the wall, sir. It's a desecration. An unholy violation." The officer stepped back and composed himself, his hands fixing his shirt bottoms.

Shahidi clenched his jaw. He wasn't expecting that. The crowd, yes. Riot police. Clashes. Hundreds were beaten and jailed, sure. But outright vandalism, mischief? That wasn't supposed to be on the menu today.

This was something he'd attend to first. An example would be made of the perpetrator in front of a large crowd, and Shahidi's reign over these people would be complete without too much bloodshed.

Perhaps that was a good thing after all. It always mystified him how Allah placed things on his menu for the day. At first glance, it repulsed him, surprised him. But upon contemplation, he could now see this as another opportunity to teach his subjects further how everything got done in the old city.

He nodded at the officer, then gestured for him to lead the way. "Carry on." This time, his tone implied impatience.

Shahidi followed the officer without another word.

When they entered the Fountain Stone, Shahidi stopped

to glance around but saw no vandalism.

He was about to ask the officer if he had been joking. Did he want to lose his job? On such a day, would his men be prone to pranks?

But the officer had crossed the floor and was already descending the stairs to the Well of Souls.

So Shahidi followed without speaking a word—yet. That didn't mean his temper wasn't sparking. It would soon flare, then ignite.

Allah have mercy on those at the end of my wrath stick.

At the bottom of the stairs, he was greeted by two more officers. One of them stood over a small pile of dirt.

Shahidi glanced around the room until he saw the marble by the wall—it wasn't fully attached anymore.

"What is the meaning of this?" His voice boomed in the underground cavern-like room. "Explanations quickly."

"Sir," the officer who had summoned him said, his voice cracking on that short syllable. "Someone pried the marble back far enough to slip behind it. They broke through the wall here." He pointed.

"I can see that," he bellowed, his anger tipping over into the red. "And where is this aggressor, this *infidel*?"

The men looked from one to the other, then back to Shahidi.

"Sir," the man by the pile of dirt whispered. "We think he's still inside the wall." He pointed in the hole. "Right in there."

Shahidi waved for the men to remain quiet as he drew his weapon. Unsure what to expect behind the broken marble slab, he cautiously approached, his stomach in knots while he locked down all outward signs of nerves.

The person hiding behind the wall could be a raving fundamentalist armed with explosives. If the worst happened, he would be dead within the minute. If he didn't die, the reprimands for allowing this sort of blasphemy to such an historical monument would be handed down throughout the ranks for months for allowing this to take place while on his watch.

By allowing it, they condoned it. By condoning it, they involuntarily became accessories. And accessories before and after the crime were the same thing to Chief Shahidi. All officers assigned to this area, this monument, would be punished with extreme prejudice.

Shahidi pointed at the nearest officer and motioned for him to ease the marble slab out of the way so that Shahidi could look behind it.

The guard hesitated, staring wide-eyed at Shahidi.

When Shahidi adjusted the aim of his weapon so it was focused on the center of the officer's chest for disobeying a direct order, the man raised his hands and moved closer to the marble slab.

Shahidi redirected his barrel at the hole behind the displaced marble wall and moved beside it.

The officer placed his hands on the marble, took one last look at Shahidi, and then shifted the marble as far to the side as possible, exposing the hole behind it.

Someone had dug a hole in the thin sheet of slate directly behind the marble. Shahidi moved closer and cautiously peered inside, his free hand raised over his shoulder for quiet.

The men behind him seemed to hold their collective

breath.

In the absolute quiet of the room, he detected the sound of movement. Someone was in the hole, and they were crawling away, moving deeper inside the monument's walls.

What the hell are they doing?

He stood back up to his full height and took in the three officers watching him, then pointed at the two men who had been waiting when he arrived.

"Inside," he whispered, jabbing a finger toward the hole. "Bring me whoever is in there. I want him alive. He will be tortured and killed like vermin in front of that crowd outside." Each word secreted from his throat was coupled with heavy guttural bass. This heresy would not go unanswered. This sacrilege would come with a price too heavy for many.

But that was why Allah put it on Shahidi's menu of the day because he was the man for the job.

It was time to serve up consequences heretofore unseen.

Even though he was quite aware that both men would rather quit their jobs and rush home, their tails between their legs, the officers had to obey.

Although neither man would make it out of the Well of Souls alive if they bolted for the stairs.

It was enter the hole and find the infidel or die where they stood, and each man was quite aware of those options.

Each officer's face was bedsheet white and covered with a sheen of sweat in the underground light as they moved toward the hole.

Shahidi didn't care one bit about how they were feeling. How did the infidel get down here unseen? How could he have done such damage without detection? Even after they found him and punished him, several officers would be punished alongside the infidel for *allowing* this travesty to take place.

Guarding these monuments was a job of honor, and the officers before him knew what they had signed up for. Their holstered weapons would offer comfort and keep them safe even if they couldn't see anything in the dark.

Since they hadn't been prepared for crawling in dark holes, no one had a flashlight with them. No one could tell if the hole was safe, either—it could collapse at any time with the recent aftershocks from the earthquake.

The officer who had held the marble back leaned close and whispered, "May we have a light, sir? Your cell phone, perhaps."

Shahidi grunted, showing his annoyance, then pointed at the candles. "Use those."

Guards weren't allowed to have their cell phones while on duty, but Chief Shahidi always had his.

Candles were lit, and both men entered the hole relatively easily, then disappeared inside.

Shahidi stood back by the stairs to ensure he'd be the first one they encountered if someone came down.

Then he checked his watch. After several minutes, the shuffling sound of someone crawling came from the hole, and both officers climbed back out into the room.

They stood and brushed the dirt from their soiled uniforms.

"We found nothing, sir," one officer said, holding unlit candles in his hand.

Shahidi's finger twitched. It would be so easy to shoot them all down here and then grab a chair and wait for the infidel to climb out before killing him, too.

He inhaled, wondering how that calmed people. Then he asked Allah for patience.

"Must I do everything myself?" he whispered. "Incompetents besiege me. When I enter that hole and retrieve the infidel myself, leave your badge and gun, strip out of those uniforms, and run from this place naked. If I lay eyes upon you when I return, your families will have funeral expenses to deal with this week."

Shahidi ignored the pale-stricken faces of the three officers as he strode to the hole. He holstered his weapon, leaned down, and crawled inside. Crouched on his hands and knees, he retrieved his cell phone and flicked on the flashlight app to examine the interior around him.

"Sir," one of the guards shouted from behind him before he had moved a meter. "Sir, it appears ready to collapse." The guard's tone was so frantic that Shahidi listened to him.

Chief Shahidi stared at the length of the tunnel—or as far as his cell phone's light penetrated—and saw no one. He edged back out into the Well of the Souls room, cursing under his breath.

Someone would pay for this.

Heads were going to roll, and he was only getting started.

"Guard this hole. No one in or out. I will return."

Then Chief Shahidi stomped out of the Well of Souls, rock dust billowing off his uniform as he ascended the stairs.

Chapter Thirteen

LEO ENTERED THE GROCERY store, pushing hard to get past several looters on their way out.

Once inside, panic filled the corridors. Down one aisle, two men fought over a box of milk. There were children, teenagers, and adults—everyone with their own needs, all grabbing at the same stuff and fighting anyone who challenged them when it appeared that there was still plenty to choose from on the shelves.

Compassion had vanished. It had been swallowed by chaos.

Leo ran along the ends of the aisles, then chose one and turned left.

A large man kicked a woman on the floor by the canned fruit section. The desire to be a hero was at an all-time low, even though he should help the woman. Under other circumstances, he would've helped her. But times had changed, and the only woman he was looking out for at the moment was Cassandra.

So, Leo looked for his own canned food and ignored the fight a few meters away.

He grabbed two beans and a large can of soup, then moved closer to the display case as a man ran up the aisle behind him.

"Get the fuck out of the way," the man shouted.

Leo had already pressed himself up against the display to give the guy some room, but if that wasn't good enough, *fuck* him.

He spun around with the can of soup raised like a weapon to see a security guard stopped in the aisle, his hands raised. He waved at Leo to move aside, then peered over Leo's shoulder.

Leo swung his gaze the other way and saw the man who had been fighting with the woman.

He was holding a large knife in his hand now, the woman whimpering and bloodied at his feet.

"I'm taking what's mine," the man said, cutting the air with little jabbing motions of the knife.

"Drop the shit and get out," the guard said, then looked at Leo. "That goes for you, too."

The man moved toward the guard, the knife leading the way. "Try and stop me, asshole."

Leo needed to leave. He had what he came for.

The man with the knife lowered his torso and bent his arms, looking prepared to fight.

The guard saw the man's posture and put his hand in his

pocket as if he had a weapon.

"The cops are coming," the guard said. "Last chance. Drop the shit and run. You might be able to avoid spending the night in a holding cell."

"How about you just fuck off and leave me alone."

"Sorry, man, can't do that."

Onlookers filled the end of the aisle now.

"Get on with it," one shouted. "Fight!"

Leo wanted out, so he hunched his shoulders and moved toward the guard, hoping he could walk right by him and out through the broken front window.

He didn't get two steps before an arm wrapped around his neck, and the guy with the knife yanked him back so hard he was lifted off his feet.

The cold blade of the knife pressed up to the flesh of his neck.

"Step aside, or I'll kill this fucker," the man screamed in Leo's ear.

"Hey," Leo said, his hands dropping the canned loot he'd been holding and clinging onto the guy's forearm at his neck. "Take it easy," he mumbled.

The guard straightened and shook his head, his hands extended outward. "Yes, take it easy. No one has to die over canned food. Let the man go, and we'll all leave quietly." The guard backed up farther. "You can have whatever you want. I won't stop you. Just let that man go."

"Ah, come on, man," someone shouted at the end of the aisle. The person actually sounded dejected. "We want to see some blood. Cut him, cut him."

"Fuck you," Leo shouted at the people taking up the

chant.

The man jerked back on Leo's neck, making him panic that he was about to get his throat sliced.

"You think I'm an idiot?" Knife Man yelled at the guard. "Disappear. Get lost. Or this guy dies right now."

The guard's face had flushed from the pressure as he backed up the aisle, hands out in front of him.

"Okay, I'm leaving."

Leo remained patient, eyes on the guard, waiting for this to end so he could leave.

What would happen to Cassandra if he got killed by some crazy looter?

The guard had reached the end of the aisle. He moved off to the left and disappeared from view.

The guy dragged Leo toward the same end of the aisle the guard had just disappeared from, then shoved Leo to the side so hard that he smashed into the shelves and dropped to the store's floor.

The man with the knife ran around the corner, screaming like a maniac.

What the hell? The guard was letting him go.

Leo leaned around the corner and saw the guard raise his hands in defense, but it was no match for the knife as it cut through his uniform shirt and entered his chest. The guard's eyes widened with fright and surprise as he stumbled back.

The man yanked out the knife, then shoved it in again. Then, once more. Blood spurted from the deep punctures.

Then the guard's legs buckled, and he dropped, blood covering his white shirt in seconds. The man pounced on him, plunging the knife into his abdomen repeatedly.

"You shouldn't have tried to stop me," the man with the knife shouted.

Leo got to his feet and moved closer, his mind reeling at the sight before him.

A sudden urge to save the guard overwhelmed him, even though he knew it was too late. The knife had done too much damage to save the man. The guard was literally on his last few breaths.

Rage surged through Leo at the injustice of it all.

Without putting much thought behind his actions, he jumped on the man who was still stabbing the guard.

Leo's weight knocked the man off balance enough that he could grab at the hand holding the knife. He twisted it upward until the man screamed and dropped it. The knife clattered to the floor beside them.

Leo braced his feet on a rack of pasta and shoved. The man collided with the shelving unit on the other side of the aisle, knocked it over, and fell to the floor on the other side.

"Kill him!" someone shouted from behind.

Leo dove at the man on the ground, driving several fists into his face. The security guard killer seemed defenseless as Leo drove punch after punch into the man's now swollen and bleeding cheeks.

So fixated on hitting the guy and releasing his pent-up anger, Leo hadn't noticed the piece of broken glass the guy had managed to grab. When the man lifted it and swung in a lazy attempt at cutting Leo, he batted it from the man's hand, snatched it off the ground, and shoved it into the killer's throat.

The man's eyes widened as blood spurted like a fountain

from his ruptured neck. It quickly covered the man's hands, cheeks, shirt, and the floor around his head.

"Holy shit, man," a tall guy said from over his shoulder. "What the fuck, dude? You fuckin' killed the guy."

Leo pushed up off the floor as the man died, choking on the blood in his torn throat.

"You're in big trouble, mister," the man added.

Leo removed his shirt, wiped himself with it as best he could, and headed for the exit. No one tried to stop him. They were just a couple of looters fighting.

He spied a rack of designer T-shirts near the checkout tills, so he snatched one and slipped into it before crawling through the broken glass.

Then he grabbed what he could carry from a rack at the front of the store and ran outside.

He didn't see Cassandra right away. When he scanned the area where he'd left her, he saw Vincent in the wheelchair on his own.

Where the hell did she go?

Farther to the left, a woman struggled as a couple of men dragged her along the ground behind them.

What the fuck?

Cassandra kicked out, and one man shrieked as he clutched at his groin.

Leo ran toward them as Cassandra shouted, "Don't like being hit by a girl?"

They released her, and she pushed up to her feet, wobbling once, then raised her hands to fight.

"Come on," she shouted. "You want to fuck me? You have to fight me first."

Leo picked up his pace until he was sprinting now.

"Hey," he shouted. "Fight me. Come on, fight me." He dropped the meager food samplings he'd been able to snatch at his feet, then raised his bloodied hands.

The taller man lunged at Leo, caught him around the waist, and they dropped to the ground.

Leo twisted and writhed under the man until he slipped out the side and looped around him. Leo was on top now, slamming his elbow into the side of the man's head. After four solid hits, the man's eyes closed, and his body went limp.

Cassandra ran at Leo and grabbed his arm. "Come on. He isn't worth it. Don't kill him."

But Leo was drunk with rage now. Something urged him to kill the man and end his life on the concrete outside the supermarket. One less piece of shit in the world. He'd killed before—not just the guy in the grocery store moments before—and something deliriously powerful drew him to do it again.

Cassandra held his arm, restraining it in the air.

When Leo glanced up, the man's friend was watching, his face a mask of shock.

Cassandra followed Leo's gaze.

"What are you looking at?" she yelled at the man. "Disappear or die. Totally up to you."

As if her words held some magic potion, the man bolted, taking his other friend with him.

Leo got to his feet and looked down at what he had done. The man bled from his nose, mouth, and left eye, where it looked like the orbital bone had broken. He was damaged in a brutal way that would take months in a hospital if he survived.

"Leo, let's go," Cassandra whispered in his ear. "People have gone crazy."

"Where? Go where?"

"A cave, a castle, I don't care. Just somewhere far from here. We can still try for the hospital because maybe Vincent's Elise is there."

"Yeah." Leo nodded like he was in a daze. "Let's go there. Drop off, Vincent. I'm done listening to his ramblings."

Leo got up and walked over to the wheelchair. He grabbed the handles and pushed Vincent toward the road.

Behind him, he heard Cassandra picking up some of the food those men had dropped.

Good. When his anger subsided, he'd need to eat.

***

Cassandra was starving. She opened a can and ate tuna with her fingers. Even though Vincent had no eyes, he watched her every bite. He raised a hand without saying a word, and she gave him a can.

Leo stopped and took a can, too.

Smoke now rose from the supermarket one city block behind them. People rushed outside, yelling that a fire had started.

"What the fuck did you do?" Cassandra asked Leo, staring at him.

He shrugged. "Nothing, the place was fucked."

"We should help them."

Leo grabbed her hand and held it firm. "Do you think these people give a fuck about you? Would they help you?"

"This isn't about them. It's about me and my conscience." She yanked her hand out of his.

"If you go to help those strangers, I won't watch out for the old man. I'll leave him in the street. If he gets hurt, it's on you." Leo glared at her. "Don't go help anyone. Help yourself. Help us."

Cassandra took a deep breath, then turned her back to the supermarket. "Where's the water? I'm thirsty."

"Sorry, pumpkin," Leo said with a fake smile. He never called her that before.

"We need water," Cassandra said. "And we need to find that damned hospital."

Vincent coughed. She couldn't tell whether it was from the smoke or the ashes in the air. Maybe he had a cold, and some of the meds were for that.

Leo nodded. "I agree. We need to keep moving." He wiped his hands on his pants like something bothered him.

Cassandra grabbed the wheelchair, and the trio moved again, not knowing what they were walking into.

Chapter Fourteen

THE AFTERNOON CAME, AND with it, a sense of gloom.

Cassandra watched as the black ash approached the buildings in this part of town, still lowering by the hour. What would happen when it reached them? Would they be able to breathe through it? Would everyone suffocate?

It hovered about six to eight meters above their heads on several elevated streets. People living in higher-level apartments were coming out into the streets as it coated their windows and likely made breathing hard.

Every road they lumbered along was full of abandoned cars and people wandering about.

Some people were more organized as they carried backpacks full of supplies from their homes as they headed out of the city on foot, while others were asking for help, wandering back and forth, unkempt and unsure what to do.

Common questions Cassandra had heard over the past hour were, "What's going on?" "Where are emergency services?" "Were we attacked?"

After several hours of walking and negotiating the wheelchair through piles of debris, the trio managed to get to the hospital parking lot.

Even though it wasn't a hot day, it felt oppressively so with that descending black cloud keeping all the heat in. Or perhaps it was working like some sort of magnifying glass and intensifying the sun's warmth. Cassandra didn't know, but if they hadn't stopped in front of the hospital when they did, she'd have had to remove some clothing to cool off.

The plan to leave Vincent in the hospital's care quickly dissolved as they neared the emergency area doors. People milled about, looking through the glass, hands cupped at the sides of their faces. Others chatted at the side.

During the entire walk up to the glass doors, no one entered or exited the building.

Then she saw why when she tried the doors.

The hospital was locked from the inside. Someone had taped a piece of paper with large letters on the glass. It stated, "NO MORE ROOM HERE. PLEASE LEAVE."

Cassandra glanced inside to see just how busy they were. Several men in civilian clothes stood guard at the door so they'd encounter resistance right away, even if someone managed to break the glass.

Behind those men, a massive queue of wounded people lined up, waiting to be seen by someone. People leaned against walls to maintain their balance. While some were seated, others were still lying on the floor.

"When a hospital is closed," Cassandra muttered in frustration, "things are worse than we can imagine."

Leo stepped up beside her and glanced through the window. "We have to leave Vincent somewhere else, then."

"Any ideas on where?"

They stared at each other for a moment. Cassandra was familiar with the city of Lausanne but couldn't think of anywhere to leave Vincent where he'd get the care he needed —at least nowhere in walking distance.

"We need water," she said, looking back at Vincent. "Leo, he has to take his medicine."

When he didn't respond, she looked over at him.

He nodded. "Fine. Let's go to the first house we see. Someone will give us water for the old man."

Cassandra nodded.

"We have nothing to lose," Leo added, starting off.

They crossed the street and rang the doorbell of the first house. After ringing bells and banging on the doors of several houses with no answer, they decided to move away from the center of town. It had become a vast wasteland of danger. They would walk more sparsely populated areas. Maybe they'd locate a hose outside a house to drink from.

Exhausted from their ordeal, they trudged along in silence now. To some degree, Cassandra was used to this life. She would typically walk the streets silently all day, searching for water or food.

She thought of her parents and wondered how they'd handle this situation if they hadn't died in that car accident that took them from her. They'd rammed into a tree at high speed, their deaths instantaneous.

At least, that was a blessing. One of the investigating officers told her to die so quickly was to feel no pain.

The funeral was held with closed coffins. Nevertheless, she wanted to see them to say a proper goodbye. After the service, she remained behind and wept, her hands on their caskets.

Then, when she was alone, Cassandra opened the lid on her mother's coffin and gawked at her remains.

She realized she shouldn't have done it the moment she laid eyes on her. There was no reason to see their broken skulls and crushed faces to say goodbye.

She spent ten days in the hospital on meds to help deal with the haunting images in her mind after that. She recalled almost nothing from those ten days. Sometimes, faint memories in her subconscious came up in her dreams, roaming around against her will. A nurse is talking to her, but Cassandra does not hear a sound. Her parents are dead. Leo, who she'd met just days earlier, was absent.

So many bad memories from those days. And only a short time before, she'd been in the hospital to have her tonsils removed. That was about a year ago.

She blinked rapidly and came back to the here and now. Stopped by the side of the road, leaning on the hood of a car, she watched Leo as he stared back at her over the sleeping form of Vincent in his chair.

They couldn't find anyone to open their door in the chaos and paranoia the world had surrendered to.

Leo pointed down the street, and Cassandra followed his finger.

A small mini-market.

She smiled at him and nodded, then headed that way.

Leo pushed the wheelchair toward it, and they met out front.

Without a word, Leo tried the doors, but they were locked. He banged on the glass, but no one answered.

Leo glanced around conspiratorially. "This place seems like a great opportunity for us." He looked above them. "That shit is getting closer, and night is coming soon."

Cassandra watched the people wandering around over a block away. Many of them looked up at the black dust as it descended even closer to the ground. By her estimation, it would be two meters off the ground within an hour—which was head level for most adults—suffocating them all.

Not waiting for Leo to decide, Cassandra picked up a chunk of concrete that had fallen from the side of the building and flung it at the glass door.

It cracked the glass, then dropped to the walkway.

The door remained intact.

Leo held up a hand, then moved to a side window and kicked a hole in the glass.

Cassandra checked people in the vicinity again, but no one paid them much attention. That black shit in the air was moving even closer.

Leo worked the hole until it was large enough to roll the wheelchair inside. Then he rolled it in, ducked under the hole's upper part, and waited on the other side for Cassandra.

After one more check of their surroundings, she bent over and entered the store.

Once inside, Leo shoved a shelf in front of the broken glass, hoping to prevent others from entering.

They rushed straight to a refrigerated unit by the front tills and grabbed water bottles. She was so thirsty she guzzled an entire bottle, spilling water out the sides of her mouth. Leo did the same.

When Cassandra calmed down and caught her breath, she grabbed another bottle and placed it in Vincent's hands. Gingerly, he lifted the bottle and drank from it. Then she fished out some of his meds, which he took reluctantly, pushing her hand away several times.

She had to guess the dosage, so she made it random. One pill from every bottle. She also took a packaged sandwich from the refrigerator and handed it to him.

Leo was already eating whatever he could find in the fridge while watching the front of the store through the window.

Vincent held the sandwich, but he wasn't eating it.

"Please, Vincent," Cassandra said, leaning close to his ear in the hopes he could hear her. "Don't give up on us now. Everything will be fine. We'll find Elise, too. But please, you have to try and eat something."

"I won't last that long," he muttered in a moment of clarity.

"Please don't say that."

"Elise is dead. I will be dead, too, by nightfall. Only then will I be free of my meat suit and ensnared mind."

"Elise is fine," Cassandra said, trying to give him hope, even though she had no idea. "We just haven't found her yet."

"He wants to die," Leo said.

Cassandra looked up at him, shocked at his callousness.

Leo shrugged under the scrutiny of her harsh glare.

"Why have we gone out of our way to drag him all over town anyway?"

"Shut up," she whispered to Leo. "That's not fair. He has feelings, you know." She refocused on Vincent, taking a deep breath. "What makes you think you'll be dead by nightfall?"

"You saw Elise, didn't you?" Vincent paused, his empty eyes aimed at Leo. "I'm right, aren't I?"

"How were you right, Grandpa?" Leo said sarcastically. "You don't know shit about me."

Vincent searched for Cassandra's hand. "I don't want them to take me. I *can't* let them take me."

"It's okay. They won't take you. We won't let them." She had no idea who *they* were.

"I need to write something down."

"No," Leo said from the front window. "Don't write shit down."

"Leo!" Cassandra whispered harshly. "What's gotten into you."

He turned away, his jaw muscles flexing.

She stared at him a moment longer, then moved down a small stationery aisle and found a notebook and a pen. When she walked back to Vincent and gave them to him, he began to scribble something with a trembling hand, making sure the letters were as legible as possible.

Leo signaled for Cassandra to come to him.

When she got close enough, he whispered, "Something's wrong."

Ready to keep the peace and not be angry at him, she nodded once, then said, "I'm feeling that, too."

She eased into his arms, smelled his neck, and felt a moment's comfort. She closed her eyes and inhaled his scent.

For that brief moment, she found peace.

Then Leo shoved her away from him so violently she lost her balance, arms akimbo, and bumped into a display rack, which kept her on her feet.

Everything happened in slow motion after that. She jerked around to see what Leo was doing and saw the blood from Vincent's neck spurting outward, covering his shoulder.

The old man had jammed the pen into the side of his neck twice, hitting a main artery.

Even though Leo had jumped into action, it was too late to stop him.

Blood flowed like a fountain and dyed the vegetable and fruit display red.

Leo had snatched the pen from Vincent's grip, but the damage was done.

Cassandra stumbled in shock at the images before her while frantically searching for something to staunch the blood flow. She found a long cloth under the counter by the cash register and ran over to apply it to Vincent's neck. She could wrap it around several times, but it soaked through instantly. The blood flowed past his collarbone and into his shirt, the man's head already dangling from chin to chest.

"Leave him," Leo said, his tone cold. "He knew what he was doing, what he wanted. Let him rest, the sick fuck."

She gawked at him. "I can't believe you just said that. He needed treatment, psychological support, not suicide." Tears ran down her cheeks as she turned her attention back to the man in the wheelchair. "Vincent, don't die on me now. Are you listening?"

But Vincent was already gone.

Cassandra leaned over him and beat his chest under some daft illusion she could restart his heart.

Leo pushed her away from the dead man.

"I shouldn't have taken him from his home," she wailed. "I shouldn't have given him the pen. I did that. Me! I killed him."

Leo wrapped his arms around her when she shouted those last words to calm her down.

"Come on, it's over. He did what he wanted."

"But how can you say that? He didn't know what he wanted. He was a sick man."

She shuddered as she looked at the lifeless body leaning sideways in the wheelchair. The note he was supposed to write rested on his knees. Blood had splattered onto it, leaving the short sentence mostly unreadable except for three words.

"LOOK FOR ME," it said.

"Look for me." She read this phrase aloud and then sobbed.

Leo watched her for a long moment, then slipped a hand in his pocket and retrieved a small bag of weed.

"Here," he held out the bag. "You need it more than I do right now."

"Keep it. I don't do drugs." She watched him, her eyes wet.

"Come on. We both need a puff to take off the edge. You'll feel better. Trust me." He lowered to the floor to sit a few meters from the dead man in the chair and lit the joint.

As if her body had a will of its own, she moved over and sat next to him, then stared back at Vincent's body.

After three puffs, she was already relaxing. How could Leo keep his composure? He seemed so insensitive, too. It was a side of him she'd never seen before. She wondered what his childhood was like. What traumas he'd faced in the past. They'd never been close to enough to go too deep.

"Do you remember when we met?" Leo spoke softly, breaking the silence.

"What?"

"That time you left your house. When we met, remember?"

"Yes. How could I forget?"

"Remember how we talked all night, and I gave you shots to drink?"

"I didn't drink everything." She smiled, then let the smoke drift from her lips. "I was throwing them next to me."

"So, when we had sex on the bar's counter, you weren't drunk?"

"Of course not. I have to be in control. I knew exactly what I was doing every second."

She leaned back, smoked, and forgot everything for a few moments. When she looked over at Vincent, shame set in. They'd done this. They'd allowed a mentally ill person the chance to kill himself. *She* did this. *She* handed him the pen.

Leo kissed her on the cheek.

She yanked away. "What the fuck? What was that for?"

He moved into her space and kissed her more passionately, violently.

She pulled away, pushing him back. Relaxed, sure, but she was nowhere near being horny.

"I can't do this right now. I want to go home, any home." Her shoulders hitched with the beginnings of sobs. "Just don't touch me like that. Not right now."

"Home?" He laughed. "Since when do you have a home?"

She shrugged, not wanting to admit that her feelings were hurt. "I want to go back to the days when we first met when I escaped from my hellhole life to meet you."

"Do you remember that one time we fought, and I tried to climb the tree to get to your bedroom window and that the branch broke off with me on it?"

Leo laughed, shaking his head back and forth while staring at the joint in his hand.

He took another drag on it while Cassandra stole another glance at Vincent. She had forgotten what it was like to be as carefree as Leo was.

A man killed himself violently two meters away from them not ten minutes ago, and Leo wanted to fuck.

There was something mentally challenging about that. Something she couldn't quite grasp at the moment.

"Babe, we have to get out of here," he said.

A scream rent the silence from the front of the store.

Startled by the scream, Cassandra got up and moved closer to the window.

"Stay away from the window," he shouted at her. "Are you crazy? You'll make yourself a target for whatever's out there."

She dropped below the window sill and glanced back at

him. "We have to see what's happening."

"No, I'll go and see and then tell you what's happening. Meanwhile, you stay safe. I can't have anything happen to you. You're too valuable."

She scrunched up her face. "People could be hurt. I don't always need protection. Someone may need our help."

Leo moved to a section of the window five meters to her right.

"The world is fucked, Cassandra. You have to stay safe and away from the shit out there to stay alive."

"Then call me crazy," she snapped at him and pushed the shelf blocking the broken window access they'd used to enter the mini-market.

A sense of danger rippled over her skin. It was in the air she breathed. People ran to save themselves from something outside. Someone howled in pain. Another person shouted something unintelligible.

The sun had lowered enough that they couldn't see the street too well, and the streetlights were out as the city didn't have electricity on yet.

Leo was beside her now. "Let me go out and have a look."

Cassandra stepped aside, and Leo eased the shelf out of the way. There was just enough room for him to crawl through the broken window without getting cut.

When Cassandra's eyes adjusted to the darkness outside, she reared back in fright.

That black dust was on the street level now.

It was moving in fits and starts, jerking to and fro. It had a form, too, an odd shape.

She blinked, unsure of what she was seeing.

Hundreds of shapes that resembled human figures were made up of millions of tiny black insects, and they were rushing toward people who ran in panic to escape the coalescing forms—or whatever they were.

She watched, clutching at Leo's arm, as the dark mass reached a tall, thin man ten meters away.

The form dissolved into a torrent of blackness, like a swarm of tiny gnats, entering through the man's eyes and mouth. The victim's scream was cut short as he was lifted a foot off the ground at the mercy of those black gnats.

Then, as abruptly as he was taken, he dropped to his knees and stretched out his arms, making spastic movements as if he couldn't breathe. The man's mouth opened as wide as it could as spheres of light rose from his throat, trapped in the black insect-like swarm's grip, the light rising toward the darkened sky. When the swarm was done with the man, and the light oozing from his throat dimmed, then died, those black gnats exited his body and flew off, likely searching for another victim.

Left soulless like a discarded shell, the man's body collapsed to the pavement, a husk of his former self.

Cassandra, unable to control herself, released an utterance of despair. Then she screamed as some form of madness enveloped her consciousness.

But those black insects could smell her fear, hear her anguish, and they adjusted their flight, spinning toward the front of the mini-market with great speed.

Her heart raced, and her legs weakened with nerves and adrenaline rush. She clutched the shelf and attempted to seal the hole in the glass window.

The black swarm rose in front of her face, ready to enter her gaping mouth and her wide-open eyes.

Something smashed into her on the last scream she'd ever utter, and she launched sideways.

Leo had shoved her away.

"Run," he screamed at her.

That one word shouted for her benefit was what killed him.

With Leo's mouth open wide, the insect swarm entered him at the end of that single, short syllable.

The horror of the moment consumed her.

Leo stood one meter away, his body convulsing as the swarm overtook him, with the guarantee that Cassandra would be next.

Someone was screaming. It took her a long moment to realize she was making that noise.

She scrambled to her feet as Leo jerked violently, tiny lights emitting from his throat.

She had to find a place to hide, but how could someone hide from a mass that floated and soared at will?

Certain her death was seconds away, Cassandra clambered to her feet and ran down the length of an aisle. Because it was a mini-market, the aisles were shorter than in regular grocery stores.

When she spun around to look back down the length of the aisle, the insects were finished with Leo. His body had crumpled to the floor, and the gnats now hovered above him —staring at her.

That was the only way she could describe it. Like the

thing had eyes, and it was watching her. But it had no eyes, no face. Yet it was an intelligent being—that she could tell. It moved with purpose, knowing what it wanted and how to get it—unobstructed.

She was as good as dead.

Like a stone propelled from a slingshot, the swarm exploded toward her.

Cassandra screamed again and ran for the back of the store in search of an exit.

One glance over her shoulder told her that wouldn't be happening.

The swarm was much too fast.

It was almost on her.

She looked right, then left, and saw a thick glass door. She dove at it and ripped it open. Emergency lighting revealed a room filled with milk and juice boxes.

A storage refrigerator for the mini-market's beverages.

Fear fueling her tired muscles, she shouldered the refrigerator door closed. The door clicked shut and sealed airtight, the thumb bolt clicking a millisecond before the swarm entered.

The insects gathered into human form and hit the glass as a unit.

Cassandra screamed at it, feeling her mind slipping.

The human form on the other side of the glass copied her expression of fear by forming dozens of tiny screaming faces.

Cassandra stopped screaming, as did the swarm.

It couldn't get in. Whatever *it* was, the thing was frustrated that it couldn't get to her.

She moved to the glass and pressed her nose to it. There

was just enough light for her to see the tiny black grains move left and right, taking whatever shape they desired.

Struck by the unreality of what she was watching, Cassandra remained motionless against the glass door, watching as the swarm looked back at her like it was waiting for something to happen. She was crammed into the cold room because, unfortunately for her, it felt like the store had a generator attached to its refrigerators.

She moved away from the glass as she shivered. There was no way she was leaving this fridge. She'd rather freeze to death than have that swarm enter her face.

Eventually, the swarm outside the glass door dissipated and floated away in pieces until nothing remained.

She waited, though.

Hours passed, and she got colder.

The one upside was—a small consolation afforded her—that it was a fridge instead of a freezer. Sure, the temperature was cold, but it wasn't below freezing. Otherwise, the juices and milk would freeze.

The urge to close her eyes and sleep for a short bit overcame her, and for a brief time, she did sleep. Curled up in the corner of the fridge, she tried to retain her body heat.

She dreamt of Vincent. He stood over her, seemingly healthy and able to walk.

He grabbed at her arms, shouting, "Wake up! Wake up now!"

But Cassandra kept dreaming.

And sleeping …

Chapter Fifteen

Mujtaba was still stuck.

Perhaps that was a blessing, though.

Soon, the men in the tunnel searching for him would discover his feet first, then yank him out roughly, and his mission would end abruptly. He'd be jailed and flogged, or whatever punishment they deemed appropriate for the desecration of the religious monument, and his delusion that Allah had sent him on a mission would die with him.

But that didn't happen.

Not yet, anyway.

His body got wedged into the cave—a claustrophobic nightmare—the candle's light he held couldn't be seen on their side of the tunnel. That afforded him some time due to his light not acting as a beacon on his pursuer's side.

Not only that, but the men searching for him sounded

like they gave up before expending the effort to get as far as he crawled.

Breathing in short gasps, happy his flame was still lit because that meant there was ample oxygen this far into the cave, Mujtaba gave up on the officers doing their jobs and pushed himself backward inch by inch until he could sit up.

The air seemed thin, though. It made him gasp for breaths. Staying hidden within the cave for any length of time wasn't an option.

Was his search over? Because when he crawled out of the hole, security personnel would be waiting for him—which meant he would be arrested immediately.

Could this have been a colossal waste of time? Did Allah send him on a fruitless errand? Was he to stew over his regrets on how he could have done things differently while lingering in a dirty jail somewhere?

It couldn't end like this. He refused to believe this was the purpose all along. But what other options were there?

He blew out the candle, closed his eyes, rested his head back against the wall, and then waited for something and nothing to happen—there wasn't anything else he could do.

A scurrying sound came from the cave floor to his left. He opened his eyes but couldn't see a thing in the inky blackness.

He smacked his head against the rock wall—the sound it made—a hollow wood thump, surprised him.

His heart beat faster in his chest, his eyes wide open, and he saw nothing as he wondered if another opening was behind him.

Mujtaba spun around and ran his hands over the wall's

surface, searching for weaknesses. Did someone use papier-mâché to cover the wood to make it look like stone? If so, why would they do that so deep in a cave? It didn't make sense—he stopped moving.

Unless there was another branch of the cave, they sealed off. A branch that *hid* something.

Kicking the thin wall covering aside would cause too much noise, so he felt along the wall for a spot where he could grab onto something and tear at it.

More voices came from the opening at the Well of Souls room again. More guards had likely assembled, searching for the man who had ruined the monument.

This meant they'd climb farther and work harder to reach him. Time was sifting through the hourglass, his liberty at stake.

If he would get through this section of the wall, it had to be now.

Fists hardened by determination and will, he pounded at the false front regardless of the noise, then pried at the thin strips of wood making up the artificial wall with the strength Allah provided.

And he was rewarded.

The wood in this cave section had been warped and weakened by moisture. He was able to snap it back and remove several pieces in seconds.

Without thinking about where the new opening led, Mujtaba climbed through as shouting erupted down the length of the cave. Someone was quite angry that Mujtaba was getting away.

He dropped a few feet on the other side of the broken

wall, then got to his hands and knees. It was still as dark as the cave, but the area seemed much more expansive, taller. He got up slowly, not knowing the height of the new space he inhabited. The candle would help, but he'd set it down in the cave and had no way to light it again.

Surprisingly, he was able to stand completely upright without banging his head. He lifted his hands over his head but only felt the air. On either side, there were no walls—just emptiness.

It gave him a sense of what the blind had to deal with day in and day out. He literally had no idea if there was solid ground in front of him or a hundred-foot drop into an old well.

He stepped forward anyway, taking small steps, hoping to eventually find a way out of this new tunnel—or whatever it was. To turn back meant a prison term awaited him.

A cold sweat formed on his forehead and under his armpits. Even his legs trembled under the stress of edging forward in such a blind fashion.

His tolerance of the darkness thinned, but he had no other option than one step at a time. Eventually, he would reach a wall or an exit—he hoped.

There had to be a reason for this room. Whoever placed that faux wall on the side of the cave knew of its existence. But what was its purpose?

Wait, what if there was no exit from this room? They could've covered it up as well. This meant he'd remain trapped until he crawled back into the cave or died.

After what seemed like five minutes but was probably less, he encountered a wall. He groped the surface and found a wooden area like the one in the cave wall.

When he knocked on it, the sound changed in the area below his knees. He breathed a sigh of relief as hope diminished fear. This had to be a way out.

He kicked at the wood, punched it, and threw his weight into it, but it wouldn't budge. Panic set in again at the thought that he'd be stuck down here where he'd starve to death and eventually be crushed during some cave-in event.

After trying everything to budge the wood, he roamed his fingers along with it, searching for a seam or a lip of some kind.

There was a flat ridge along the top. With his fingers pushed to the back of that ridge, he pulled toward him to pry it from the wall.

He was rewarded with a popping sound.

Then the wood pried back, and he saw it for what it was —a cupboard door. The popping sound was the small catch releasing.

Tiny shafts of light illuminated the room beyond, just enough that he could see the cupboard opened into a small box-like enclosure. He crawled through, then laid out flat and stretched his arms to open the top.

After being in the dark for so long, the wash of light forced him to close his eyes. He blinked away the brightness, forcing his eyes open again to get his bearings.

Candles were lined in a neat row above his head, and next to him was a red cloth with Greek letters. A triangle with a Christian painting of the resurrected Christ was in the middle of the fabric. The material rested on a marble slab with candles lining both sides and a fresh bouquet. There were images of the resurrection and Christ to the left and right.

He was in a church of some kind.

Mujtaba pushed up and crawled out of the box, his hands trembling, elbows and knees weakened by the ordeal he'd just endured.

He'd landed in a Christian monument of some kind, but at least that cave of certain death was behind him now.

He glanced around, and after not seeing a single person, he moved silently to the next room.

With the map of Jerusalem in his mind and the interior of this church being Christian, he estimated he was in the Resurrection Church or the Church of the Holy Sepulcher. It was the only Christian site close enough to the Dome of the Rock to be connected underground. This placed him in the center of the Christian faith—the tomb of Jesus.

If he recalled correctly, it was consecrated somewhere in the early 300s A.D.

He ducked when voices reverberated off the massive walls, moving closer. It was difficult to determine if they were outside the temple or inside.

How could a dark-skinned Islamist get out of Jesus' tomb without being noticed?

It seemed Allah was thrilled with throwing him test after test.

The voices were closer still, so he ran for the large, red curtain suspended near the back, having no idea what lay behind it.

When he pulled it back, Mujtaba was amazed to see such opulent artwork. The hallway beyond the curtain had a large chandelier hanging over a spot cordoned off with red ropes—access was strictly forbidden.

He admired the paintings around him, mouth open in amazement. In the church's raised dome, a large painting of Christ gave him chills. Even though he had little to do with Christianity, being faithful to Allah made him experience awe at the sight before him. How could he not have reverence for a place so important to millions of people worldwide?

Peeling his eyes from the glorious visions of Jesus, he turned back the way he came. He must locate an exit and get outside without bumping into anyone.

Where was everyone, though?

He moved to the right and saw the supposed tomb of Joseph. Without realizing it, while trying to escape the building, he'd circled the center and stopped by a wooden door on a side wall where several bags were piled haphazardly.

Maybe they'd organized a charity event of some kind. It would be just his luck if those bags were filled with clothes. Using the police uniform to gain access to the holy sites worked, but now he didn't need it to exit—he wanted to be rid of it. Questions would be raised, and if he were ever stopped and asked for ID, his cover would be blown, his escape for naught.

So he ran for the bags and tore them open. Sure enough, they were filled with clothes.

Allah saved him yet again. Allah be praised.

He found something that would fit him and quickly changed into a T-shirt and shorts. Before throwing away the police clothes, he checked the pockets and found a gold ornament. With great care, he held it up to admire it. Such a stunning piece was sent to him directly from Allah. He could've attacked any random officer, but he didn't. He took the clothes of the one guard who had such a piece of jewelry on him that would beguile any man's eye. As if it would break into a thousand pieces, he placed it gently in the pocket of his new shorts.

Then he stuffed the police clothes in the bag and tied the top before heading toward the exit sign on the sidewall.

Careful not to rush outside into a melee, he checked the window beside the door. Crowds of Christians fought to enter the church in fear of that black dust floating much lower now. Even the sun had descended in the sky as nightfall would be soon.

Then what?

As far as his eye could see, there was a human wave of people moving like a breeze, fighting to enter any building to escape that hovering blackness.

The wooden doors to Mujtaba's left were closed and firmly secured by thick chunks of wood laid across their center.

He glanced back outside, searching for a police force, but saw no such uniforms.

Why was the door locked? The temple was so large it could accommodate all these people in peace.

The voices came to him again.

Mujtaba spun around and saw several men of the cloth staring out another window by two massive wooden doors.

They hadn't noticed him yet, which would normally be a blessing, but his desire to learn why they weren't letting the faithful inside the church for some form of protection, however rudimentary, drove him to put one foot in front of the other in search of answers.

When he neared their position, he chose the man who had the darkest skin in case he spoke Arabic.

"As-salaam Alaikum," he said in the formal way of greeting another Muslim, which really meant, *Peace be upon you.*

The man looked at him with a puzzled expression on his face.

When he didn't respond, Mujtaba continued in Arabic. "What's going on here? Why's the door closed?"

"How do you not know?" the man said in perfect Arabic. "Muslims, not Christians, hold the keys to the temple." The man glanced out the window and pointed at something. "Do you see the ladder those elders are holding?" He glanced back at Mujtaba. "As soon as the keyholder arrives, they take it out of that small window and unlock the church. At night, they lock it and give the key back. The door regularly opens at four in the morning, but no one has appeared to open it for us today, and now it's dusk. We are still waiting."

After accessing the Well of the Souls, crawling through that cave and resting, and then accessing the separate tunnel, Mujtaba had lost any sense of time. How many hours had he been lingering in the tunnel?

"With so many people outside waiting to enter," the man continued, his gaze fixed on the people outside, "we are afraid we will be trampled." He stopped talking and faced Mujtaba. "How did you get in here?"

Mujtaba ignored the man's question. "Is there another

way out?"

"There's only one entrance and one exit."

"Really now? What happens in the event of a fire?"

"The same."

"Isn't that dangerous?"

The assembled priests turned to look at him. Perhaps they weren't challenged that often.

"The temple burned once, and it collapsed. They restored it, and it's still standing today. There are many precautions in place to prevent a similar act."

Mujtaba jumped when something thumped into the enormous wooden doors. People were kicking at the door, desperate to gain access.

The priests stepped back as one as the pummeling of the wood resonated throughout the nave. The crowd of believers had turned into a crazed mob. As the thumping and hammering increased in pace, so did the volume of the people outside the building.

Something cracked, like wood splintering.

Behind him, the priests dispersed as if blown by the wind, their black robes billowing up as they hastened toward the rear of the church.

Mujtaba followed them, scampering toward the back as well. If that crowd created a broken ingress, the risk of being trampled was too high to remain loitering at the front.

The banging increased in volume and intensity, even as he distanced himself from it, accompanied by frantic screaming.

Something was happening beyond those massive doors, and it wasn't good.

He stopped halfway up a row of pews and stared at the doors, frozen to the spot as if mesmerized by those screams. Even the priests edged out of hiding to stand by the red curtain, their collective gaze on the front doors.

Then, as if God Himself hit the mute button on the Earth remote, everything fell silent outside. The screams died abruptly, and the door clicked open.

Mujtaba would swear his heart stopped at that moment, along with his breathing, however briefly, as he stared at the doors.

They opened with a heavy creaking noise, but no one slipped inside.

Where had everyone gone? It was impossible to imagine hundreds, if not thousands, of people just wandering off in seconds.

Too curious for his own good, he moved toward the open door.

One look over his shoulder confirmed the priests were gone. They'd left the comfort of the red curtain to hide somewhere deeper within the church.

At the door, he stretched out a hand and gripped its edge.

After a deep breath, he pulled it all the way open.

A mountain of people lay on top of each other—not a single one moving. They all wore frightened expressions in their final moments.

Every last one of them appeared to be dead.

They had died collectively, in mere seconds, just outside the church walls. The swell of bodies had to be in the thousands. They filled every square centimeter of cobblestone, every alleyway, every nook and cranny.

Not a soul moved.

This vision caused his stomach to clench, and he vomited, most of it hitting the pile of bodies nearest to his feet.

The church door kept him upright as he held it for support. Breathing like he'd run a marathon, wiping bile from his chin, Mujtaba lowered to his knees as millions of tiny insects merged in front of him.

What the Hell is that?

The insects moved in a pattern until the image of a human face materialized. The mouth opened in a scream.

Mujtaba reared back, praying he didn't pass out.

Something from within forced him back to his feet. He staggered momentarily, then stepped outside, drawn toward the black entity. A hand squished under one shoe, and he stumbled over an elbow with the other.

When he could stand upright without wobbling, he understood his mission as it unfolded in his head.

It was all about the evil.

His job was to uproot it from the world as the old man had told him in the vision. This great responsibility was bestowed upon Mujtaba, and he had to be strong to endure.

The human face, consisting of a million tiny insects, watched him as he took a step back. Would that entity dare to enter a place of worship? The church may not be a mosque, but it was a place of worship, a place of God, where evil wasn't just not welcome. It was banished.

He stared at the black swarm as it watched him.

"I dare to look evil in the eye," he whispered. "If you dare, come into the house of the Lord. This is God's home.

Enter at your own risk, you vile inimical spawn of Satan."

The being expanded so that the facial image became bulbous and seemed about to explode.

With every passing second, the being swelled until it finally shattered into a million tiny pieces and took off in another direction.

Mujtaba clasped the gem in his pocket, feeling stronger than ever, even though his body shook from head to toe, and he was soaked in a full-body sweat.

He was in the right place at the right time.

Praise Allah that a mountain of dead people surrounded him, and yet he was the only one left standing.

"Praise Allah," he whispered as he lowered to the floor and laid on his back. "Thanks be to Allah, for Allah is great. Prayers and peace upon Muhammed." He lay there and waited for his body to calm down from the shock of what had just happened.

And the realization that the mission Allah had sent him on was intact.

He had been chosen.

He was the one.

The chosen one.

And he could not fail Allah, for he would give his life in His service.

Chapter Sixteen

LAUSANNE, SWITZERLAND

Cassandra opened her eyes and gasped at the cold taking over her limbs.

Startled and confused, she thrashed around to get her bearings, and it all came back in its glorious colors of horror.

The black cloud-like thing outside the glass door of the refrigerator was no longer there. She got to her feet and moved closer to the door, every ounce of her body stiff and shivering. When she curled her fingers into a fist—with effort—she could barely feel them.

One look outside the glass refrigerator door revealed no one waiting for her—human or otherwise.

She placed a pale grip on the door's handle, popped it open, and stepped out into the main store.

Once in the warmth of the building, she gingerly lowered herself back to the floor, every part of her body seized by chills. She should be dead, but somehow, she'd made it.

From where she sat at the end of an aisle, with dim morning light forcing its way through the front windows, she saw Vincent's bloodied body on the left and Leo's to the right.

Her eyes were filled with warm tears as she stared at them.

What was happening? What was that thing that killed them and chased her? Would it return to finish the job?

After so many hours curled up in the fridge, her toes and fingers were still numb but not frostbitten, which was good. Soon, she'd be warm enough to move around like usual.

She waited on the floor, stretching her legs and arms, clenching her fingers slowly, listening and watching for any signs of trouble.

Then, she made an effort to get up. Once on her feet, she headed toward Leo's body, using the shelves on either side for support. It was apparent that he was dead, but she had to check.

As she drew near, she saw the empty look in his eyes, his mouth open in the final scream.

"Leo," she whispered. "Don't leave me alone here." She cried while staring down at him. The thought of checking for a heartbeat repulsed her as his skin would be cold. "My love …"

She lowered to her knees, gently stroked his hair, and then found the courage to close his eyes. She couldn't stand the feeling that his corpse was looking at her.

"Why did you sacrifice yourself? It should've been me. Why did you leave me all alone in this world? Why?"

She never imagined that this man, who always cared about himself first, would give his life for her. How many people could say it and then follow through?

A memory of the two of them under the stars by the lake came to mind.

"You know," Leo said that day. "I'm not a good person."

"What do you mean?" she asked, intrigued.

"I mean, I have a hidden dark side when I'm with you. It may be hard to understand, but that's how I am."

She smiled at him. "You're my dark prince."

He didn't seem to be in a light-hearted mood. "Haven't you ever noticed how we're never with other friends? How about meeting one of my relatives? This is something you haven't done. Why do you think that is?" Now, he smiled strangely.

Cassandra stared at him, studying his face, and then she laughed.

"Are you an ax murderer or something?"

"It's okay to find it funny." He shrugged. "That's why I'm here. You keep me good. When I'm with you, the dragon is banished."

"That sounds like a fairy tale." She gave him a sweet, gentle kiss on the lips.

What darkness was he referring to? He was her knight—well, her dead knight now.

She lay next to him and closed her eyes. A few seconds was all she needed to forget, to turn back to the time when she slept next to him under the stars. After a moment, she turned to the side and caressed his face, wanting to remember the shape of the face she loved so much.

When her fingers touched Leo's cheek, she gasped.

He was still warm.

How long did it take for a body to become cold? When did rigor mortis set in?

Her imagination had to be playing tricks on her because she didn't want to believe he was dead. The warmth was nothing more than a ruse, hallucination, or delusion.

Yet, believing that, she still touched his neck and pressed down lightly to feel for a pulse.

Nothing came to her. Then she placed a hand on his heart. She sat up straighter. There was movement in his chest.

A frown creased her forehead. Was he dead or not? And if not, why lay there all night with his eyes open? How was that even possible?

Confused, she got up and eased over him to rest an ear on his chest.

He was alive.

She detected a rhythmic beat, a pulse.

"Leo, Leo," she gasped, getting up on her hands and knees.

She grabbed him by the shoulders and shook him.

Leo didn't react.

She slapped him—still nothing.

She glanced around for something to help her. There were bottles of water next to Vincent's body. She grabbed a bottle and poured it over Leo's face. He didn't react.

Maybe if she found a strong smell to put it under his nose. Didn't people wake up when they smelled salt or something?

But all the store had was bleach. There was table salt in little containers, but she couldn't detect much of a smell from it.

So she grabbed the bleach, poured some on a cloth, then placed it under his nose.

Again nothing.

It was as if he'd fallen into a deep sleep, a coma. What else could she do?

Waking him was beyond her limited knowledge. She needed help, which could only be had by leaving the minimart.

What if that black entity returned? Would she make it to the fridge in time?

She approached the front window, remaining hidden behind the shelf they'd positioned in front of the broken glass.

Then she tilted her head and tried to see what was happening on the street out of the corner of her eye.

She gasped, a hand rushing to cover her mouth.

The street was quiet, but it was full of people lying on the ground like Leo, eyes wide, expressions of fear sketched upon their faces.

It was as if she were the only one left alive in the entire city. She stayed in that position for several moments, watching the street, but none of the bodies moved in the early morning sunshine.

She could try to wake people, but she had no success with Leo, so what made her think she could wake others?

Could this all be some kind of trap?

She quickly dismissed the idea as paranoia because everybody—all strangers—would have to be in on it for that to work.

Whatever felled these people, she wanted no part of it.

Without thinking about what to do next, she pushed the shelf out of the way, slipped out through the broken window, and ran behind a parked car to hide and wait.

Her hands clenched and unclenched. Her breathing came in rapid gasps, and she wondered if she would hyperventilate. Leo needed her, these people needed help, and she was cowering behind a car.

Some kind of hero I turned out to be.

She forced herself to get up and look over the edge of the car to see if anyone was coming after her.

No one was. And that black entity was nowhere to be seen.

The sky was clear today.

Someone had thrown away a pop can—or dropped it when they were attacked. She picked it up and threw it over the car and into the road. If this were any sort of trap, that noise would provoke someone or something to emerge, but nothing did.

There was only silence when the can found a new resting place.

When she placed her back to the car, indecision still rife in her thoughts, she caught someone's face pull back from a living room window.

They'd been watching her.

She scanned the windows of other houses and saw nothing. Then she turned her attention to the house to her right.

More faces, but this time, they didn't look away.

Terrified people peeked out of their doors and windows all up and down the street.

Fear kept them inside.

She was outside and willing to figure out what had happened—why weren't they?

Slowly, she pushed up to her feet, bolstered by the people watching her, and dragged herself to the closest unconscious man lying a few meters away.

Like Leo, this man was in his twenties, blond, thin, and dressed in pajamas. She knelt beside him and took his hand, feeling for a pulse.

There had to be dozens of pairs of eyes on her at that moment.

The young man's pulse was there, steady but weak. His chest moved like he was in a deep sleep.

She slapped him hard, but he didn't react.

What could cause everyone to enter into some kind of coma? That black entity did this to them. But what was *this*?

She got up and went to the next person on the road. The slap had the same effect.

Cassandra wiped at her eyes. No one had come out of their homes yet. She looked at them, glaring at the houses behind her, then screamed in despair. How dare they not come outside and help.

"Everyone is unconscious," she shouted, sobbing now. "We need a doctor. Please, someone, come out and help me."

No one moved. There was no sound but the sound of a soft breeze in her ears.

She lowered her head, feeling as helpless as a lifejacket in a burning building.

The distinctive sound of a door opening came to her.

She looked up, wiping the tears away to see where the sound came from.

A man had stepped outside of a house two doors down.

Gradually, others exited their homes, coming out one after another, watching each other. Several people couldn't bear the sight in the street and retched.

Cassandra walked away and headed back inside the mini-market to tend to Leo.

He was exactly where she'd left him.

She lay down next to him again. She didn't know what else to do. He was still breathing, which gave her hope that he'd wake up soon.

"Do you know what happened?" a man asked, startling her.

He'd entered the store after she didn't push the shelf back in place. He moved closer but stopped a few meters away. "I saw you outside. It was brave what you did." The man watched her, his eyes kind, soft.

"I don't know if I'd call it brave." She got back to her feet, her body weakened by the ordeal.

"Are we safe now?" he asked, his voice trembling.

Cassandra gave him a disparaging look. "How the hell should I know?"

"I'm a doctor. Will you let me examine him?"

Hope bloomed in her chest as she stepped back and gestured at Leo. "Please, yes."

The doctor opened Leo's eyelids and used his cell phone

flashlight to check for something. Then he checked Leo's pulse.

Outside on the street, people talked. Some cried loudly, while random screams sounded as people discovered loved ones. Twenty-four hours ago, this road would have been full of people, cars, and the dull chaos of everyday life. But now, there were tears, sorrow, and despair.

"It appears your friend is in a coma. But without a full examination, I can't tell you more at this time."

"Will he live?" she asked.

"Without doing proper tests at a hospital, I can't know what's happening."

She glanced toward the front window. "Everyone else around here needs a hospital, too."

"Well, if we hurry, we can be the first ones there. He may need medication. Here, help me lift him."

"Where will we go? The hospital was full and locked up yesterday. They'd be overwhelmed today."

"My doctor's office is just down the road. I can check him better there."

Cassandra stared at the man for a long moment. Was he really a doctor? Will they actually go to a doctor's office? Or was he showing concern for some ulterior motive to get close to her?

Living on the street had taught her to rely on herself and no one else. But this had to be different.

Decision made: she bent over and put all her strength into lifting Leo with the doctor. An unconscious man weighed a ton.

They could get upright, but she almost abandoned the

effort because he was too heavy.

"Take his feet," the doctor said as he grabbed Leo by the armpits.

Cassandra wrapped her hands around Leo's ankles and lifted them. She gave a final look at Vincent as they wobbled out of the store.

Once outside, they set him down to catch a breath. Then the doctor lifted Leo on his own and hefted him over his shoulder, staggering a few steps for balance.

"That's not a good idea," she hastened to say. "You'll hurt yourself." *Not to mention Leo when you drop him*, she didn't add but wanted to.

The doctor sauntered forward without saying anything, stepping over bodies in the street.

The smell oozing off the bodies got to her as they walked. Several people had released their bladders and vacated their bowels where they lay.

Cassandra had read disaster novels and seen movies with such themes, but to experience it live was like nothing else. The smell in the air wasn't just fecal matter. It was also terror and misery.

The formerly beautiful city was at war without knowing who the enemy was. Everyone was disoriented, frightened, desperate, and lost about what to do to move forward.

The doctor continued to carry Leo on his back without stopping for a break until they arrived at a newly built apartment building with most of its windows still intact.

Somehow, the doctor made it inside the building and placed Leo in the elevator before he recalled the electricity was out.

He turned to Cassandra. "I can't carry him up three floors," he said through gasps for air.

His face dripped with sweat as he gently eased down to sit next to Leo and placed his head back against the elevator wall.

Leo was still in the same state. Nothing had changed. Cassandra felt deep loneliness take hold of her. Without Leo somewhere alive in the world, she would be orphaned a second time.

"He won't wake up—"

"We can't know," the doctor said. "Did you happen to see what caused everyone to slip into this coma state?"

She shook her head. "I hid all night. The noises scared me." She met his gaze. "I'm not as brave as most people."

He nodded and got back to his feet. "I've rested enough. Let's do this."

The doctor lifted Leo again and started for the stairs.

"Damn," he muttered to himself. "I should have taken an office on the first floor."

They made it to the third floor without a break. On the top step, the doctor faltered and then set Leo down.

A large sign said "Dr. Oliver Traves" on the door across from the stairs.

Oliver searched his pockets for something, probably looking for the key. As soon as he found them, he opened the door, grabbed Leo again, and stepped into a pleasant reception area. Artwork adorned the walls, and the furniture was neat and proper, with the requisite light reading on the coffee table in the waiting room area.

"Stay here," he said, then moved down a short hallway

and disappeared into a door on the left.

Cassandra obeyed, but only for a moment. She wanted to see what he was doing with Leo.

She examined a painting hanging over a black leather sofa. Then moved the magazines around, finding nothing of interest.

This was ridiculous. She couldn't wait any longer.

She strode down the hallway to the door the doctor had entered and shoved it open, startling the man.

"What are you doing?" the doctor asked, spinning around to gawk at her.

Cassandra scanned the room. There were two hospital beds, two large lamps above each, and two trolleys with tools. Next to each bed was a heart monitor. Leo was already connected and showed a steady heartbeat. The doctor had placed something on Leo's left hand, and there was a tube up Leo's nose. Everything looked doctorish, which calmed her down for the moment.

The doctor glanced back at Leo, the irritation at being interrupted easing from his face.

"I will run some tests. Fortunately, I have a generator for situations like these."

Cassandra approached Leo, sat beside him, and then took his hand. He seemed so calm as if nothing was wrong.

The doctor inserted a needle into Leo's arm and withdrew blood. Cassandra bit her lip and looked away.

"He didn't feel a thing," Oliver told her, then took the vial of blood and exited the room.

More than a half-hour passed before the doctor returned holding papers.

"From the simple tests I conducted, everything's fine with this man. Other tests need to be performed in a hospital setting. I don't have the necessary equipment." He gave her a firm look, his lips pursed. "We have to get him to a hospital."

Cassandra gave him a bewildered look as if he was speaking in another language.

"Everything is closed around here, locked up. Did you see how many people were out there? Please, Doctor, there has to be something else you can do."

"Call me Oliver." He cleared his throat. "Well, assuming everything's fine with his brain and internal organs, I could use a few supplies to keep him alive for a while, at least until we figure out what happened to everyone." He moved to a side counter and picked up a pad of paper. "One of us has to go get these supplies, and I suggest it's you. If the patient goes into convulsions or has some other issue, I will need to be here for him."

Cassandra wasn't sure she should do what he was asking of her. How could she leave Leo alone with a man she had just met, a doctor or not?

On the other hand, Oliver was her only hope.

"Okay." She nodded at the doctor, then moved to stand beside Leo, kissing him gently on the lips. She hoped this wasn't their last kiss.

When she turned around, the doctor was waiting with everything written down on paper.

"Where will I find these items in the hospital?" she asked, taking the paper and examining the list.

"You have to find a medical supply room. They'll give you what you need if someone's there as they know my script pad. Good luck." He gave her easy directions to the nearest hospital, and Cassandra strode from the room, a small amount of hope in her step.

She ran down the stairs to the main floor, but on the final step, she wasn't sure how she would physically do what was asked of her—both legs trembled violently from anxiety and fatigue.

Everything had happened so fast that she didn't have time to process it. She'd gone through scary situations since choosing the street life, but nothing compared to this—the carefree days of yesterday seemed so far away.

She wiped at her eyes, took a deep breath, and ran for the building's exit.

She couldn't just sit and cry. People were dying, and she was grieving for yesterday's gone by.

Leo needed her help, and she'd help him. He'd do anything for her so she'd be there for him.

Knowing that she committed to doing whatever it took to deliver this medicine back to the doctor.

Anything—even if it killed her.

Chapter Seventeen

CASSANDRA EXITED THE QUIET building. She would avoid the hospital they went to yesterday. It had been locked up with a security detail. Getting in wouldn't be easy—likely impossible.

Instead, she headed north toward the hospital Dr. Traves directed her to.

The shops were all looted by the time she made it to the Place de la Palud. The once-busy street with four- and five-story buildings now looked like something out of a horror movie. Large piles of corpses—they may still be alive like Leo, but they all looked like corpses—were scattered everywhere, their eyes wide, frightened expressions on their faces.

Most of the windows in the stores were broken from the ongoing looting.

She considered how reckless it was as a woman to be walking the streets alone, then dismissed the thought because she had to do this for Leo.

She rocked from side to side to avoid stepping on the mass of bodies in the street. Sometimes she grabbed a road sign, sometimes, she leaned on a building.

She slowed when she saw a lone man bent over up ahead. He appeared to be searching the pockets of the dead—ironically just below the "Fountain of Justice."

Money didn't matter at a time like this as everyone was just *taking* what they wanted, but would it matter later, when it was all over?

Whatever the case, Cassandra couldn't bear to watch the man act like a vulture feeding on the corpses.

"Hey," she shouted at him. "These people are someone's brother or mother. What the hell are you doing?"

The man straightened up and turned to stare at her. After a moment, he shrugged, mumbled something under his breath, then continued looting the pockets of the fallen.

Unless she was physically prepared to restrain him, she could do nothing, so she cursed him and moved on.

Electricity hadn't been restored yet. The traffic lights were still dark.

It felt like the powers that be had disowned Lausanne and left it to fend for itself. How far-reaching was this catastrophe? Did it extend outside Switzerland? England? Russia? North America?

She had no way of knowing for sure but prayed that it wasn't global.

Should she be carrying some sort of weapon? That

thought alone raised her anxiety.

She reached the Escaliers du Marché and climbed the winding wooden staircase. The cobblestoned street to her left was too steep to traverse on foot, so they installed the stairs a few hundred years prior. It led directly to the city's cathedral, where she'd find the hospital across from it.

Ascending the dozens of steps, she panted for air and then stopped before reaching halfway. A melody emanated from the church organ above. This encouraged her to climb faster to reach the Cathedral of Lausanne.

She'd been here before but had never entered the structure. After the death of her parents, she had avoided churches, whatever denomination they were.

Closer now, near the top of the wooden stairs, she saw dozens of people milling about—alive—outside the church doors. Several bodies were lying around in that unusual coma state, but seeing others alive gave her hope.

Why were they all here, though? Were they drawn to the church for prayer out of fright? When death seemed near, almost everyone turned to God.

Instead of bypassing the cathedral on her way to the hospital, she entered and asked around. Perhaps someone might know what was going on.

She pushed through the assembled crowd to get inside the enormous gothic church. She passed a sign with the official name, The Cathedral of Notre Dame of Lausanne, and the date of A.D. 1170 when construction of the cathedral began.

She'd heard somewhere that church entrances were made to look like the doors of paradise. If that were true, then

Heaven was crowded today. Under the volume of the imposing church organ, she heard cries and prayers. The assembled crowd was desperate and terrified. The massive organ usually united the faithful in joy, but now it seemed to unite them in sorrow.

She couldn't go any farther, and maybe there was no point. The holy building was filled with the faithful. No scientists, doctors, or authorities were milling about consoling the people.

The church organ stopped, and from somewhere near the front, she heard a male voice trying to calm everyone. At first, she couldn't decipher what he was saying because of the general din of the crowd, but when the people realized someone was talking, they quieted.

"What happened is beyond what we could have imagined," the man's voice boomed. "Satan reached the church's threshold but didn't dare enter."

Satan? Cassandra looked around to see if anyone else was as confused as she was. *Could he be talking about that black mass of faces that floated after her in the mini-market?*

"Those inside the temple were spared Satan's wrath. Those outside fell into the fury of his wickedness and are all in the sleep of Hell. We must repent our sins for God to help us resist the work of Satan. God has never forsaken us and won't forsake us now. So, let us pray for our loved ones who are in this dark sleep and pray for those still awake. Pray for salvation." His voice rose on those last three words, echoing throughout the massive building.

Cassandra didn't want to hear anymore. She got that the black swarm hadn't entered the temple, so she and Leo would be safe there. Maybe they'd be safe in any church.

Cassandra stumbled back toward the exit, but a woman stepped in front of her and clutched her arm before reaching the door.

"He told you to look for him," she said, her eyes wild.

Cassandra reared back, puzzled. "Who are you?"

The woman had short wavy hair and thick black eyebrows and wore a long straight dress adorned with a pearl necklace. Cassandra had no idea who she was.

"You have to find him," she blurted. "Don't leave."

"Find who?"

The woman seemed quite annoyed, an arrogant expression crossing her features.

Then someone shouted near the front of the church, and Cassandra turned to see what was going on.

When she looked back at the woman, she was gone.

Chills rose all over her body, and she hugged herself to stave off the worst of it.

Had the woman been talking about the note Vincent wrote? The one that said, "Look For Me." If so, she left his body back at the mini-market.

But how was that possible? They'd been alone in the mini-market. Cassandra scanned the crowd, but the woman was gone.

Shaking her head at the absurdity of it all, she exited the church and headed toward the hospital.

It had to be a coincidence, a case of mistaken identity. Cassandra just reminded that woman of someone else.

Entering the cathedral had cost her valuable time. She had to remain focused.

After stepping over bodies in the street, she made it to the hospital. Unfortunately, the situation was exactly as she had predicted. Those who could carry their loved ones had shown up at the hospital entrance and were stuck there. The line had to be over two hundred strong.

How would she get inside now?

She walked the perimeter of the building in search of an alternative entrance. On the east side, garbage bins were lined up along a brick wall, which meant an exit door would be nearby.

She slipped between the dumpsters and found a set of double doors a few meters along the wall. There was no handle, no knob. She tried to pry it open with her fingers tight against the edge, but it didn't budge, locked from the inside.

She would have to wait and hope that someone used these doors soon.

Where the shadows were deepest, she sat on the concrete in a tight corner behind the doors to wait. Head back, eyes closed, she controlled her breathing in an attempt to remain calm, to relax.

When the doors burst open, and a woman stepped out with a garbage bag, Cassandra jerked awake.

She climbed to her feet in a rush, blinking rapidly, then grabbed the propped-open door.

A hand smacked onto her shoulder before she got two steps inside the building and yanked her around.

"What are you doing?" the woman asked.

"I have to get inside."

"There's a line out front. Go to the queue with the

others."

"I don't have time to wait."

The woman appraised her. "You look fine. You're not carrying a body. Why do you want in here?"

"I found a doctor to help my friend and me. I'm not here to be a burden to anyone. I just need a few supplies." She withdrew the list Dr. Traves gave her. "Please, he's all I have left. If something happens to Leo …" Her eyes filled with tears.

The nurse studied her face, took a deep breath, and released her arm while looking down at the list.

"Come with me," she said, then pushed past Cassandra. "I better not get in trouble for this," the woman muttered.

Once inside the hospital, the nurse pointed to a small room. They stepped inside together, and she held up a uniform similar to hers.

"Put it on over your clothes. You'll need it to get into the other building." The nurse explained to Cassandra how to get where she was going and then stared into her eyes. "Now listen, I didn't see you. You didn't see me, either." She patted Cassandra's shoulder, then slipped out of the room.

Cassandra got dressed in the uniform, exited the small room, and headed to where the woman told her to go.

In the next building, they were out of beds. People were left on stretchers, and the floor in the hallways piled next to each other. They had gathered on chairs, cabinets, and wherever else they could find.

Doctors, nurses, paramedics, and interns examined people, gave them needles, extracted blood, asked questions, and talked to them as Cassandra strode by in her new hospital garb.

She made it through the busier areas, then followed a nurse up a set of stairs. The nurse entered a door on the other side of the corridor.

While debating if she should follow her inside that room, the door opened, and the nurse edged back out, pulling a cart filled with small boxes on top of it.

Cassandra moved quickly in the other direction when she strode toward her, peeking into the rooms.

What had happened at the hospital? Did that black swarm enter the building? If not, why not? Did it remain in the streets, avoiding hospitals, churches, and houses?

She was passing room 272 when she glanced inside and froze at what she saw.

It wasn't possible. How could what she just saw be explained?

Stunned into paralysis, she waited until her heart wasn't in her throat, a hand on her chest, then eased backward a notch to glance inside that room again.

She gasped so suddenly that she choked on the air. Her eyes watered at the sight before her because the people in the room couldn't be real.

It was impossible.

Unless God had a hand in them being there—that could be the only answer—otherwise, she had gone mad.

Cassandra placed one foot in front of the other and stepped inside to see if it really was her long-dead parents, seemingly alive and healthy again, in hospital room 272.

Chapter Eighteen

JERUSALEM

Mujtaba lay on his back, staring at the vast ceiling of the Church of the Holy Sepulcher. Was it possible the Christians moved the Ark of the Covenant from the Temple of the Dome, carrying it through the tunnel and into the Christian's central chapel? What if they had stolen it? And if so, where would they hide it?

He rolled sideways to see several priests watching him, unsure how to act around him. Finally, one of them called for the Arab who had spoken to him earlier, then offered a hand to help him to his feet.

Mujtaba was baffled and surprised by the kindness of a non-Muslim—a Christian.

"Come, my child, get up," the man said in Greek.

Mujtaba took his hand and stood.

"Do you want something to eat?" the priest asked.

Mujtaba looked at the others, then focused on the Arabic man. Even though he understood English, he decided only to use that man as a translator. Speaking to one man would keep things simple.

"I am Nassir," the Arabic man said. "The priest asked if you want food."

Mujtaba nodded, too exhausted and hungry to continue his search at the moment. Food would be good.

The priest gestured for Mujtaba to follow him, and Nassir fell in behind them.

Once seated at a small table, the priest brought him bread, cheese, and olives, gave him a water glass, and then sat across from him.

Nassir sat on a chair by the wall.

Mujtaba looked at the priest and said, "Bismillah," which was the invocation used by Muslims before an undertaking like eating. He figured Nassir would translate if they wanted to know what he said.

The expressionless priest said, "Christ God, bless the food and drink of the faithful. He is always Holy, now and forever and ever. Amen." He made the sign of the cross.

Mujtaba attacked the bread as if it had been days since he last ate. He avoided eye contact with the priest, who seemed to watch him.

Then, the priest glanced at Nassir. "How did a Muslim find himself in the House of the God of Christianity fighting that evil entity?"

Nassir translated.

Knowing he'd have to explain, Mujtaba was prepared.

"Allah sent me."

"How did you get in?"

"Allah brought me."

The priest frowned but didn't pursue that line of questioning. Instead, he asked, "What was that thing out there?"

"Satan."

The priest gasped. "How can you know for certain?"

"A person who believes in Allah can recognize evil when he sees it."

"Can you describe what you saw?"

Mujtaba set down the bread, finished chewing the piece in his mouth, then nodded. "A black entity consisting of human faces, the souls Satan has damned. It enters the people standing outside the church." He grabbed an olive, bit into it, then spit out the pit.

"Why didn't it hurt you?"

"Allah protected me." Mujtaba ate another olive.

"My child, it would help if you told us more. What is it you were looking for?"

The priest's voice was soft and soothing. Mujtaba recognized the kindness in the priest, but he was an old man and wouldn't understand much of the search he'd been sent on.

"Priest of Christ, I feel your love and kindness in how you conduct yourself. For your own safety, I mustn't tell you more. If you want to help me, point me to the nearest egress point, and you'll never see me again. Continue to believe in your God. I pray He will help you." Mujtaba stared at the priest while Nassir translated.

The priest responded, and Nassir faced Mujtaba. "If you please, stay longer, learn to trust us. Perhaps you'll share this secret of yours. Otherwise, you are welcome to leave whenever you want." The priest rose from his chair, a look of disappointment crossing his features now.

Mujtaba got up from his chair, too, then grabbed more bread and stashed olives in his pocket.

"I'll be taking my leave," he said.

Nassir nodded, whispered Mujtaba's words to the priests, and then led Mujtaba to the exit.

Once outside, he turned back to Nassir. "Thank you," he muttered. "May Allah be with you."

"Thank you, my unknown brother, but I have become a Christian."

Mujtaba nodded. *Traitor.*

He left the building on foot without knowing where he was going. His knowledge of the area was limited. When he started his quest in Saudi Arabia, he didn't have a particular plan in mind. He could have gone to Lake Tiberias, but how exactly would he look in the lake without equipment and money?

He considered his train of thought from earlier. What if the Christians had actually stolen it? How would he find the locations where they could have hidden it? His knowledge spanned Islam, not Christianity. He could've asked that priest but couldn't risk such a secret.

He needed to locate a library, go online, and gain more knowledge. Otherwise, he'd end up walking in circles.

As he walked, he avoided looking at the bodies piled

about the landscape, the people Satan left behind. Today, the sky was clear of black dust, but he suspected it would return when the darkness fell, and more terrible things would happen. He would need to find shelter before dark.

After an hour of walking, he stopped at a tourist information building, but it was closed.

Mujtaba scanned the area, but the only people nearby were laid out on the ground, unmoving.

No one would see him break in, so he pried the door open with relative ease as it had been slightly damaged in the earthquake. The small interior was equipped with a table, two chairs, and a wall of shelving adorned with advertisements for hundreds of locations tourists could enjoy.

At the front window, which looked out onto the public side, was a bench with two seats and a computer where the employee would book the events and sell tickets.

He sat at the computer and pressed the button to turn it on, but nothing happened. He pressed other buttons, but still nothing. After checking to see if the computer was plugged in, he realized that there was still no electricity.

He flipped through the brochures in search of where a library might be. He was able to locate the address on a city map, so he took the brochure with him and left the tourist building.

From the map, the library appeared to be three and a half kilometers away. Going on foot would take more time than he wanted to expend. He needed a bike and began a search for one as he started walking in the general direction of the library.

Allah rewarded him half a kilometer away. An

abandoned bicycle lay on its side, discarded by an owner likely in desperate need to survive—it would no longer be useful to them.

He mounted the bike and glanced around at the unfortunates scattered as far as the eye could see. There were so many tourists with no one to take them off the streets, put them in a warm home, or care for them. Like stray dogs, they all lay about where they had fallen. At some point, someone would have to pick them all up. But when?

Mujtaba placed his feet on the pedals and rode with the map as his guide. He preferred to stay on the main streets for safety, but things were different when he exited the downtown area. Cars had crashed on the road, blocking his access several times. A long line of cars that had been out the previous night was now dented and demolished, and a few were upside down. One had caught fire, then burned itself out —yet smoke still rose from the engine block. There were unconscious people and corpses alike scattered in and out of cars, filling the landscape with a depressing visage.

He closed his eyes while straddling the bike, whispered a prayer for strength, and then moved on, meandering around everything from bodies to cars and toppled baby strollers. He focused on his direction, eyes on the street before him without looking left or right.

After an hour, due to the rugged terrain, he arrived in front of the large rectangular building that housed the library. He set his bike aside and went to the entrance. The door was locked, so he knocked, hoping someone was inside.

"Anyone in there? Please, open up," he shouted in Arabic and then English.

He knocked again, then stopped when he thought he heard someone approaching.

A paper covering one of the windows bent down, and two fearful-looking eyes stared out at him.

Then, the distinctive snick of the door's lock clicking open came to him.

The door shot open, and a hand lashed out.

Mujtaba frowned and clutched the hand, which gripped him back, then yanked him inside the library before he could protest.

Chapter Nineteen

LAUSANNE HOSPITAL
Room 272

Cassandra made it through the door of the hospital room without collapsing. She leaned against the wall and stared at the man—her dad?—then focused on the woman—her mother?

Sebastian and Chloe Christen.

Her heart felt ready to split apart. Neither one had turned her way yet, so she removed the chain from her neck and opened the heart-shaped locket.

In profile, they were the same as in the photo. But how was that possible?

Her parents—her dead parents—were standing not two meters from her, both looking like they were in their thirties.

Both living and breathing like all other conscious and awake human beings.

Doppelgängers?

Impossible. Together? In the same hospital room?

Or did they *actually* die in that car accident? Could they have buried imposters?

All these questions and more raced through her thoughts as she considered that black swarm. Did it have something to do with this?

Maybe she was losing her mind, and this was some sort of illusion.

The air seemed to thicken around her, and she couldn't catch a breath. There was a slight tremor in her hands as her body broke out in a cold sweat.

Then Sebastian glanced over his shoulder, saw her, and ran to her side, his arms open.

"My love, my sweet daughter," he whispered into her ear as he hugged her. "I didn't expect to see you so soon."

He held her as tears ran down his face. She was thoroughly confused and distraught.

Chloe moved close and embraced her, too.

Cassandra gave in to the group hug she had been longing for since she was eighteen—since her parents were torn from her life after that car accident.

Nothing could explain this—it had to be an illusion. Whatever it was, she didn't want the hug to end.

How could she have put so much stock in a parental embrace? Yet, at this moment, at this time, it meant everything to her.

Cassandra sobbed. She never wanted to be lost again,

orphaned, or left alone to fight this world. Thoughts of her mother smiling in the spring sunshine and her father splashing them with water in the summer rushed through her like a gale-force wind.

"Don't cry, dear," her mother said. "Please."

Her mother wiped her tears as her father stroked her hair.

Then, her mother led her to the bed and gestured for her to sit. Cassandra stared at them numbly, not knowing how to react. From somewhere within, a tiny voice whispered for her to *wake up*, to get out of this delusional dream that she didn't want to end, but she ignored that voice.

"Something serious has happened," her father said, concern creasing his brow. "You have to find that man, Vincent."

She frowned. That was one of the first things he had to say to her. Really?

"I'm crazy, aren't I?" She paused, studying their faces. "I've escaped from some mental hospital, or I'm high on some LSD-laced shit, and everything I've seen in the past two days is a trip, right?" She stared at them. "You two aren't real. You can't know who Vincent is." She looked away, focusing on the floor. "What's happening to me?"

"Cassandra, listen." Her mother moved in front of her. "This is important. Look me in the eyes." Her mother held her shoulders, then forced her head upward. "Something terrible happened. Something upset the balance of our two worlds, our planes. You have to be careful. Some entities are dark and evil. Vincent sent us here to wait for you, to talk to you. He said you tried to help him, that you were kind."

"Vincent is dead, Mom. He killed himself in a mini-market with a pen." She laughed, searching her mother's face. "I can't believe I'm having this conversation with my mother."

"His body is dead, Cassie."

Cassie. Her mother's one nickname for her. Only her mother ever used it.

"He killed himself so Satan's black spawn wouldn't take him."

Something came back to her from their time in the mini-market, something Vincent had said before asking her for a pen. He'd taken her hand and said, *I don't want them to take me. I can't let them take me.*

At the time, she had no idea who *they* were. But now, based on what her mother had just said, she understood what he meant—that black shit, Satan's spawn.

"How would Vincent know I would be here?"

"Vincent just knows, but it's dangerous for him to appear before you in this setting. They'd find him."

Now thoroughly confused, she asked, "Is that why you're here? To send me a message?" She looked from her mother to her father, then back to her mother. "You're not here to stay?"

"We're here because you've kept us here. You haven't let us go, so we remain close to help you through your purging —grieving is the more common word—before heading to our final destination."

"But how—like, how is this possible?"

Cassandra's shoulders hitched, and she wept again while her parents looked at each other, nodding and staring as if communicating with their eyes.

"We are all in danger right now," her father said. "According to what Vincent said, your mom and I need to go to a safe place, a place with God's presence. Only there will we be okay. So, we're heading to the temple next, as we feel there'll be more of us within. We must leave now, and you, my sweetheart, must find Vincent. Don't do anything else."

Cassandra shook her head. "No, don't leave. Wait, I have so much to tell you. Don't leave me again."

"You have nothing to tell us that we don't already know," her dad said. "We're always with you, just on another plane."

"I have to find medication for Leo. That's why I'm here." Cassandra was about to say more, but her mother raised a hand, cutting her off.

"No, Cassie, you shouldn't do that. You have to leave him behind. This is the reason we were told to come here."

"Are you saying I should just let him die? He's all I have." That thought felt like a betrayal.

"Leo is not who you think he is." Her father moved in front of her. "You need to stay away from him, or you'll hurt us all. Please don't do it, don't help him."

"This doesn't make sense. Did my parents come back from the dead to give me boyfriend advice? Really?" She wiped her cheeks and stared at them. "Leo was there when you weren't."

Behind her, out in the corridor, someone paged a doctor, and an alarm tripped, the beeping incessant.

"Yes, he was." Her mother placed a hand over Cassandra's heart. "But now you have to let him go. The fact that Vincent found us and sent us here has already been extremely risky. There are rules."

"What rules?" She cleared her throat. "Wait, where did he find you?"

"We went home in search of you and discovered Vincent waiting there. Coming into this form again, down here, we didn't know we were still dead—at least dead in the sense that we're not alive on Earth." She shrugged. "I hope that makes sense. Basically, we didn't remember we were dead before this. But then Vincent woke us, we remembered everything, and he explained what was happening. We had no other choice, even though we're now in danger."

"Danger? From what?"

"You've seen it," her father said, his tone serious.

Cassandra shivered. Yes, she had seen it.

"We have to leave." Her mother eased back. "We don't have time. When night falls, it'll be back, and it'll be bad—worse, much worse."

Her father took her hand.

"My love, we'll see you soon."

He hugged her, kissed her cheek, and moved away to be beside her mother.

Then they filed through the door and disappeared as if nothing had happened.

Cassandra dropped onto the empty bed, not knowing what to think. Her eyes were swollen from crying, and her limbs were heavy.

What was going to happen at night? Would that balance of two worlds be upset again when that black swarm took shape? How many more people would be caught by that thing, only to be left on the ground comatose?

She didn't know what to do next.

Leave Leo and find Vincent? If so, how?

If Vincent could find her parents, why couldn't he just pop up now and talk to her? They said something about it being too risky. What did that mean?

Vincent's note said, *Look For Me*.

That strange woman in the church said *he told you to look for him*. Then she added before disappearing; *You have to find him*.

And now, her parents were pushing her to speak with Vincent.

One thing was for sure. The night would soon be upon them, and she didn't want to be outside when it came. Determining a safe haven before then could quite possibly save her life.

In the meantime, she wanted to help Leo and search for Vincent.

Not knowing what the hell was happening or if she actually just spoke with her dead parents, Cassandra got up off the hospital bed and left the room.

She had to be proactive, so she decided what needed to be done, and she was prepared to do it.

Consequences be damned.

Chapter Twenty

A woman who appeared to be in her thirties, her black hair tied up in a rubber band, pulled Mujtaba inside the library and then slammed the door shut.

The expression on her face emoted surprise, but her brow remained scrunched in puzzlement.

Words flowed from her in a rush of Hebrew, but Mujtaba didn't understand a thing. When she saw the confusion on his face, she switched to English before he could stop her.

"What were you doing *out*side?" She glanced over his shoulder. "That black smoke is floating out there."

"That black smoke you're referring to isn't out there anymore. It's gone."

She glared at him dumbfounded.

"How did you escape it?" Mujtaba asked.

Her hands visibly trembling, the woman motioned for him to follow her. She led him out to what looked like the main hall, where over a hundred younger people—university types—were spread apart to make room for Satan's coma victims.

The bodies lay among them in a creepy collage of cadavers.

"It was just outside those windows." The woman pointed. "We heard the screams." She looked back at Mujtaba and shuddered. "We were about to close the library for the day. Students were studying, so some in the religious sector prayed in Aramaic and Greek. Then the mass just went away." She turned to study the people watching her speak to the newcomer. "We stayed inside, praying it wouldn't come back. Some fell asleep, while others stayed awake to watch over the others. When the sun rose and the mass was gone, we gathered outside in short trips to wake those people up, but that was in vain." She pointed at the bodies. "They're breathing but not waking up. We think they're in some kind of coma. What can you tell us? Is help on its way?"

Mujtaba shrugged. "I don't know how I could help. I've been praying non-stop, too."

"Well, you're alive. You're not in this coma thing." She flicked a hand at the bodies on the floor, likely in frustration. "You must've found shelter of some kind."

He tilted his head and examined the library anew. "Was this ever a religious building?"

The woman shook her head.

All eyes were on Mujtaba.

"That black mass didn't touch me because I was in a church of God. It left the priests alone as well. I assumed it was because of the church, you know, a sacred spot."

"That settles it. Inside, we're safe. Outside, we're not."

He raised a finger. "But only when the mass is present. I just biked here from town without an issue."

"Right, okay." She held out her hand to shake his, and the quivering calmed somewhat. "I'm Rita. A pleasure to meet you."

They shook hands. "I'm Mujtaba, and I came here in desperate need to study the word of God. We're missing something with this smoky mass thing, and I feel the answers are in the scriptures. Do you have religious books in English?" Was his story believable? Her nodding told him so.

"Yes, follow me." Rita stepped away, and he followed her past shelf after shelf until he saw the inscriptions in English.

"This is the area. Read whatever you want. I'll head back to my people to console them that there are other survivors. I'll come to check on you soon."

"I thank you, Rita. Deeply."

Her eyes downcast, she backed up a few steps, then pivoted and walked away, leaving him alone in a mass of religious literature.

Mujtaba took a deep breath and searched the spines of many books. He tried to recall the visions he had before starting his mission. Maybe he'd missed something. He rested his head back against the shelves and closed his eyes to concentrate on the journey that had brought him here.

It started three months ago. Glass had broken somewhere

in his house, waking him—but it turned out to be a dream. In that dream, he went to the living room of his house and saw someone sitting in an armchair. He approached cautiously, wary of an attack, until he stood in front of the man, demanding to know what he was doing inside his house.

As soon as Mujtaba saw the man's face, he jerked awake, his heart racing.

This went on for many nights. Every time he reached the chair in the living room, he saw the same man and woke up.

Afraid to close his eyes at night, the old man's image haunted him. It haunted him because the old man in the living room chair had no eyes. They'd been gouged out with some jagged tool—that's how terrible the man's face looked.

He prayed to Allah to give him strength and guidance, but it was in vain. What could a man with no eyes have to tell him? What was the purpose of the dream? Did it mean Mujtaba was leading a blind life? That he had no direction?

Finally, he decided to confront his fears, face the man in the dream, and talk to him.

So he sat in the same chair, fully awake, closed his eyes, and addressed the old man aloud.

"Who are you? Why are you stalking me?"

No answer was forthcoming. Yet he persisted until he fell asleep. Then, once again, he saw the old man.

The man opened his mouth, saying, "Once you believe the impossible, you'll be ready to listen."

"What do you want from me?"

"You have a mission—to find what is lost."

After those words, the man disappeared, and Mujtaba snapped awake.

It had been the first time they spoke to one another, but it wouldn't be the last. The man returned in his dreams to repeat those exact words repeatedly, like he wanted to tattoo them onto Mujtaba's consciousness.

Mujtaba was full of questions. He didn't know his heritage. Could it be possible that he was descended from a prophet? Did religious blood flow in his veins?

When he saw the old man in the chair again, he asked, "Why me? You said, 'Find what is lost.' What am I looking for?"

The man added one more line that night. "You are the last descendant of Aaron." Then he disappeared.

When he woke later that morning, Mujtaba laughed at the thought.

Aaron? Really? The prophet, high priest, and brother of Moses?

If memory served him correctly, Aaron was granted the priesthood by the Pharaoh for himself and all his male descendants—which would include Mujtaba if what the eyeless man said was true—and he became the first High Priest of the Israelites.

A little voice within him asked, *What if it's true?*

If he was a descendant of Aaron, how did that matter? What could he do? Find what was lost—the Ark of the Covenant.

That had to be it, so he came on this journey.

Him? A Muslim descendant of Aaron? That meant the blood in his veins was of a religiosity not seen in the modern world.

How interesting that such a quandary could exist.

Many years have passed since Aaron's time. The movements of populations, religious texts, and translations are not something quantifiable.

About a month had passed since his last visit with the man in the chair. It was on the last visit that the man had said two words. "Taboot Sakina." The Taboot-e-Sakina, or the Ark of the Covenant.

Now Mujtaba knew what he was looking for, but he had no idea why.

Did Allah send that man?

Unclear on so many points, he decided to leave his village to search for the ancient artifact. As a devout Muslim, he couldn't imagine he would be the Mahdi, a messianic figure in Islam who is to appear at the end of times to rid the world of evil and restore the divine Kingdom on Earth. He was just Mujtaba and would allow the visions to guide him … until they didn't.

Then the earthquake came, and the black entities further validated the visions and his decisions.

But what if there was a crisis of faith, something cataclysmic worldwide? Perhaps a Mahdi *was* needed to right things when they were so wrong.

Mujtaba began his journey weeks ago after respecting the Hadiths and listening to the Imams in his village, having no idea what was coming.

And so far, the old man hadn't reappeared to him since he left on his quest.

He picked up a large version of the Christian Bible. He flipped through it and then placed it back on the shelf. This wouldn't be easy.

He was about to go in search of Rita to ask her for directions when he saw the spine of a book with a title on it that made sense. He grabbed it and held it tight.

"The Ark of the Covenant."

Indeed, many others were searching for such a religious relic before him. But if his visions were accurate, he was the one who would find it—only he could find it.

"Are you okay back there?" Rita asked, moving toward him.

Startled, he only responded with a nod.

"What are you holding?" She leaned down to read the title. "The Ark of the Covenant." She met his gaze. "What? You think that'll save us?" Her tone was a mix of humor and disbelief.

"What if it can help?"

She scoffed. "Well, for starters, it doesn't exist. And if it did, it would've been destroyed years ago. People have searched for it for millennia, but no one's found it."

"What else can you tell me?"

"Me?" She touched her chest. "Not much, but my friend Sam would know more. Come on." She gestured with a wave to follow her. "I'll introduce you to him."

Mujtaba didn't expect that. "He's here? In this building?"

Rita was already walking away, waving a hand over her shoulder for him to follow.

"But I don't get along well with people," he whispered under his breath.

Rita stopped at a corner, looking back. "Are you coming?"

He nodded, then followed her out of the religious section

of tomes.

When they returned to the assembled crowd, she called out to Sam. A young man got to his feet and started toward her.

Rita led them to a small office. Once inside, she faced Sam.

"This gentleman here claims that the Ark of the Covenant may be able to help us through this mess."

Sam, a young man in his mid-twenties with a sunburned face behind a thick beard, stared at Mujtaba in amazement.

"That's an interesting theory, given that it's believed the Ark of the Covenant had superpowers of some kind. Maybe something inside it could beat this evil we're facing today."

"What sort of superpowers did it have?" Mujtaba asked, having never heard of such a thing.

Sam glanced at Rita, who nodded for him to continue.

"It's widely known that God gave specific instructions for its construction. It's said to contain a golden pitcher with manna, the Prophet Aaron's belongings, and the tablets of the commandments. It was made of acacia wood and gilded with pure gold. They had two gilded poles that passed through two rings for its transport. On it were two golden cherubim, and from there, God communicated with Moses through light.

"Whatever obstacle they encountered along the way burned, from bushes to scorpions. As soon as they set foot on the Jordan River, the river dried up and remained so until everyone crossed. In wars, they had it with them to win the battle. No one could touch it except Aaron and his descendants."

Mujtaba gulped. That was why he had to be the one to

find it. However, according to Islam, the history of the Ark was vastly different. The Ark has existed since the time of Adam, who brought it from Heaven to Earth. Inside the Ark was the Black Stone, located in Kaaba; Moses' stick; the ring of Solomon and Zulfiqar; the sword of the Prophet Muhammad; and later, the authentic Torah.

"And where do they say the Ark is suspected to be?"

Sam spoke with his hands. "Look, a lot's been written about it, but no one really knows. Recently, I read that some people were looking for it on a mountain in Japan because they had a similar ritual. Others say it's in Zimbabwe, and many replicas are out there. As I said, no one really knows."

"Okay, what do you surmise is the most popular belief about its location?"

"Some say in the Al-Aqsa Mosque, in the Dome of the Rock, on Mount Nebo where Moses saw the Promised Land and has his tomb."

This confused Mujtaba. Did the Muslims have one location for Moses' tomb, and the Christians have another?

Sam continued. "Then in Ethiopia, they say even today that they have it in France, England, Italy, Egypt, and I don't know how many other places."

The young man avoided answering his question because none of those locations were the *most popular*, so he asked differently. "How about if you were going to search for it? Where would you go first?"

"I'd go to the Al-Aqsa Mosque," Sam said without hesitation. "Right where the temple of Solomon was built. Tunnels have been discovered, but don't give archaeologists access to them."

"And if you were unsuccessful. Where to next if it wasn't there?"

Rita was still beside them, her head swiveling as she followed the conversation without saying a word.

"Off to the Dome of the Rock."

"And after?" Mujtaba prodded.

"Mount Nebo would be my final place." Sam frowned, one arm crossing his chest, the other hand caressing his chin. "What does all this matter, though? It's not going to be found. Let's be realistic. If it's out there, the powers that be will be using it for their own selfish needs and keeping it from the likes of us."

"Would they find a way to destroy it?" Rita asked. "Or use it to stay alive while the rest of the world perishes?"

"You know what we should do?" Sam glanced at Rita, then Mujtaba. "We should pray. Our Father already saved us once. Maybe He will save us a second time."

"Would you sit with us?" Rita said. "Pray with us?"

Mujtaba shook his head. "I really must be going. Thank you for your help." He slipped between them and headed toward the door he'd entered through. "Please, come and close the door behind me."

He was more confused than before now. The scripts, the locations, and the traditions were all different. How would he ever locate the Ark in such a short time if no one knew where it *actually* was? He was a Jewish man who grew up as a Muslim and was now looking for Christian sites. What a paradox.

He was confident that something had to exist in the Dome of the Rock, and it was transferred to the Temple of the Resurrection. But from there, where did it go?

Once outside, the door closed and locked behind him. Then he heard Rita's muffled voice wishing him luck.

He turned and waved at her, a smile on his face. Then turned back and withdrew the map to study it again.

The Greek Patriarchate and the Armenian Patriarchate were not far from the Temple. How did he not see that earlier?

He had to go back.

It was almost noon when he mounted his bike and got peddling again.

More people were on the streets now, but these people were upright, walking among the comatose victims, crying, holding one another. It seemed that Satan didn't get as many as he likely wanted, although the city was still so empty it felt like a new beginning.

That old man in his chair, his eyes missing—is this what he wanted to prevent? If so, why not tell him sooner? Mujtaba could have been more organized, at least enough to know what he was looking for and why he was looking for it.

Once he entered the old city of Jerusalem, struggling to avoid crashing over the piles of bodies strewn about, he decided to visit the Greek Patriarchate first.

Tracing the alleys by bike was challenging, but he wanted to keep it for now in case he needed it later.

As soon as he arrived at the entrance, he was disappointed. A large, iron, hermetically-sealed door left no room for access or breaking in. Other buildings were close, and there would be people inside them. Unarmed, he had no hope of gaining entry.

So, he decided to move on and search the Armenian Patriarchate instead. After one last look at the iron door, he returned to his bike and turned it around.

Three uniformed men stood twenty meters away, staring at him. One of them was pointing his way.

It was the guard from earlier. The one he'd knocked out and relieved of his uniform.

He had completely forgotten what he had done to get to this moment—well, not *forgotten* per se, more like forgotten to consider those actions and move around the area with more stealth.

So he leaned back and knocked on the large iron door with his fist.

"Help," he shouted in English.

The three men stomped toward him.

The door he banged on remained closed.

He thought of escaping on the bike, but what if they were armed? He could catch a bullet in the back for his efforts.

Luck had sifted through his fingers like salt. There was nothing left to do but raise his hands.

The guards surrounded him, and then the man he hit earlier reared back and punched him in the cheek.

It stung badly, but he deserved it and could take it.

"I didn't do anything," he said, trying to plead innocence, a hand covering his wounded cheek. "What's going on here?"

Then the men shoved him over and fell on him, punching, jabbing, and kicking until he curled into a ball on the ground.

His arms were yanked back, and handcuffs were clamped onto his wrists

He shouted, "What did I do?" through lips already swelling. "You're making a mistake. You must let me go."

Another round of punches answered his plea for clemency.

Things had gone from bad to worse, and he figured these three men would be responsible for him not finding the Ark, thereby killing the rest of humanity in one single act of violence and incarceration.

Or was this his fault to begin with?

Had he failed in his mission to act appropriately as befitting a descendant of Aaron?

It was in Allah's hands now.

"Praise be to Allah," he whispered as they dragged him to the police station.

Chapter Twenty-One

LAUSANNE

Cassandra stumbled down the corridor, wondering what part of reality involved seeing her parents alive again. And what was that warning about Leo for? How could they think Leo was a problem?

It was such a profound visit that should have been filled with hugs and love, and *I miss yous*.

Leo had been her knight, the one who was there when she was alone. He'd been there when she'd despaired at the loss of her parents—those same people warning her to forget about him now. It just didn't make sense.

She refused to get too attached to people after her parents had died. That sort of devastation came once, and she couldn't stand it a second time—it would kill her. Which meant she couldn't bear to leave Leo helpless, to abandon him.

There was something significant about Vincent, though. If he directed her parents to her through some fucked-up animation of their spirit, how did he know where she'd be and when? And if he needed her to end this nightmare somehow, wouldn't it end for Leo, too?

That led her to conclude she had to find Vincent first—however improbable that sounded. The man she knew to be Vincent now lay on the floor of the mini-market, the blood from his torn neck still pooling around his head.

But *if* she found this man, and once he explained what was happening, she could head up to the church to see if her parents were where they'd said they would be. If all that happened was real and she wasn't losing her mind, then she could head back to Leo's side.

And all that had to take place before the sun went down. Being on the street after the sun went down wasn't something she wanted to test.

Still in the nurse's uniform, she entered a storage room. She didn't take long to locate several of Doctor Traves's list items. Before being discovered, she quickly stole over a dozen small bottles and hid them in her pockets, socks, bra, and underwear, then sauntered back out into the corridor.

There was no way she'd be able to exit through the main doors with all those people camped out front. She had to leave through one of the back doors of the hospital.

Cassandra found the stairs and descended to a lower floor, where she passed a room filled with people sleeping, or they were in a coma-like state like Leo. Someone said something to her, but she didn't acknowledge them.

Without slowing for anything or anyone, she found the doors near the trash cans and exited the building, then removed the nurse's uniform from over her own clothes. With the nurse's blouse, she wrapped many of the small bottles for the doctor, tucked them under her arm, and left the hospital property.

She had no idea how to find Vincent, if that was even possible, and wasn't willing to walk back to the house where he used to live. But what other choice did she have?

So she headed that way reluctantly. Some form of transportation would be nice but limited to her feet pounding the pavement, she just walked.

If she wanted to keep her sanity and composure, she had to stay focused on her goal and avoid listening to the cries and pleas of the people lingering around her on every street, around every corner.

It took her thirty minutes of stepping over bodies and ignoring people, even one man screaming about his lost wife, to make it to the Parc de Milan. From there, she vaguely remembered which house might be Vincent's.

After several wrong turns, she finally found it. Timidly, she climbed the steps to the house. When she reached the front door, she entered with caution.

"Vincent?" she called, the skepticism in her tone clear. There was no way anyone would answer.

And no one answered.

Why would they? The man killed himself in front of her. How the hell would he make it back home?

Her parents, alive in that hospital room, gave her some

sort of twisted hope that Vincent was alive, too. If they could perform such a miracle, couldn't Vincent?

The living room and kitchen were one large room on the ground floor. Another room, which appeared to be an office, branched off to the right. She entered it to see what was on his desk.

Papers were scattered everywhere, notes from a frantic pen scratched across most of the pages. She tried to read what was written, but they were difficult to decipher.

Then she saw something that made her gasp.

Her name was written on something.

She snatched up that paper and read three words: *chaos, black, balance*. Below that, it said, *the war of the black shadow, Cassandra*.

She shivered. How many Cassandras could he be referring to? Did Vincent write that? Or Elise? She folded them up and slipped the paper into her pocket, then searched the office for more but turned up nothing else of interest.

Back out in the living room, she studied the books on the shelf. There was a lot about divination, hypnosis, and psychiatry. She couldn't connect it all.

She climbed the staircase that had a track with a chair attached to it on the right side—specially designed for Vincent's wheelchair—and examined the two rooms on the top level. They reminded her more of hospital rooms than anything else. In the bathroom, she opened the cupboard, searching for other medications she hadn't noticed in her hurry the first time. She drank water from the tap and looked in the mirror for a moment.

Her red hair was dirty and messy, and she looked

exhausted. The shower was behind her. She wanted so badly to take a bath. Leo would be fine until she got back.

Decision made, she stripped naked and turned on the water. It was still hot, which she was grateful for.

Once the tub was full, she eased in and stretched out, then sat motionless for several minutes, letting the hot water ooze the stress from her limbs.

With her eyes closed, she tried to relax and not think about what had happened to everyone outside, but the memory of meeting that black swarm invaded her thoughts constantly. She opened her eyes, soaped herself up, rinsed, and dried herself off. Once she was dressed again, she left Vincent's house.

If she was truly supposed to locate Vincent, where could he be?

She had to believe that she had actually had a meeting with her dead parents in a hospital room earlier today, buying into that mad theory that the dead man could be located and talked to.

Cassandra shook her head to clear it. This was insane. Whatever happened to the world was affecting her as well. If it didn't make you unconscious, it messed with how you think, feel, and see things—it caused illusions.

Determined to focus on reality and stop wasting time, she stomped forward, heading toward the doctor's building to deliver the bounty she stole from the hospital.

Along the way, she would pass the city cemetery where her parents were buried. It wouldn't hurt if she visited their gravesites for one minute to ensure the ground wasn't disturbed.

Could they have crawled out after all these years? Is that how they made it out alive?

Now she knew whatever happened was fucking with her head. How could she be asking herself such a ridiculous question?

They were dead, and she couldn't possibly have seen them, let alone had a chat with them about finding a man with no eyes, a man she barely knew.

What was so important that she had to find Vincent anyway? How could he help?

The entire walk to the cemetery, the paper from Vincent's desk in her pocket with her name on it burned a hole through her thoughts.

Maybe there was something to it after all.

Maybe Vincent *knew* something and would impart that knowledge to her.

Just maybe … if she could find him.

But her prospects were looking more grim by the second.

Chapter Twenty-Two

Late afternoon descended upon Lausanne as Cassandra made her way to the city's cemetery. With the sun setting in the next few hours, she wondered what everyone was still doing, wandering around the streets, gawking at the bodies strewn about. They should be seeking shelter, looking for places to hide. The day was coming to an end. Weren't they afraid?

Getting back to Leo later today was less plausible. Finding somewhere safe for the night was what she'd be doing as soon as she finished a visit to her parents' grave.

As she neared the cemetery's road, some kind of crowd waited around the front gates. It looked like they were waiting for a celebrity to appear, or perhaps some metal band wanted to perform amongst the graves.

Cassandra got closer, then edged past them to get to the

entrance. People were kind and allowed her through. Once she reached the inside of the cemetery, she saw why the group of people had gathered.

A man stood on a platform by a large tree, gesticulating to the crowd fifty meters away. People stared up at him without saying a word.

Something about it reminded her of a sermon on the mount.

Cassandra moved closer to hear what the man was saying. She focused on the man's features when she got as close as twenty meters. Something about him was recognizable.

Her head reared back in surprise when she recognized the man—well, not *him* in particular, but he resembled Vincent—just a younger, more robust, handsome version. Below him, a delicate-looking blonde woman with enormous eyes surveyed the crowd.

Wait. That woman. They were the same as the photos in Vincent's house.

Could it *actually* be a younger Vincent and Elise, just like she'd seen a younger version of her parents at the hospital?

In her stumbling around, wondering where she'd locate Vincent, did she walk directly to him?

"… and I know you're all confused," the young Vincent went on. "I know you expected things to be different, but you have to concentrate. Close your eyes and think. What's the last thing you remember from your life? If you can't remember it, you won't be able to understand, and you'll end up wandering aimlessly. Difficult times are about to come, and I need you to be aware, especially if that darkness descends again."

When Vincent roved the crowd with his eyes, he stopped on Cassandra.

After a slight nod her way, he jumped off the platform and strode to stand in front of her.

Their eyes locked on him approaching, but she didn't move.

Startled by her memories of him, the last image of a pierced neck, she shivered when he stopped inches from her.

"Don't be afraid," he whispered. "Come with me a moment." He took her by the hand and led her farther into the cemetery, searching for a more private location to talk.

Elise followed close behind.

"I'm sure you're full of questions." He spoke in a calm, steady voice, which she appreciated.

Cassandra just stared at him in fear. First, her parents, and now she was talking to the younger version of the man who killed himself in the mini-market last night. And he had his original eyes! How was all this possible?

"Don't be afraid, or perhaps I should say, don't be afraid of me. I present no danger to you."

"Vincent? Is it really you? Am I talking to you, or is this some sort of mad delirium? I can't tell if I've entered some story called *Cassandra in Wonderland* meets *The Walking Dead*."

"This is a new reality. The sooner you accept it, the better for everyone involved. Once it gets dark, that vile entity will attack again."

"Okay, I'll bite." She stared into his eyes, marveling at

how pretty they were. "Tell me what I'm supposed to know."

Vincent sat and motioned for her to sit on the rock ledge beside him. Elise sat on the other side of him, watching them silently.

Vincent cleared his throat. "It was about a year ago when I started to have hallucinations. I heard voices, thought I was dying, had panic attacks, then seizures. Finally, after a marathon of medical examinations, I found Elise, a psychiatrist, to talk about my problems." He glanced at her with a kind smile. "The doctors thought I'd gone mad anyway, so it all worked out.

"During our sessions, I experienced vision problems. Gradually, Elise became more than just my psychiatrist—she became the partner I wish I'd had throughout my life. Elise referred me to a neurosurgeon as she understood my problem wasn't just a psychiatric one. After even more tests, I was diagnosed with a degenerative disease in the brain that didn't even have a name. Apparently, I was the first to have it."

He glanced back at the assembled crowd, and Cassandra followed his gaze. The people were getting restless as the sun moved lower in the west.

"My condition deteriorated constantly," Vincent continued. "Elise had read about a new experimental drug. I agreed to try this treatment because she would be there every step of the way. After a few treatments, I was better and felt somewhat human again. I was happy, I was dating Elise, and I was living life with hope."

He stopped to smooth out his pants while staring at the ground.

Cassandra just stared at him, wondering how it was

possible.

"Eventually, the problems started up again, but this time they were different. It was as if I had opened a rift in the future. I kept seeing a car accident and a picture of someone messing with the brakes of a silver car. I felt the man's hatred and anguish, and I could even see the tattoo with the lion in his hand. I saw it repeatedly, and it didn't matter if I was sleeping or awake. I discussed it with Elise, and she told me that the disease had probably reappeared and I would have to go for tests." He glanced at Cassandra. "However, a week later, I saw a silver car coming out of the lake on the news. The driver, a woman, drowned inside the vehicle. Authorities initially ruled it an accident, but they discovered someone had tampered with the brakes."

Vincent shook his head, his eyes glazing over. "I knew I wasn't crazy, but I couldn't get Elise to believe me. So, we agreed to more tests. That's when I learned that that experimental drug we could try. When that didn't work, they elected to stop the treatment, give me painkillers, and load me up with antipsychotics. Elise and I were utterly disappointed and devastated. All hope was gone as we returned to my reality, my visions.

"Although I still knew what I saw, I knew it was true. I wanted to go to the funeral for that woman, and I convinced Elise to come with me. Now, Elise didn't know what I was going to do."

They exchanged a glance, and Elise gave her head a subtle shake.

Vincent cleared his throat and continued. "When they were lowering the coffin into the ground, and people were saying a few words before throwing soil on it, I stood and said, 'Let the soil that covers you, my unknown lady, be light. I wish the one who cut your brakes, the man with the lion tattoo, will never find peace and surrender to the authorities.' After these words, everyone turned and stared at her boyfriend. He shouted that I didn't know shit and ran away. Elise and I escaped the area before the mob of mourners descended upon us.

"Elise was furious with me, but at the same time, she couldn't believe what she'd witnessed. After that, the visions intensified, often to the point where I couldn't separate truth from reality. I saw an enormous explosion in my head, over and over. It burned my eyes until the doctors told me they were diseased and needed to be taken out to stop my pain. Those visions tormented me, and even though I lost my eyes, I could see better than ever before—just on the inside." He stopped and touched Cassandra's hand. "It was about three months ago when I saw everything. I prepared Elise for what was to come. I met with an important Muslim man named Mujtaba in his sleep to prepare him for his journey, and I told Elise about you and Leo."

Cassandra reared back for the second time since seeing him. "The future?" Cassandra muttered. "You saw all this happen months ago? You knew about Leo and me?"

"I know it's a lot to take in, but you must believe me. In fact, I *need* you to believe me."

"Why did I find my name written on paper in your home?"

"Because you play an important role in everything yet to happen."

"Then tell me what'll happen and how Leo's involved."

"It's better to tell you what happened than what *will* happen."

She nodded at him to go on, then glanced up at the sky. Darkness was approaching rapidly, making her stomach clench.

"There was an explosion in Cern. For some reason, I'm unaware that this explosion upset the entities' balance on a higher plane of vibration. It was the particle accelerator. They created black holes or opened the door to Hell—I don't know. Basically, any soul that was earthbound and hadn't found its way home yet returned to Earth in human form."

"What do you mean by any soul that hadn't found its way home yet? Earthbound? Do you mean they were forgotten?"

"I mean any soul bound here by emotion. Intense love or intense anger will often imprison a soul on Earth as they feel they have unfinished business here. Sometimes, the people left behind, their relatives, can *feel* their presence. It's because they're earthbound and still living with them, even though they're dead."

Cassandra fingered the amulet with the picture of her parents in it. "You mean, like, ghosts?"

He nodded and glanced down at the amulet. "Yes, your parents were earthbound, too. They were staying close to you, wanting to watch you grow up. Many of those who are earthbound have no recollection of their deaths. In fact, some even think they're still alive."

"Is that a problem, per se? Wouldn't families unite again?"

Vincent frowned. "I wish the issue were that easy, but bad souls are out there."

"Bad souls? How do you mean?"

"Why did I commit suicide yesterday? Have you thought about that?"

She shook her head, afraid to answer. She had theories but didn't want to disrespect him by voicing one that might be misconstrued as ridiculous.

"I did it to avoid being caught up by that black dust. I had to do anything to avoid becoming one of their victims. That black dust came from below and spread after the explosion, covering everything at night. It is filled with evil entities, and they're intelligent. It stole the souls of hundreds of thousands of people to get stronger. All the bodies you've seen cast about the streets are healthy and alive, but they lack their souls now. These black dust entities will return this evening to get more souls in an effort to become even stronger. The bodies on the street will now remain in their comas until they die. There's nothing anyone can do. That box was opened, and the contents can't be put back inside. It's like, what's been said cannot be *un*said, what's been seen cannot be *un*seen."

Her stomach filled with acid as the sky lost light by the minute. "Is there a way to fix it all? Can't we put Humpty Dumpty back together again?"

Vincent stared off into space for a moment, then turned to her. "There might be. I'm working on it."

She waited another moment, then said, "Well, will you tell me?"

"To right this upset, I'm hearing we need a truly holy

act."

"A holy act?" She frowned. "What the heck does that mean?"

"Think of Jesus and how he died on the cross for our sins. We would need someone to perform some sort of act that would be wholesome in every way. Someone without moral blemish, someone noble and religious, someone willing to be crucified for the rest of us." Vincent shook his head and stared at the ground. "But I fear in this world that that won't happen anytime soon."

Cassandra stared out at the tombstones, all representing the passage of time, the ending of the life of a loved one, a son, a daughter, a father, and a mother.

"What about Leo? Will he stay in a coma until death?" She looked back at Vincent. "Is there nothing I can do for him?"

"Unfortunately, Cassandra, Leo will be one of the first to rise if he hasn't already. His body will fail and be cast aside, but his soul will rise. And when it does, steer clear."

"What do you mean?" She leaned away from him, studying his face. "How can you say that? Leo is a good man. He can't be swayed to become part of that black dust shit."

Vincent stared off across the cemetery, appearing to focus on nothing. "It's better you learn who and what Leo is on your own terms."

Cassandra stared at him in amazement. "I can't leave him behind. I have to help him even if it hurts me."

"Cassandra. Give it a day. His body won't die today, I assure you. Visit with your parents. Especially when you don't know how long they'll be here."

Something else was tormenting her, and she couldn't let it go. "How will I distinguish who's alive from who has been resurrected from the dead? What about whether they're good or bad? You both look so *real* to me."

"There's no way to tell us apart." Vincent glanced up at the sky now. "But what I can tell you is you mustn't be found outside in the dark. You have to go to a temple or a church. The evil entities don't enter places with a divine nature, whatever that place may be. So, hurry now. Leave us. Come another time. We can talk more."

Cassandra bolted to her feet and looked west. The sun had dipped over the lip of the horizon.

She turned back to Vincent and Elise, overwhelmed by everything he'd said.

"You're running out of precious time." Vincent waved at her. "Please, go now."

She stepped backward, then after a few meters, she turned and ran from them, moving around the people who hadn't dispersed yet and exiting the cemetery as the last of the sun left them, and the area fell to dusk.

Cassandra ran up the road, sprinting for the closest church, the whole time wanting to wake up from this nightmare. Entities on their plane of existence? Stealing souls in the streets to gain power? What the hell had happened to the world? Had Hell been unleashed upon them? Was this a version of Armageddon, according to the scriptures?

An elegant woman sidled up next to her, matching her pace. They looked at each other before slowing to a stop on the road.

"Guilt is perhaps the most painful companion of death,"

the woman said, then turned to the right and continued on her way, leaving Cassandra to stand alone on the darkening street.

She shook her head, then got moving again, hoping her parents would be in the Lausanne Cathedral when she got there.

Having run out of time, she had to relinquish the idea of helping Leo today. She would head there tomorrow when the black dust swarm dissipated in the morning sun.

Her mind went back to her parents, to her *earthbound* parents, who were stuck here so they could watch over her. That created a need in her to spend time with them while they could still see each other. She had to convince them to leave her to head home.

But what was home? Heaven?

Her thoughts ran wild—all this was too much to take. She glanced up and checked the sky as the sun's light dimmed rapidly. The cathedral was at least twenty minutes away by foot. She ran harder as small swarms of blackness flew above the sky like the awakening of early bats flitting around.

She'd do it in ten minutes. She'd be safe inside the church if she could maintain this speed.

Was ten minutes too long, though? What if they had locked the doors when she got there?

Pulling from internal reserves she didn't know she had, adrenaline fueling her limbs, Cassandra ran for her life— literally.

Chapter Twenty-Three

JERUSALEM

Mujtaba was locked in a cell.

The visions, the mission, and all the thoughts that Allah was directing him were gone. This was the end of the road. Whether he was a descendant of Aaron or not, he'd failed.

No matter what he said, they wouldn't listen to him. He tried to explain that his mission was above their laws. And who was following laws now anyway? The world was over, and trying to enforce the law, jailing people to be tried in court one day, was ridiculous. There'd be no court, no bailiff, no judge. More than half the population were outside, lying in the streets, breathing their final breaths while in a soulless coma.

He had to regain his strength and find a way out of there.

How would he find the Ark of the Covenant while locked behind bars? Yes, he'd failed—so far. But he could still follow Allah's plan if he liberated himself.

Mujtaba curled up in a corner and watched the movements of his guards. He'd counted ten others inside the detention center. He studied them, too, in case one of them would want to help him escape. Many of them were young, some in their teens. What made them choose a path that led to jail at such a young age?

On the other side of the cell was a man who appeared to be in his sixties and sat bent over, his head in his hands. Perhaps he'd be willing to help them escape, although Mujtaba had no plan.

He pushed up to his feet, his ribs still sore from being punched and kicked, and walked over to sit next to the older man. The eyes of the others were on him, watching where he was going. Everyone had to be considered a threat, especially a man with blood caked on his lips and bruising visible wherever his skin was exposed.

The older man didn't raise his head to see who had sat next to him. It was like he hadn't even noticed someone was there.

Mujtaba wanted to engage him in a conversation, but a guard passed their cell, so he remained quiet until the guard passed.

But the guard didn't pass—he stopped out front and shouted a name. There was a disturbance in the cell, and the older man beside him raised his head to see what was happening. His features looked European, so Mujtaba chose English to ask him a question.

"Why are you here?"

"I wandered into a place I shouldn't have been. At least that's what they told me. Although, I don't understand. I'm here every spring, and I'm usually welcome. I don't know what's changed." He spoke English with a German accent.

"My name is Mujtaba." He stuck out his hand.

The man took it, and they shook. "Oskar."

"Oskar, we must find a way to break out of here." Mujtaba kept his voice low as he glanced around to see if anyone watched them.

"Are you crazy?" Oskar said in a forced whisper. "I don't want to get involved in anything like that. When they check my papers, they'll see who I am and let me go."

Mujtaba leaned away from the man, appraising him. "Are you rich?"

"No."

"Politician?"

"Let it go," he said with a half-smile. "I saved thousands of them." Oskar shook his head. "Instead of locking me in here, they should have shown me some respect."

Mujtaba stared at Oskar in amazement. Was he serious, or had he lost his mind?

Oskar went on. "You must have read about me, and if you haven't, you will have seen my photo. You know, I was famous at the end of World War II. I saved more than six thousand people from Hitler's rampage."

Mujtaba had no idea who the man was. Then a name came to him.

"Oskar Schindler?" Mujtaba whispered, knowing it couldn't be true.

The man before him had to be mad, totally insane. He'd probably watched that Spielberg movie and was telling everyone he was Schindler. That was why they picked him up off the street and plucked him down in this hellhole. If he didn't die soon, he'd end up in an asylum.

Several police officers came and stared at the detainees, then whispered to themselves. They spoke loudly in Hebrew while locking eyes with Oskar.

Mujtaba didn't understand a word, but by the expressions on the faces of the other prisoners, it was something serious.

A slow migration brought all the prisoners to the far side of the cell, leaving Mujtaba and Oskar alone as if they were infected with something highly contagious.

Another police guard approached the cell without saying a word. He opened the door and waved for Oskar to come with him.

Oskar winked at Mujtaba, then got up and exited the holding cell. As soon as he saw the door closing, Mujtaba ran at it but was too late.

"I didn't do anything," Mujtaba shouted. "Get me out of here."

No one paid any attention to him except one of the other detainees.

"Will you shut up?" the man said in an irritated tone. "If you're so innocent, why are you in here?"

"How'd he get out?" Mujtaba pointed at the retreating Oskar.

"He's one of the dead." Several people frowned at that statement, but the man kept talking. "I heard them discussing another man who once killed Yitzhak Rabin. Something serious has happened, like some time warp for the dead. Or someone is playing an elaborate prank on us all."

Mujtaba remained skeptical. It had something to do with that black entity thing. But how were the dead allowed to roam as if they were still alive?

It was impossible, and he'd be delusional to believe such a notion.

More determined than ever to leave, he shouted for the guards.

Time was running out.

A man in uniform stormed toward the bars. "If you don't close your mouth, I'll force it closed." The man's tone was laced with venom.

"I need to tell you something. It's a matter of life and death."

The guard hesitated, but there must have been something in Mujtaba's desperation that made the man step closer.

Without hesitating a second too long, Mujtaba said, "I fought the black Satan yesterday in a Greek church. Find Nassir and the priests and ask them. Terrible things will happen unless you get me out of here. I believe I've been chosen to stop this black madness."

The guard stared at him, eyes filled with contempt, then just walked away without uttering a word.

Mujtaba prayed that the guard had gone to get the keys, but when he returned, he was joined by the men who had hit him earlier. They entered the cell without a preamble, shoved him to the ground in a corner, and kicked and punched him until he lost consciousness.

***

When he opened his eyes, he saw nothing—no light. It was different somehow, like they'd transferred to a different cell so he'd be isolated.

The pain created a new reality, like a new consciousness. It seemed that was all he was aware of. Everything ached all over, and he was sure one or two ribs had been broken.

Things had gone from bad to worse. There was no chance of succeeding in his mission now.

He picked himself up, gasping and grunting with the effort, then limped to the wall. Using his hands as guides, he roamed the wall until he found a door, then banged on it for several minutes.

No one answered, and he heard nothing outside the holding cell. It was as if he was the only one alive in the entire building.

What if everyone had died or were subjected to that coma state? He'd be locked in this dark room for weeks until his body failed and he died of starvation.

How did it all come to this? He had no sense of time as he didn't know how long he'd been unconscious. What if the sun dropped and the black Satan mass found him in the cell? Couldn't it ooze through the cracks under the door? If that happened, he wouldn't have any help or means of escaping it.

A shout escaped him, sounding like a wild animal. Finally, out of options, he knelt and prayed to Allah to ask for help and guidance.

What seemed like an hour passed before he heard something on the other side of the door.

Hope surged in him. They weren't all dead yet. Perhaps he'd get out of here sooner rather than later.

He moved up to the door and placed his ear against it. There were no voices, just the footfalls of someone drawing closer, then the sound of keys.

Were they coming to release him?

A key slid into the door of his cell.

He stepped back to avoid being hit by it. The door opened, and a dark figure carrying a flashlight aimed the beam at his face. He put his hand up to ward off the intensity of the light since he'd been in total darkness up until that moment.

Another man entered, grabbed his arm, and without a word uttered between the two of them, they dragged him from the room.

Eyes half-closed and limping, Mujtaba tried to walk while the men supported him, the flashlight lighting their way.

They turned right at the end of the corridor and continued until they stopped at an old wooden door. The man with the flashlight used a key to open the door, then shoved Mujtaba inside and plopped him down on a chair by a table. They handcuffed him to the chair, turned on a dim lightbulb overhead, then exited the room without saying anything.

There was nothing to look at other than the table, chairs, and light bulb. The four walls made the room appear to be a perfect square. The sparse furniture was made of wood and secured to the floor with braces and screws. He wasn't going anywhere until someone came to release him.

Footsteps pounded toward the door. It opened, and one of

the guards who'd been hitting him earlier stepped inside. He was accompanied by another man holding a flashlight again.

The man who'd hit him moved to the center of the room and stared down at Mujtaba, who reared back to avoid more fists. They locked eyes with him as he wondered what this was all about. Were they going to beat him some more? Release him? Or just kill him?

Time stopped as neither man looked away from the other. Then the guard slapped the table so hard it felt like the floor vibrated.

"Who are you?" he asked, breaking the silence.

"It doesn't matter," Mujtaba replied, shaking his head.

"I won't repeat my question."

Pain sucked, but Mujtaba was not cowed by their alpha male display of clenched jaws, raised voices, and angry glares—Allah was with him.

"I am a child of Allah, just like you," he stated matter-of-factly.

The guard made a signal to the man with the flashlight. He moved closer, reared back, and drove a fist into Mujtaba's face. It knocked him to the extent of his handcuffs. Being secured to the chair kept him from falling, but the pull on his wrists stung and may have split his skin.

Mujtaba spat blood, his anger flaring slightly. "You are a tough man, punching a secured prisoner."

"Who are you?"

"I thought you wouldn't repeat the question."

Flashlight Man moved closer.

"Okay, okay," Mujtaba said, scrunching his body to avoid the man's fist. "I'm the one who was sent to defeat that black swarm. By keeping me here, I can't complete my mission."

"You are blaspheming the name of God," the man across from him shouted and slapped his hand on the table again.

Mujtaba didn't blink this time.

A knock on the door interrupted them.

Flashlight Man opened it a crack, whispered to whoever had knocked, then eased the door closed.

The two men stared at each other, and then Flashlight Man said, "Chief Shahidi, they want you upstairs. It's urgent."

Shahidi gave Mujtaba one last look, then stormed out of the room.

Flashlight Man closed the door and leaned back against the wall.

Mujtaba stared at him, trying to meet the guard's gaze.

Time passed silently, and Mujtaba was quite aware of what that meant—sunset was approaching.

His face stinging where he'd taken the recent blow, he mumbled, "What's your name?"

The guard didn't move or say a thing.

"Please, I need your help. I must leave." Mujtaba cleared his throat. "The night will come, and when it does, that black swarm will take the people it didn't take yesterday. I can help, but not if I'm tied up here. Please."

The guard remained motionless near the door.

Mujtaba decided on another approach and was about to ask more questions when Chief Shahidi opened the door and stepped back inside the room.

"Get those cuffs off him," he said.

Without hesitation, the guard pushed off the wall and moved behind Mujtaba, releasing the handcuffs deftly.

Was this a good or bad thing?

"I won't forget what you did," Shahidi said, his neck corded, a vein throbbing on his forehead. "I'll be watching you, looking for you." He rotated his neck as if loosening it. "This isn't over."

The guard placed a hood over Mujtaba's head and pulled him out of the chair and toward the door.

Mujtaba obeyed without protest. They had to be letting him go. After passing through corridors that smelled of moisture and mold, they climbed steps until he was pushed down onto another chair and his hood removed.

They took his fingerprints, and when a third man approached, a needle in his hand, he tried to get up, but they held him down on the chair. One man wrapped an arm around his forehead, yanking it back, exposing his neck.

Mujtaba grunted in protest until he felt a needle enter his thigh. Even if he wanted to pull away, they held him too tight.

"What was that?" he asked. "What the hell was in that needle? I didn't authorize any sort of meds!"

No one answered him. They lifted him from the chair and patted him on the back as if they were all old friends. One of the men gestured at the door, and Mujtaba took his first few steps unaided by a guard.

Once outside the room, Sam—the young man who had told him the story of the Ark of the Covenant in the library—stepped in front of him.

Sam wore a military uniform and glared at the others as

if he were superior to them. Mujtaba couldn't tell rank, but Sam's opinion obviously mattered.

"Are you okay?" Sam asked.

"I'm not sure. I guess." Mujtaba touched his swollen jaw and moved it around. "I'm surprised to see you here."

"They mistreated you?"

Mujtaba rubbed his neck where they injected him. "They were just doing their job, I'm sure," he muttered.

"Follow me." Sam moved away, and with hesitant steps, Mujtaba walked behind him, still flanked by two guards.

The corridor was narrow and paved. White paint was peeling off the walls, and framed pictures of soldiers adorned each side. Mujtaba followed Sam until he slowed, opened a door leading to a stairwell, and then turned and watched him.

Sam gestured at the stairs. "Well, are you leaving, or are you just going to stare at me?"

Mujtaba moved past the man.

"Go up," Sam said.

Mujtaba hit the steps two at a time, hoping to leave the building before anyone changed their minds.

Sam followed close behind. "Two floors," he said.

After two floors, they exited the stairwell and stepped onto the main floor of the police station.

Sam pointed to the front doors, where an EXIT sign was lit in a bright red light above them.

Mujtaba didn't have to be asked twice.

He strode to those doors and stepped outside, the late afternoon sun caressing and warming his face. There was less than half an hour of daylight left. He'd lost so much time— too much.

And now, more people would die, which was something he'd have to bear on his conscience.

Without hesitating one more second, he jumped off the front steps of the police station and ran for a church.

Chapter Twenty-Four

LAUSANNE, SWITZERLAND

Like clouds rolling in for an evening storm on a brisk wind, the black entities coalesced in the air above as Cassandra made it to the church on time.

Out of breath, her legs shaking, she stopped a few meters from one of the side windows.

The courtyard was jammed. A large crowd of frightened people were clambering to access the church but struggled to get in as it was full.

Several people made the sign of the cross and prayed on the steps and front lawn of the church as the black dust hovered above them, slowly lowering from the sky in concert with the lowering sun.

Cassandra scanned the crowd for her parents. She pushed

people out of the way, shoved forward, holding her hospital stash close to her belly, and finally found them standing by a stained glass window.

When her mother saw her coming, she opened her arms. They hugged, tears coming from both of them.

Cassandra eased back after a moment and then hugged her father.

"Dad," she said, pulling out of his embrace. "We don't have shelter. We need somewhere to hide."

"I know, but something will happen. We'll be able to get in soon."

Cassandra glanced over her shoulder. The black mass was only a few meters above everyone's heads.

"We need to be inside." She turned back to her parents. "Now."

Her father nodded at the window.

She understood what he was suggesting.

"Dad, that's hundreds of years old."

"It's that or let that thing take us." He jerked a hand at the floating blackness.

Cassandra stepped into place with one more look at the swarm less than a meter above them, lifted her foot, and then kicked the glass.

Nothing happened—except the people on the other side of the window backed away to avoid being sprayed by it when it broke.

She kicked the glass again without looking at the moving shadow in the sky above them.

Still nothing.

The crowd behind her turned into a roiling frenzy.

Someone bumped into her, jostling her to the left, then right.

Cassandra lunged at the window and snapped her foot outward, thinking she had moments to live.

The glass broke, shards cascading inside the church.

There was no time to think or mourn over the loss of that stunning window. All she thought about was diving through it and getting to the other side.

Hands reached out and helped her over the sill as her father pushed from behind. Then Cassandra's mother rolled inside, and finally, her father.

Their timing had been exact. Someone screamed behind them, then someone else screamed.

The broken window's opening got jammed with heads and shoulders as panic set in. People bent and twisted to gain access to the sanctity of the church, but by doing so in such a panic, no one was able to climb inside.

From inside the church, standing on its stone floor, Cassandra stared at the hole that was once a stained glass window and saw the horror on people's faces.

Someone got yanked out by someone else stronger and more eager to get in.

The blackness was waiting.

They were seized, and some light was forced from the person's face. The man who had replaced the other person was too wide to force his way in, and when he looked over his shoulder, something attached itself to his face.

Then he was gone, too.

"Don't look," her father said, pulling her close to him and shielding her eyes. "It's taking their souls. We're safe, though. We're safe."

"Are you okay, Mom?"

"Don't worry, we're fine." Her mother stepped closer.

The screaming outside dimmed several minutes later, then stopped altogether. Whoever had been outside the church had been cut down in minutes.

It was over.

Inside the church, a mournful silence descended upon the survivors.

Cassandra lowered to the floor, her legs too weak to support her.

Her parents joined her, and once they kicked away the pieces of glass, they rested their backs against the wall under the broken window.

People throughout the church now cried and whimpered to themselves. This tragedy affected everyone one way or another.

She stared at her mother and father to keep her mind off what was happening to their world. How far-reaching was this disaster? Was it just Lausanne? Or was it happening all over the Earth?

She stared at her parents. She wanted to tell them so much, but this wasn't the best time—maybe a little later. So, she just sat next to them and existed with them.

When she opened her eyes, more time had passed. It had gone full dark outside now, but the church was lit up with candles.

Most sat on the floor, the pews, while others lay where they could find the room.

The black swarm attacked when the darkness fell, but now that it was closer to midnight, were they safe to venture outside?

Cassandra wasn't willing to try it, but since the church was so crowded, some people had wandered into the courtyard to sit. Finally, others left the church entirely, likely headed to their homes, leaving Cassandra with a bad feeling.

Her parents were discussing how everyone was waiting for the sound of the bell tower, a tradition for over six hundred years.

So even now, the bells rang as usual, and then everyone quieted, listening for the sound of the night watchman's call.

Then it came.

"I am the night watchman, the time …" the voice stopped mid-sentence.

Everyone froze. Cassandra could only guess what had happened, but no one wanted to confirm it.

Cassandra couldn't bear it. She looked at her parents, concern on her face, then got up and pushed toward the door leading to the bell tower.

When people saw her heading that way, they made room for her to pass.

She opened the door and looked back at her parents. An old woman stepped closer and handed her a candle. It seemed like, at the moment, she had the undivided attention of everyone in the church.

Cassandra looked away, then climbed the old steps one by one. She passed the first floor of the bell tower and continued to the next, then up the other five.

When she made it to the top, exposed to the night air, the nightwatchman was sprawled on the final few steps, unconscious.

That dangerous black swarm had gotten to him. He'd rang the bell, which might have summoned it, and it took his soul like everyone else who was outside in the dark.

Her curiosity drove her forward. She continued up the last stairs, stepping over the sleeping man. She glanced over the stone ledge on the top level, her body outside and unprotected.

The dark swarm was below her at this height. It moved in odd directions, searching for conscious victims to incapacitate. Did that mean whoever had left for home recently had been taken, too? What about the people in the courtyard? Did everyone go outside too soon?

She took a deep breath and turned to go back down to the safety of the church when a black shadow took shape directly in front of her.

Cassandra stopped moving, her eyes on the shape while it watched her. Her heart beat in her ears, and panic swelled through her, making her want to grab onto something to remain upright.

How would she get past it to descend the stairs? Why was it watching her? She feared she wouldn't be able to handle having her soul ripped from her body.

Perhaps the only way to escape it would be to throw herself over the ledge, to fall from the bell tower. She had to do what Vincent did and kill herself. Once dead, her soul would leave her body the way God intended. Then Lucifer wouldn't get his grubby hands on it.

Although, escaping this thing by suicide wasn't something she was willing to do if getting to the stairs was still an option.

The black shadow thickened and formed a body right in front of her. Cassandra stared mouth agape, then snapped her mouth shut. Her body was unmoving, her legs shaking with the rush of adrenaline.

The shape became something she knew.

She found her voice as the candle wavered in her hand.

"Leo?"

"Vincent was right," the blackness whispered.

It had intelligence? The black dust could think, too?

The dark shadow she saw resembled Leo. It moved toward her, his dust hand extended. "Come, walk with us, my love. I've always owned you, been there for you, and I will again, my Cassandra …"

She panicked and aimed the candle at him. The light made him recoil, his dusty eyes squinting shut.

She dove for his feet, sliding headfirst under his essence. Some of it touched her flesh, and she recoiled at the feeling. At that single touch, a dark window opened in her mind, and she saw Leo for who he truly was and who he had always been. The darkness in his soul was unlike anything she ever thought possible. He hated her, despised her, and had only remained close so he could kill her later.

All those thoughts assaulted her in the two seconds of contact, and then she was past the entity's reach, hitting the top stair and moving over it. She used her hands to slow her descent back inside the church.

The hard stairs bombarded her ribs and stomach, but she made it halfway down the first flight before slowing and turning her head to look over her shoulder, still sprawled on her stomach.

The blackness was gone.

Stunned and in pain, her right wrist hurting now, she twisted around on the bottom step and got to her feet on the landing. After taking a moment to catch her breath and shake her head at the thoughts she'd had to endure, she limped down the rest of the stairs and entered the main section of the church again.

All eyes were on her.

She wiped her face, grateful she was still alive, grateful Leo wasn't a part of her life anymore.

"It's still out there."

Her words traveled from mouth to mouth in seconds.

Those at the church entrance tried to close the door to those who were just outside it. Others in the courtyard ran for the shelter of the church.

"We will all die," someone shouted.

"There's no room for others in here," another voice bellowed from somewhere to her left.

"No," a man called. "My wife is out there."

"Mom, hurry up. Come in."

No matter how many people shouted, the conclusion was the same. The church couldn't accommodate more people. In the end, whoever was the fastest made it inside.

The doors were closed with great effort, stranding dozens of screaming people outside.

No one was ready to sacrifice themself for anyone else. There was no charity or faith or hope in this church today.

And the church doors remained closed and locked until the next day.

Chapter Twenty-Five

JERUSALEM

The sky had darkened—the night was coming—as Mujtaba stumbled along the road, faint light painting the clouds a mirage of pinks and reds in the west.

Mujtaba's heart raced—the night was near, too close. Would that Satan-swarm return? Would he find sanctuary in time?

From behind, someone called his name.

Mujtaba spun around to see a familiar face jogging up to him. The man from the church.

"Wait up," his friend said.

"Nassir?"

Nassir slowed and tried to catch his breath. "See?" He panted, then placed his hands on his knees and took several large breaths. Once righted again, he said, "Our roads meet again, and you have a lot to tell me before nightfall." He gently patted Mujtaba on the back, staring at the wounds on his face.

"You look rough, my friend." Nassir gestured at the road, and they continued along the road with haste.

Mujtaba glanced over at his friend. "Did you help me get out?"

"Not alone. I had Sam's help."

"But how?"

"We will exchange information soon, yes?" Nassir kept his gaze forward, continuing to walk fast.

Mujtaba's time was measured, his purpose specific. Whatever Nassir had to say wouldn't alter Mujtaba's course. Allah was the wind in his sails, and there were no signs it was abating.

Nassir continued. "We'll find a safe place, and I'll tell you everything I know."

"But Nassir, you're considered a traitor since you renounced Allah the Almighty."

"Traitor?" Nassir ran sideways to gawk at Mujtaba. "Betrayal has nothing to do with my decision as a Muslim to become a Christian."

"Anyone who leaves Islam is considered a traitor, so I cannot understand why you'd help me."

Nassir faced forward as they jogged along, the light dimming even further. "I don't owe you an explanation about my personal faith. Our goal right now is to reach the Church of the Resurrection before that evil blackness descends upon us."

The road was full of empty cars with nary a movement. The authorities hadn't collected any bodies yet, likely because many of those *authorities* were unconscious, too.

A grouping of bodies at least ten high was piled by a fence, making Mujtaba shudder. It was as if he was starring in a horror movie about the end of the world.

This wasn't a good omen of what was to come. He needed to hurry, his task was necessary, or the rest of humanity would perish.

They'd slowed to a brisk walk, but it wasn't fast enough—they had maybe twenty minutes to sunset, perhaps less.

Nassir picked up his pace. Mujtaba followed his gaze and saw the swarm hovering only meters away now. Then he caught up to Nassir, and they ran alongside one another.

A strange feeling came over Mujtaba just outside the temple, like his body was numbing. A thousand pins penetrated his skin, his heart pounded, and he fell behind Nassir while trying to calm down and catch his breath. Soon, Mujtaba was left behind, bent over, his hands on his knees.

"Are you coming?" Nassir shouted back to him. "We're out of time!"

"You go." He waved at him. "I'll be right behind you."

Nassir proceeded toward the Holy Temple, his fear of dying overpowering any noble sense to help Mujtaba. The temple lights, which received electricity from a generator, were lit up, with the Satan swarm slowly gathering around its walls.

"Open up," Nassir shouted, banging on the wooden door. "I brought Mujtaba with me."

Mujtaba ambled closer. Though he was feeling

marginally better, the choice to gather himself together inside the church or stay outside and perish was a simple one.

"They locked us in," someone shouted from beyond the door, their voice muffled, but the fear easily detected in their tone. "I can't open it. Hurry, find refuge as soon as possible."

Nassir lowered his head, hands pressed to the wooden door, looking defeated.

"May God be with you," the muffled voice shouted.

Mujtaba stared at Nassir.

This was the end.

They'd been banished from sanctuary, and Satan's swarm would be on them in mere minutes.

Then Nassir spun around and jumped toward Mujtaba.

"The Patriarchate! We can go there." Then he was off running. "It's not far. Come on. Hurry!"

Mujtaba followed as they ran through the city's dark alleys. They passed other people searching for sanctuary, knowing full well that many of them wouldn't make it.

They arrived at the Greek Catholic Patriarchate two minutes later. Mujtaba was exhausted, his injuries and sore ribs making running a nightmare of pain and fatigue.

The large iron carved door was closed and locked up tight. Just opposite was a building that belonged to the Orthodox Patriarchate, which was also locked.

Mujtaba glanced upward. Satan's swarm was one meter above them. "We're in serious trouble." It was so close now that he could taste the evil hovering in the air, Satan's breath licking the back of his neck.

"Last chance," Nassir shouted, then pointed. "The main building."

Nassir ran down a cobblestoned street—where he got his stamina from, Mujtaba could only guess.

When Nassir stopped in front of the main building, he lost hope. He desperately knocked and pounded on the door while shouting to be let inside.

His pleas were met with silence.

Mujtaba grabbed Nassir, spun him around, and placed his hands on Nassir's shoulders. "Where else can we go? We've got but minutes left."

Nassir's eyes focused, then beckoned Mujtaba to follow.

"The Armenian Patriarchate."

They ran, and by the time they got there, screams throughout the dark city of Jerusalem were heard coming from all directions.

Somehow, fear and adrenaline gave them the strength to run even faster.

With the swarm close enough to touch now, they ran up to the door of the Armenian Patriarchate only to realize that it was locked, too.

The act of climbing the iron fence to enter the protected courtyard wouldn't work as the fence had barbed wire along the top like the perimeter of a prison, not to mention the swarm was low enough now that they had to bend over to avoid having their heads touch it.

Then Mujtaba saw one last attempt at safety.

Because the swarm lowered like a descending cloud as the light in the sky waned, if they got to lower ground, it would afford them precious minutes to get inside somewhere, anywhere.

"This way," Mujtaba shouted at Nassir, then ran hunched

over, his ribs screaming in protest.

Nassir followed close behind as Mujtaba headed along the Patriarchate's fence line, which declined on a gradual downhill. At the bottom, they were able to stand up again.

Down here, the swarm was a full meter above their heads and slightly higher than the fence.

To their left was a small shop that offered refreshments for thirsty tourists. It was closed now as the owner was probably one of the bodies strewn about at their feet.

Without hesitating, knowing any form of hesitation meant death, Mujtaba climbed onto one of the Coke refrigerators that held juices and sodas, then launched himself over the fence.

He landed in the gardens of the Patriarchate and screamed at the pain, clutching at his chest when he landed and rolled.

Nassir landed with a heavy thud beside him, grabbed Mujtaba's arm, and forced him to his feet.

They ran toward the entrance of the building on the inside of the property, Mujtaba wondering where he found the strength amidst the pain.

Holding Nassir back, they managed to reach the end of the Armenian garden, but he just couldn't go any farther.

Nassir ran ahead in search of unlocked doors but found none.

He knocked on the back door over a dozen times, his fists bleeding now, but no one answered their call.

It was as if the Patriarchate had been locked up and deserted.

***

Nassir understood his choices in life had led him to this place at this time. After his many years devoted to Islam, he converted to Christianity after the attack on the Twin Towers in New York.

That was an unspeakable abomination in the name of Allah. There was no way Allah would have ordered such an attack. It was Osama bin Laden's madness that brought shame to Islam. Fundamentalists in all religions did that, causing the faithful to be hated, ridiculed, and chastised for the madman's wrongdoing.

Since then, he'd always felt his past would catch up with him. One day, Osama or one of his cronies would arrive and take him out for his betrayal. Nightmares came and went. Allah would send them. His death always lingered around the next corner, forcing him to watch his back to see if his past had caught up with him.

So, when he knocked on yet another locked door, which didn't open, he knew this was Allah's doing—the past had arrived to clean up a mistake.

The mass of swirling blackness that made him think of gnats or tiny black flies had reached him.

Nassir spun around to say goodbye to Mujtaba, who was now sprawled out on the ground, gasping and wincing like he was having a heart attack.

Fear overwhelmed him as the blackness gathered into a shape in front of him.

A man with legs, arms, a torso.

Nassir prayed aloud, banking on his faith being enough

to save him. He closed his eyes and waited, the prayer rushing from his lips.

He opened his eyes and saw a familiar shape standing before him on the final word. He jumped back, bumping into the locked door, his mouth and eyes wide in terror.

"Osama bin Laden," he was able to whisper before the black flies dissolved their human form and gushed toward his face.

Like hundreds of tiny knives, the thing pierced his body through every orifice, then exited through his eyes and mouth.

Nassir dropped in front of the door, now soulless, an expression of terror imprinted on his face.

***

Mujtaba watched Nassir's attack, completely helpless. Hidden behind a large Armenian cross-stone called a Khachkar, he closed his eyes and prayed to Allah. He didn't want to see any more of this reality.

It was an evil that all religions had prophesied, an evil without flesh and bones that can take with it all that is good from the souls of men and women.

He couldn't accept what he saw in front of him.

And where was Allah in all this?

He immediately banished the thought. He would lose everything if he lost faith in such a trying time.

Satan's swarm was close. He felt it in the air, in the marrow of his bones, but he didn't want to look at it for fear of what form it would take.

He would die with his eyes closed. It would be better that way.

And so he prayed, "In the name of God, the Merciful, the Compassionate. Praise be to Allah, Lord of the Worlds ..."

Satan's blackness swarmed around him for hours, waiting him out, but Mujtaba didn't open his eyes.

He remained focused, rigid in his belief, motionless behind the holy Khachkar, locked in fervent prayer for hours.

He fell asleep sometime after midnight with his forehead on the ground and pressed into the dirt. Then the dreams came, and they were just as maddening.

Chapter Twenty-Six

LAUSANNE, SWITZERLAND

The morning found Cassandra curled next to her parents on the church floor.

Moaning and weeping were the first things she heard upon waking. Survivors' guilt had to be eating away at some of them for having locked the doors, leaving others outside to suffer.

What would they face upon opening the door this morning? More bodies piled high? When would the bodies begin to die? Eventually, they'd start to decay in the streets, and the downtown core of most cities would be uninhabitable due to the horrid smell of the dead piled everywhere—if people were still alive to inhale that smell by then.

Cassandra rolled away from her parents, got to her feet,

and then stretched—her body had stiffened on the hard surface throughout the night.

She found space between a pair of sleeping children and adults to make her way to the massive front doors. Others seemed to be waiting for someone brave enough to open them.

Without speaking to anyone, she unlocked the door, opened it, and took a few tentative steps outside, the eyes of dozens of people on her.

The sun's rays spilled inward, basking the floor in a glorious yellow glow—the church's interior filled with light. Dazzled by the sun's brightness, her eyes half-closed, she glimpsed an eerie picture.

Several hundred people were lying on the ground, their eyes open. It was as if the hill on which the church was built was paved with human bodies, an expression of terror frozen on most of their faces.

She exited the church slowly. Some of the folks locked inside last night followed her out. Soon, the cries and whimpers of grieving family members could be heard from all around the church area as a crowd gathered outside, gawking at the bodies.

Cassandra pushed her way through the crowd to get back inside the church. When she reached her parents, her mother looked visibly upset, and her father held her arms.

"Mom, Dad, we should go somewhere to talk," Cassandra said.

They nodded, got to their feet, and followed her to the back of the church, which wasn't as noisy. In a rear corner, Cassandra stopped and turned to face them.

"What can you two recall from the time before you met up with Vincent?"

They exchanged a glance, then her mother said, "We have no memory of that time. It's as if we just woke up without knowing what day it is, what month, what year as if we hadn't aged."

Her father nodded in agreement.

"Anything in your memory regarding your car accident?" she asked.

"What accident?" her mother asked, frowning.

Cassandra tilted her head and placed her hands on her hips. "It was how you both died. A car accident."

Her parents exchanged a glance.

"How long ago?" her father asked.

"Just over a year now." The pain of loss hit her, twisting her insides. Then she decided on what to do. "Mom, Dad, I need you both to stay here. If what Vincent said is true, you won't be safe outside. But I have to meet him again. We didn't have enough time yesterday, and I don't want to lose either of you." She was so close to having a breakdown but held it at bay. She had to remain strong for them. "Can you promise me to remain inside the church where you'll be safe until I return?"

Her father nodded. "Go, we'll wait here."

Without another word, Cassandra turned away and strode out of the church unimpeded. She could hold back her tears until she was outside in the morning sun.

After skirting bodies along the roads and passageways, she found herself in the Place du Chateau a short time later. It was also littered with people trying to wake up the unconscious horizontal crowd covering the cobblestones.

Thirty minutes later, she entered the cemetery where her parents' bodies were buried and where she had spoken to a dead man the day before.

Her mind still reeled on the city behind her—the city had fallen to an evil black force, likely a spawn of Hell.

Without overwhelming herself, she avoided thoughts of the future. How could they realistically rebuild after all this? How many people were still alive? Without society, without a social structure, would humanity collapse into chaos?

Bodies lay lifeless—soulless—where that horrific entity found them. On the sidewalks, in their cars, on balconies, and on the street, where people once ran carefree to spend time with loved ones.

That time was over, and a new era had been ushered in.

One of death and horror and loss.

By contrast, what she found in the cemetery made her question her sanity. How could this happen when the entire city was dealing with such devastation?

The scene was something akin to a social event. A crowd had gathered, a crowd of well-dressed attendees chatting in hushed tones. All that was missing was a waiter handing out glasses of champagne.

Cassandra realized who they were before having to be told. These people were the unforgettable souls who once inhabited the plush-lined coffins belowground. The people who had been sleeping, awaiting Judgment Day.

It gave new meaning to walking on someone's grave—someone's *own* grave.

Vincent's voice traveled to her through the soft din of the

walking dead, and she moved closer to where he spoke about restoring good souls to the human world.

When he saw her, he stopped talking and stared. Others turned to see what he was looking at.

It reminded her of the time after her parents died. Everyone at school would watch her with pity—the unfortunate girl whose parents were killed, and then she went crazy. Every time she passed by a group of students, they'd whisper about her. She hated their pity, hated the comments —she hated everything.

Vincent jumped down from his elevated position on a stone wall and approached her.

He touched her arm. "I was waiting for you."

"You were right about Leo. I couldn't see it. I couldn't even imagine it. How could he be so evil?" She shuddered and wrapped her arms around herself. "He wanted me dead." She stared at Vincent's eyes and studied his face. "I touched his essence, or whatever he's made of, and caught a glimpse of his hatred."

Vincent nodded slightly. "After what happened, many masks will fall. But don't let your guard down. You have to be careful, Cassandra. You can't trust anyone. Leo may come again, or he'll send others for you."

"What about the people hiding in the church? What will happen to them?"

"The dark souls, those with evil intent, can manipulate the blackness to take shape now. They use that to inhabit a body during the day to trap people like us, then take their souls when darkness falls. You can't trust anyone because you can't possibly know who you're talking to, friend or foe."

She stared at him. "What?" Cassandra held up a hand. "Are you saying we have to hide at night to avoid the black dust, *and* during the day, we have to avoid people who are reanimated versions of that black shit, like, in the flesh?"

He nodded. "It's already happening. The evil is getting stronger, and men like Leo fuel it."

"So, what can I do to stop it?" She stepped back. "Wait, *can* it be stopped?"

"I can't tell you that." His face slackened as he glanced downward. "I don't know everything." He looked up into her eyes. "You must proceed on your own. Perhaps you'll find a way to stop it."

What a wasted trip. She came all this way for nothing.

"Vincent, I have to get back to my parents. I left them in a church. And to be honest"—she looked away—"I was hoping you could tell me what to do next. Now I feel like I'm at a dead end, and that's starting to piss me off."

"You're not at a dead end." He placed a calming hand on her shoulder. "You're in limbo. They are two different things."

"I was never good at waiting."

"This is your chance to shine. Go do something with your life that'll leave a legacy."

She snapped her head toward him. "What does that mean? Leave a legacy? What the fuck?"

He got up and walked away without another word, leaving her alone.

Cassandra stared at his back as he retreated, her hands clenching in frustration.

Then, she decided to go back to the church. At least she could spend time with her parents. While there, she would contemplate what to do next.

When she passed the cemetery gates, her mind found its way back to Leo. How did he so mislead her? How had her emotions blinded her so severely? Was that what they meant when they said love was blind?

She picked up her pace and came upon a man attempting to retrieve a body.

Another man shouted about removing all of the dead bodies in the street, convinced they'd died and would start to rot and smell soon.

"Stop touching them," Cassandra said to the man, dragging a woman by the ankle. "If they're not familiar to you, don't touch them. What right do you have to move these people? Their loved ones may come along to fetch them and wonder where they'd gone."

The man released the woman's ankle and turned to glare at Cassandra. "So what, just leave them all here?" He shook his head. "No fucking way, little miss." He snatched up the woman's ankle again and dragged her toward a house.

What the hell is he doing?

The other man kept shouting about the dead and how Jesus was coming later that day.

"Where are you taking her?" she asked. "To another pile of dead bodies?"

The man grunted something, then stopped again to stare at her. "Why are you sticking your nose in my business? Who the hell do you think you are?" He shook his head. "Do you see cops around? Huh? Can you call emergency services and get a reasonable response time? I don't think so." He took a step toward her. "So, mind your own business before I drag you into my house and fuck you into tomorrow. You can scream all you like, little girl, and no one will come to help." He waved a hand at her. "Just fuck off and flit away, little birdie bitch, before your pussy has to cash checks your mouth is spending."

Cassandra had started to vibrate when she understood what this vile creature of a man was doing. He was taking unconscious, warm female bodies into his home and doing what he pleased with them.

"What you are doing is—"

"Shut up, bitch. How come you're still talking to me?" The unknown man had worked himself into a fury now. He dropped the woman's legs and stomped toward Cassandra.

She couldn't fight this man—she didn't know how to have a real fight.

She had to get out of there to de-escalate, but how could she leave others to his perverted whims?

When she stepped backward, her hands raised out in front of her, the man produced a knife.

Then he rushed at her from five meters away.

"Hey, what are you doing—"

Someone screamed close to her left as she jumped back out of the way of the lunging man.

The person who screamed landed on the stranger with the knife and knocked it from his grasp, and then they dropped, arms and legs akimbo, to the concrete.

The screamer crawled away in a scramble for the knife, snatched it up, and spun back around, stabbing the man's hand.

Pain and surprise made the pervert shout out. Then he stumbled away, clutching his bleeding hand, his face a mask of raw anger.

The woman he'd been dragging became a forgotten token as he fled the scene, scrambling onto the porch of a house, then inside, the door slamming behind him.

"Are you okay?" her savior asked.

"Yes, thanks to you." She nodded, her nerves making her whole body shake. She glanced at the woman left behind. "That was the best place to stab that man."

"Why's that?"

"Now, he can't be dragging random women into his house as his hand is gravely wounded."

"Gerard," the man said, extending his head. "My name's Gerard."

"Cassandra." They shook hands. "Pleased to meet you." She pulled away. "I'm off to find someone, and I'm running late." Even though she'd taken a few steps back, she kept her gaze on the man.

Having calmed down after the scuffle, Gerard whispered, "You will be the death of me, but you will be worth it." Gerard moved in the opposite direction.

"What does that mean?"

"Another time, perhaps. I'm sure I'll see you soon."

Confused, Cassandra walked toward the church, her mind racing. Through all this chaos, she just had a chance encounter with a sick man and then an interesting man, and they both left an impression on her. The sick man left her body shaking as the adrenaline left her system now. The interesting man—Gerard—left her wondering who he was and what he could have possibly meant by what he said.

Gerard had stopped in the street when she glanced back over her shoulder.

He was watching her.

That seemed creepy with all the dead bodies lying around.

She picked up her pace, and after meandering through several streets, she reached the church. The doors were open as people dragged their dead family members inside, praying they'd wake up and return to who they were inside the sanctity of the church—proof that hope may be dim, but it hadn't died.

She saw her mother from afar and watched her. Then her mother glanced toward her, and their eyes locked. Cassandra stepped around the bodies and the people, praying fervently among them, then made it to her mother and hugged her tightly.

"What did Vincent tell you?" her mother asked when they pulled away.

"Nothing. Absolutely nothing." The hopelessness in Cassandra's voice was evident. "It was a complete waste of time. Mom, is there somewhere we can go?"

Her father moved into view from the side. He looked at her and nodded. "I can't stay here all day, every day." He turned to his wife. "I mean, we were in the hospital when we met Cassandra, so we know we can be outside. To live in the church in fear isn't an option for me. That's more like a prison sentence."

"So, what would you have us do?"

"I want to see that stuff we're hiding from at night."

"Dad," Cassandra jumped in. "Are you crazy? I can't lose you twice. Please, just think about what you're saying."

"What will it do to me?" He shrugged. "I'm already dead."

"Dad," Cassandra said, staring up at him. "It'll take your soul, and you'll disappear forever this time."

"What if it can't, you know, because we were already dead?"

"You're willing to risk that?"

"Yes, now that the sun's up. Wherever that thing is, it's weak."

"How would you know that?"

"Because it's hiding. It would also own the daytime if it were still strong."

"Why you, then?" Cassandra asked. "Answer me that."

"If not me, then who? And as I just said, there's no way I can stay hidden in this temple forever."

"Okay, where would you find this thing?" Chloe asked, her arms crossing over her chest.

Cassandra felt he had a point. Though she couldn't stand the thought of losing him, in her heart, she knew he was right.

"I'll follow the bodies. They'll lead me somehow." He took his wife in his arms and hugged her. "I need to go alone," he added in a whisper.

There was no way Cassandra would let him go alone— she'd follow him at a distance to see what he was up to.

Her father pulled back from the hug, nodded at Cassandra, then started for the church's front doors.

Cassandra nodded at her mother, then started after her father, thinking he wouldn't find anything and return empty-handed.

This was a stupid idea and a waste of time, but what else would she do?

She stayed back in the shadows and followed her father through the streets of Lausanne for over half an hour before he slowed and then crouched over a man's body. She watched from afar as her father pulled his arm back and punched the man in the face.

What the hell?

She gasped, hands rushing to cover her mouth. When her father got to his feet, he spat on the body, then stomped away furiously.

Once her father had disappeared around a corner, she ran up to the man on the ground—the one who caused her father to strike him while he was so defenseless.

He appeared to be in his sixties, thin, with a large, curved nose and sunken eyes that rested under thick gray eyebrows. She studied him with thin hair around his temples and a gray fringe above his brow, sure she knew him from somewhere. Her father knew the man—that much was for sure.

To avoid losing track of her father, she had to leave. She'd memorize the man's face and think about it later.

Cassandra ran for the corner he had disappeared around and saw that he'd stopped to lean against a wall while staring at all the bodies. Or wait, was he looking for someone?

She remained behind the wall, waiting to see what he would do, contemplating whether she should just walk up to him and ask him what the hell he was up to.

While she peered at him from twenty meters back, he quickly dropped to his knees and searched the bodies close to him. It didn't take long for someone to notice and call her dad out.

"Hey," a man shouted. "What are you doing?"

Her father kept going through the pockets of a man's jacket, then his jeans. After that, he spun sideways and searched the next body.

The man who had shouted shook his head and moved closer to her father. "Hey, what's your fucking problem, buddy?"

"I'm looking for someone," her dad shouted back.

"Sure, everyone's looking for someone. But in their pockets? What do you expect to find in there? Money? Drugs?"

Her father got to his feet. "I was checking for ID, not that it's any of your business." He stepped backward, then turned, and walked away.

After strolling along another block, he stopped outside a large building and examined the front. He nodded at some inner thought, then headed for the door—it was locked. He kicked it hard, but it didn't give. Clearly irritated, not at all reminiscent of the father Cassandra knew, he grabbed a couple of stones and threw them at the glass like a child dealing with a tantrum. Then, he gave up and walked in another direction.

Stunned by her father's behavior, she could not explain it away. Did he have a dark side like Leo? If so, would the black gnats come for him?

She continued to follow him, and at one point, after he

turned a corner, she lost him.

The Tour de l'Ale rose before her, but her father was nowhere to be seen. The staircase that led to the entrance was empty, so she ran down the main road a little farther, but there was no trace of him.

He was gone.

Upset that she had lost him, Cassandra wandered back to the tower stairs. At the base, she glanced around again, and then, one step at a time, she climbed toward the tower entrance.

He had to be there.

The inside was relatively empty. In one corner sat half a dozen bags of soil for planting something, and beyond that, a spiral staircase led to the top of the tower.

Cassandra hesitated. Did he come in here and climb those stairs? If so, why would he do that? What was up there?

Since that was the most likely scenario, she should wait for him to exit the building.

On the other hand, she'd be waiting long if he didn't come in here.

Screw it—she'd climb the stairs to get an aerial view of the area in the hopes of finding him wandering around somewhere.

By the time she placed her foot on the bottom step, the sound of someone descending from above could be heard and felt as the iron staircase vibrated with movement.

Cassandra scurried away and went back outside to hide. If it were her father, she'd continue to follow him. Then she'd come back later to figure out what he'd been doing up there.

As expected, it was her father. He emerged from the tower's base, stopped at the door, and glanced around. Was he looking to see if anyone was watching him? Did he suspect her, or was he being paranoid?

She waited half a minute, then followed him again as he hurried down the main road—not in the direction of the church.

When he finally stopped for a break, it was in front of a vandalized bank. The windows were broken out, there was graffiti about the end of capitalism, and a security door was sitting ajar.

Her father glanced over his shoulder, then jumped several bodies to get inside.

Cassandra moved closer after he disappeared from view. When she reached the window's ledge, she peered inside.

Chairs and desks were overturned, computer screens pulled from the bases, some missing, others were broken and smashed on the floor. Papers were scattered about as if a tornado had passed through the bank's interior.

Her father stood at a door near the back elevators, yanking hard on the knob. He stepped inside when he got it open, and the door closed behind him.

Cassandra jumped over the same few bodies her father had, ran across the bank's interior, slipping and almost falling on several pieces of paper, then opened the same door and followed him inside without making a sound.

Beyond the door was a gray corridor, the emergency lighting working well. It was only about three meters long, and it was empty.

She hurried down the length and peeked around the edge.

Her father stood at a door with something in his hands. He inserted a key. A lock clicked, and he pushed the door open. She waited until it closed, then ran the length of the hall.

A sign on the door said, SAFETY DEPOSIT BOXES in capital letters.

She tried the handle, but it was locked. She wasn't getting inside unless she knocked and revealed herself to him.

Afraid to be caught in the hallway, she headed back down the length of the corridor but then came to a sudden stop at the sound of metal clanging and her father cursing.

She glanced back. It sounded like he'd accessed one of the boxes, didn't like what he saw, and threw it to the floor.

She tried to listen for another sound, but nothing came to her.

Heart in her throat, she made it to the end of the hallway, stepped back into the bank proper, then climbed over the bodies and went outside to wait for her father to come out.

Cassandra had no idea what he could be doing. After what had happened to everyone, bodies lying in the street, a mass of some sort of black evil cloud taking people's souls, what could be so critical that her father had to go through a safety deposit box?

Did her mother know where he'd been headed? Was this something they wanted to hide from her?

After about fifteen minutes of waiting, he exited the front of the bank and headed back the way he'd come. She followed him at a distance but had to stop when he sat on a terrace.

He placed his head in his hands and didn't move for ten

minutes. Was he crying?

Then he got back up and started walking again, this time much faster.

After more trudging along, he slowed in front of a four-story building that had been partially knocked down in the explosion from a few days ago. He moved closer to the entrance, where the door was broken open. Bodies had piled up outside in their quest to gain access before the swarm got to them.

She followed him inside, then sprinted to the same door, bounded through it, and heard him on the stairs.

So she took the stairs two at a time with her shoes gently landing on each step.

Out of breath and trying hard to remain silent on the fourth floor, she peeked around yet another corner.

Her father had just knocked on an apartment door. The door opened after a moment, and her father stepped inside with the door closing behind him.

"Bloody hell," she whispered as she approached the door and placed her ear to it.

What the hell is he doing?

Muffled voices came through the door.

"I can't believe my eyes," a man said. "Should I have expected this? So many people are living again, and yet so many are dying."

"You owe me an explanation," her father said.

"Seriously? What more do you want? I spared Cassandra for you. You were out, but she lived."

"You bastard, you let her live for your own selfish reasons."

Cassandra swallowed hard and placed a hand over her closed mouth. Nothing made sense? Was her father involved in some sort of conspiracy?

There was a commotion behind the door, like they were fighting, scrapping.

She was torn. Should she intervene or wait?

She pressed her ear against the wood as hard as she could, but only the sounds of a scuffle came to her, coupled with grunting.

Then, the door was ripped inward, and her balance was lost.

Since her weight was pressed forward as she leaned into the door to listen, she dropped inside the front foyer of the apartment when one of the men was trying to shove the other out the door.

Cassandra hit the floor so hard that her head bounced at an odd angle, and her consciousness was lost in a single fall.

Chapter Twenty-Seven

Cassandra grunted, then touched the side of her head before opening her eyes. She tried to get up, but a hand eased her back down.

"Dad?" she muttered, wincing at the headache.

She rolled to the side and discovered she was on a couch, likely in the apartment where she'd been eavesdropping at the door.

The man standing over her took a moment to come into focus. She blinked several times until she saw it was that man she'd met on the street. The one who saved her from the knife-wielding creep and said something about her being the death of him—Gerard.

She frowned. What was he doing here?

"I followed you," Gerard said. "Something about you intrigued me."

"Yeah? How's that?" She laid her head back down and closed her eyes to stave off the headache.

"You challenged a man twice your size. He had a knife. He rushed you, but you stood your ground for that defenseless woman. And yet, no one would know. You didn't do it for credit." He fell silent, then added, "I'd call that bravery. The kind that wins medals in a war, and believe me, we're at war right now. The war to survive."

She opened her eyes. "You're the brave one. You fought that armed man." She glanced around. "Where's my father?"

He frowned. "Is that who you were following?"

Cassandra eased her legs off the edge of the couch and sat up slowly. "Why were you following me?"

Gerard studied her face like he was trying to decide what to tell her. "I saw you following that other man—your father. You entered this building, and I waited outside. After ten minutes, a man ran outside and disappeared up the street. Then the man you were following exited—your father—but I didn't see you anywhere. I waited another ten minutes, then came looking for you. When I got to this floor, the apartment door was open. I found you lying on the couch right here. So, I watched over you and waited until you woke up."

"Thank you," she said softly. "I mean, I think so."

"Are you feeling any better? Can you remember what happened?"

For a moment, she was drawn to his deep blue eyes.

"I'm okay." She tried to get up but plopped back down, caught her breath, and looked around the apartment. The occupant must be rich to afford such expensive items. Even the couch she sat on must have cost a fortune. She spied ornate glass showcases on the far wall with sculptures on display within.

She tried to remember what the men were arguing about before the door opened, and she blacked out.

"Are you okay?" Gerard asked, sounding concerned.

She nodded, then regretted it as pain swept through her head.

What did *spared Cassandra* mean? Was she saved from the car accident that killed her parents?

Then, another thought made her stare at the far wall. Could her parents have been *killed*, and the accident wasn't an accident at all?

She pushed off the couch and reached her feet this time. Wobbling once, Gerard's hand now on her forearm, she scanned the apartment again. The living room wouldn't help as everything was pristine displays and expensive furniture. There were no desks, credenzas, armoires, or cabinets where essential items were often stored.

"What are you looking for?" Gerard asked.

Cassandra hesitated, as she didn't actually know what she was looking for.

"I need to find out who lived here. I need his name and how he's connected to my father." Cassandra glanced away as she headed toward the bedroom. Once inside the new room, she found a library just beyond it. This room had shelves from top to bottom, with books from another era. The place smelled of old paper, and the dust in the room swirled slowly, stirred by Cassandra's entrance.

Her gaze stopped on a glass case positioned in the center of the room. She approached it as if it called to her. Some special swords were on display without a label to identify them. It made her think of a scythe.

The temptation was too great—she had to hold it. So she opened the showcase and grabbed the blade by the handle. Turning it, examining it, she detected a huff of breath behind her. She spun around, holding the sword up.

"Oh," Gerard said, his hands raised. "It's just me."

Cassandra smiled and lowered the sword. "I got carried away. Sorry." She averted her gaze.

Cassandra headed past him and back out into the living room with the sword still in her hand.

The sun had reached the western part of the sky, filling the pit in her stomach with acid.

She needed to leave to return to the church and find her father to learn more about what was happening. He owed her an explanation, the sounds of his quarrel still echoing in her mind. But to get to the church on time, there wasn't enough time to perform a full search of the apartment.

"Thank you," she said to Gerard as she headed for the apartment's door, tossing the sword on the couch. "I appreciate your help."

"Where are you going?"

"To find my father and speak to him about what happened here."

Half running, half jogging, she arrived back at the church before the sun completely disappeared. The black swarm hadn't wholly formed in the sky above yet, giving her time to walk the last block to catch her breath.

Voices from within the church echoed down the quiet cobblestoned streets still covered with bodies. It was a creepy picture to witness.

When she knocked on the church doors, they were opened, and she was granted entry. It wasn't as full as the previous evening. Either people had been out wandering through the day and hadn't returned yet, or they found alternative places to wait out the darkness.

She scanned the faces, searching for her parents, but couldn't see them right away. Candles were lit everywhere, and a group of people was praying near the crucifix at the front of the church.

Someone seemed to be arguing on the far right side of the nave. A man's voice, quite similar to her father's, stated something, then went silent.

She headed that way as a man accused someone else of everything being their fault.

Upon closer inspection, she discovered it was her father, and he was arguing with a tall man that Cassandra didn't recognize.

Cassandra stepped in between them and glared at her dad. "What happened today? Why did you leave me in that apartment?"

"This man can't seem to adapt to the new reality," the tall man said from behind her.

Cassandra turned around to address him. "I wasn't talking to you."

The man held out a hand. "I'm Simon."

"Cassandra," she said, not taking his hand. "Why so formal?"

The man shrugged, his face forlorn. "Just don't want to forget the niceties that made us a civil society. Sebastian wants to forget, though."

Cassandra spun back around, but her father was gone now, melting back into the surrounding crowd, disappearing on her once again.

"I have to go find him," she muttered, then stepped away.

It took her fifteen minutes to locate her mother asleep on the end of a pew, but her father was nowhere to be found. She lay down next to her and wondered where her father had gone this time. What was he up to, and why was he intentionally avoiding her?

Something banged near the front of the church, startling Cassandra to sit up and look.

People were rushing to close the doors and lock them.

Then, she saw her father talking to someone else from the corner of her eye. Before she got to her feet to confront him, people were banging the doors to be let inside.

Darkness had fallen.

It had started again.

Cassandra remained on the pew by her mother, arms crossed over her chest, eyes closed.

She wanted the night to end.

She wanted it all to stop.

But that was looking less and less likely every day.

This was a new reality—their new reality.

Chapter Twenty-Eight

JERUSALEM

The sun appeared, the first light of dawn penetrating the blackness. Exhausted, eyes shut while still trying to rest, the sun's warmth caressed Mujtaba's eyelids.

After a night of terror, forcing his eyes closed until he slept, he recognized the light for what it was and then dared to open them. To his relief, nothing coalesced in front of him —the darkness had returned from whence it came—for now.

He got to his feet, grimacing at the stiffness in his joints and muscles after spending a night on the ground.

Then he glanced at Nassir near the back door of the Armenian Patriarchate. The man appeared lifeless, an expression of terror on his face. Mujtaba moved closer and leaned over him, closed his eyes, then whispered a prayer to

Allah to find Nassir's soul and let it rest. May Allah forgive him for his transgressions.

It was time to leave. Mujtaba's mission was elsewhere, and the evil was spreading. He made it to the fence, and it took some serious effort to get back over it from the inside without being impaled by the barbed wire.

His goal today was Mount Nebo, where Moses saw the Promised Land. He had to find a way to get there and consider how he could possibly cross the border into Jordan.

Then it came to him—Sam. He had to go back to the police station, find Sam, and convince him to help.

He took the road toward the police station, passing all the people Satan had taken the night before. The road was void of upright human beings, though. There was no company outside. Whoever wasn't lying in the street remained sequestered in their homes or churches, peeking out at the street. A warm breeze wafted by him, carrying a rank smell of soiled pants mixed with something decaying.

Some of the soulless lying in the streets had died, while the others who were still alive were soiling their pants where they lay.

An hour later, his stomach growling for sustenance, he made it to the police station. No one manned the front gate. He stepped around the gate and was about to knock on the door when it opened abruptly.

Chief Shahidi jumped out, grabbed his arm, and yanked him inside, slamming the door behind him.

"What happened?" Shahidi shouted, shaking him.

Mujtaba glanced over Shahidi's shoulder. Police officers were scattered around the floor, some with their eyes wide, most staring at nothing.

Mujtaba pushed Shahidi away and glared at him. "Where's Sam?"

"You think I'm going to tell you?" Shahidi looked him up and down, then focused on his eyes again. "Almost everyone is dead." His shout had a shrillness to it that grated on Mujtaba's ears.

Mujtaba pushed past the man and shouted, "Sam? Sam?"

He entered the main office, where the officers had desks and work areas for writing reports, and saw most of the policemen from the previous afternoon on the floor.

What the hell happened in here?

Shahidi chased after him. "Hey, where are you going?"

Mujtaba ran for the stairs. He needed to find Sam, and Shahidi could prove an obstacle.

He hit the stairs running, dropped one floor, and shoved open a door leading to a back alley.

Behind him, he heard Shahidi speaking to someone—likely on a police radio—then the voice was cut off when the exit door slammed shut.

Did Chief Shahidi still have officers outside? Did the man just call them to come after him?

Without waiting to find out, Mujtaba ran to the end of the alley and bounded into the road. When he glanced over his shoulder at the front of the police station, the door was open wide, and five men stood looking in both directions. When they laid eyes on him, they gave chase.

Mujtaba ran.

He didn't know where to hide, then thought of the Church of the Resurrection. He might find safety there, but it was too far away. He'd never make it.

He saw a sign for a Jewish Synagogue to his right and decided to risk it. Perhaps it was a sign from Allah.

He entered the alley beside the synagogue and pulled on the first door he came to. It opened, and he bolted inside. When he turned around to lock it, he couldn't—the door required a key.

So he searched for a weapon but only found a metal candle holder, which wasn't much. He held it over his head in the corridor, his heart racing—but no one came.

They didn't follow him inside.

He lowered the candle holder to his side.

After catching his breath, he moved over to a window but couldn't see his pursuers. Where had they gone? How could he lose them so easily? And why were they chasing him in the first place?

Mujtaba started toward the back of the building. It may be a safe haven for now, but he couldn't stay. He cautiously pulled open the first door he came to. It revealed a dark staircase leading to the level above.

After listening for a moment and hearing nothing, he climbed the stairs slowly. At the top, he found two rooms, both empty. One room looked down to the street at the front and the other to the rear.

When he peered out at the street, he spotted six men watching the synagogue, waiting for him to come back outside.

At the back window in the other room, he peered outside and saw two armed men standing there guarding the rear exit.

What the hell had Chief Shahidi told them? That he was

some sort of criminal? A murderer?

Being stuck inside the synagogue wouldn't last. They'd come in after him soon enough. He needed a diversion. Then he needed to escape out the back and run for it.

Fire.

Would that work?

Mujtaba ran back down the stairs and stayed to the side, where he found a door that led to an office.

It was locked.

He raised his foot and kicked the wood right beside the doorknob. It buckled but didn't give way. He kicked again, then again. On the third kick, it cracked enough that the door popped open.

Inside, he rifled through the desk drawers until he found a lighter and two packages of matches. On the way back out into the main area, he stopped when he spied a small pile of newspapers.

Praise Allah.

Back in the main section of the synagogue, Mujtaba shoved several old wooden chairs into a pile in the center of the spacious room, then rolled up newspapers and shoved them beneath them.

After one more look over his shoulder, he flicked the lighter several times and ignited the paper. It caught fast, and flames licked at the dry wooden chairs.

Surveying his bonfire as it was slow to start, he scanned the room, searching for other things to burn, and found two cardboard boxes just outside the office door. He ran over to them and discovered they were full of Jewish pamphlets advertising an upcoming event.

He hauled them both over to the fire that was still struggling to get going and strategically emptied one box into the several spots at the base of the chairs.

Within minutes, flames licked as tall as Mujtaba.

The fire was going quite well now.

He jogged to a side window, the smoke making him cough, hoping he could catch a breath of fresh air. The window was nailed shut.

He dropped to his knees and hacked so hard he wondered if he'd be bleeding soon. The pain in his chest made his eyes water, and he found himself moaning. Could it be possible to break a rib from coughing?

Someone yelled from the front of the building. Something about the fire, but he didn't hear it over his coughing.

Wouldn't that be a waste of Allah's trust if he succumbed to the smoke and died after Allah had entrusted him with such a monumental task?

He needed to leave the synagogue immediately. There was no way he could spend another minute in this building.

Hunched over to avoid the accumulating smoke near the ceiling, he ran for the back door but pulled up short. The fire had reached the sidewall and was now licking up the side of the back door.

Going out the exit at the rear of the building was now cut off.

He screamed inside his head and spun around. The front door was chain-locked shut. There was no way he was getting out that way.

Using the side door he'd entered the building through

would send him into the waiting arms of six men out front. Everything would be a waste of time if he did that.

Through a window?

The windows upstairs weren't as fortified.

In a last-ditch effort to leave the burning synagogue, Mujtaba ran for the stairs, taking them two at a time. The air in the back room wasn't as smoky, and he could take a couple of lungfuls of cleaner air.

The window opened with ease.

When he looked down, the two men he'd seen earlier in the back were gone.

He eased his right foot out the window, and it touched the roof on the other side. Supporting himself by clinging to the edge of the sill, he pulled the rest of his body outside, inhaling blessed clean air—which made him cough again. This time, it was accompanied by even more pain as his ribs ached for him to stop.

Someone was yelling from the front of the synagogue. The building was going up fast, which he hadn't expected. A small fire, sure. A few chairs, maybe a little of the floor, but not this. Not the entire building engulfed in flames before he even had a chance to exit.

Maybe they'll think he died in the fire. Maybe the people chasing him would leave him alone after this so he could finish what Allah set out for him to do.

His foot slipped when he turned around to look at the ground below to see how he'd get off the roof.

He frantically grabbed at the windowsill to correct the imbalance but missed.

Arms akimbo, then pinwheeling, Mujtaba teetered over

the roof's edge and dropped into space.

The ground came up fast, knocking the wind out of him. Like being body-punched by a giant, he grunted and scrunched up his eyes at the pain, begging Allah to spare him a broken bone.

How could his chest hurt this much?

An engine drew close. He tried to open his eyes and lift his head but only rolled his head to the right.

A man dismounted a motorcycle. Then, the man stood over him and placed his hands under Mujtaba's arms to get him to his feet.

Mujtaba grunted in protest, clenched his teeth, and screamed, the pain spiking in several places throughout his body.

The unidentified man shoved him toward the motorcycle and made him get on, then hopped on the front and shouted over his shoulder, "Hold onto me, or you will most certainly die in this back alley."

Mujtaba shoved his arms forward and leaned on the man's back, his hands clutching at cloth.

The bike's engine revved, and they pulled out of the back alley.

No one shot at them. No one stopped them.

Chapter Twenty-Nine

SEVERAL HOURS LATER, MUJTABA tried to open his eyes. Waves of agony swept through him, and he squeezed his eyes shut.

The last thing he remembered was the burning synagogue, the upstairs window. Then, falling, and someone grabbed him. He held on until the motorcycle stopped, happy he'd been able to maintain consciousness for the entire ride.

The man had ushered him inside a building where his lungs felt burned from the smoke at the synagogue. Once settled, he coughed himself unconscious.

A hand touched his shoulder. "Remain on the cot," the man said softly, soothingly. "I gave you painkillers and an ointment where the heat burned your neck and hands. The fall from the second floor might have caused a concussion, too. Rest easy, brother."

He recognized that voice. "Sam?" he muttered.

"Yes, Chief Shahidi called me when you left the station. That's how I knew where to find you. We'll talk soon. For now, just sleep some more. It'll be dark in a while, but I think we're protected here."

Mujtaba didn't like the doubt he detected in Sam's voice, so he pushed up onto his elbows and opened his eyes. Another cough threatened to rise from his chest, but he suppressed it with a short grunt.

It looked like they were in a cave. Religious symbols were set up at the entrance, letting anyone know who entered that this was a holy place. Candles flickered, and closer to their position, a clay oil lamp—an Israeli lamp—brightened their area. A Christian cross, the symbol of the fish and the palm tree, one crescent of Islam, and the trident of Shiva were painted on the soil.

"What have you done?" Mujtaba mumbled, staring at the symbols.

"The black souls don't enter churches no matter the religion." Sam shrugged. "So I filled the front of the cave with as much religiosity as I could." He met Mujtaba's gaze. "If you know something, like how to stop this shit, tell me. Otherwise, we'll end up dead like the rest of the poor souls out there."

Mujtaba realized at that moment how much of a fool he'd been. What made him think he could find the Ark on his own? People had searched for centuries and hadn't found it. How was he supposed to locate that exact thing this week?

He figured it was destiny with Allah on his side that he'd be guided to its location. If he were the Mahdi, the second coming, a descendant of Aaron, then wouldn't this be a rational conclusion?

He laid back down and fixed his eyes on Sam. "Long before all this happened," he swallowed, "I saw visions that led me on a path." He closed his eyes. "Visions of an explosion in a factory in Europe somewhere. It would cause a horrendous evil to escape. Those visions gave me direction and hope. I was informed that I had to find the Ark of the Covenant to fix what had gone wrong." He paused, crestfallen in his failure. "I chose different religious sites, praying Allah would show me the way. But, alas, it would appear I have failed."

"Mujtaba, I understand that your faith is unwavering and your intentions were noble, but what you're saying seems far-fetched."

"Then why hasn't Satan taken me?"

Was everything nonsense? Were the visions a delusion, and he was fodder for a mental hospital instead of Allah's faithful servant? He couldn't bear the thought that it was all in vain.

"I don't know why Satan hasn't taken you yet. Perhaps you've been lucky so far. But Mujtaba, we won't be able to figure out anything until we leave this place."

"Where are we?"

"In the cave of Zedekiah. It's an underground quarry that spans five city blocks under the Muslim Quarter of the Old City of Jerusalem. There's a tunnel that will lead us to Jericho."

"Wasn't it once called Solomon's Quarries?"

"Yes, indeed it was."

"Why Jericho?"

"I have access to a shelter outside Jericho. It has everything we need to survive long enough to figure out what to do next."

Mujtaba opened his eyes and glared at Sam. "You may not understand. We are out of time. What about those people who were chasing me? I don't know them, and they weren't wearing uniforms—therefore, they were not military or police. So, who were they? If it weren't for them, I wouldn't be here. I was trying to escape them when the building caught fire, and I fell—"

"Listen, when you left the police station, Shahidi radioed me and gave me a general direction of where you were running. He saw those men watching you and warned me. When I heard the commotion and saw the fire, I figured you would come out the back." Sam shrugged. "So I took out the two men standing watch back there and waited for you."

"Took out?"

"I shot them."

Mujtaba frowned. "Murdered them?"

"They aren't real people, Mujtaba."

Now, he was baffled. He blinked a few times rapidly, staring at the rock ceiling. "What are they then?"

"Part of the evil that's making everyone fall into comas. We are witness to the darkness creeping upon the daytime now."

"I don't follow," Mujtaba said, thoroughly confused.

Sam adjusted himself and leaned back against the cave wall. "When the attacks started at night with that black wind, we all hid and stayed alive. So far, I've figured out that it's some kind of entity or a collection of souls."

"Like an evil entity that came from Hell."

Sam nodded. "Indeed, like that. But Satan doesn't want to wait until the darkness falls to continue claiming souls, so he sent reanimated beings up to walk in the sunshine."

"Reanimated beings? Is that possible? Or are we talking about demons?"

"These demons have been chasing people in the streets, entering buildings through the daytime, and taking as many souls as they can gather. Like it's some sort of soul convention, and prices are slashed for this week only."

"Not sure I can conjure humor at such a time."

"I understand. It was a dumb analogy anyway." Sam cleared his throat. "The black wind has much more force, power, strength, and a hive mind. When darkness falls, be well hidden or else. But these demons of the day are limited to the physical constraints of the human body, so in the day, there's still some hope, however fleeting."

It all sounded so confusing. How were they supposed to know who was alive and who wasn't? Who was coming after them, and who wasn't? The only logic he could abide by was that they were likely demons if he was being chased.

"We would need to catch one of them to find out more," Sam said.

Mujtaba shook his head. "We don't have time for that. I must continue to follow my visions, even if I sound delusional."

"Well, we can't move much anyway. You aren't well enough. Your lungs are damaged. You may need oxygen. You've been beaten up and burned." Sam shook his head.

"You may have the will, my friend, but you don't have the strength." Sam waited a moment, then added, "Let's stick to my plan and head to the shelter as best as we can in your current state. We can move slowly and rest often, and when nightfall arrives shortly, we'll be protected in here."

"How do you know this tunnel leads to Jericho?"

"Because of King Zedekiah."

"The man this cave is named after?"

Sam nodded. "He entered this cave en route for Jericho while fleeing a besieged Jerusalem, running from henchmen of the Babylonian King Nebuchadnezzar. They caught him, killed his sons in front of him, then gouged out his eyes. Zedekiah lived out the rest of his life in prison as a blind man."

"People were mad barbarians years ago."

"Mujtaba, we still are."

"And this water leaking from the cave roof—it doesn't concern you?"

Sam chuckled. "No, not at all. It's a natural occurrence that is dubbed Zedekiah's tears."

They sat in silence for several moments.

"Something tells me we need to leave without delay." Mujtaba pushed himself up until he was sitting. His body hurt everywhere. The pain he could handle. Death was something he wasn't interested in yet. "Let's not go together, though. You should leave first. Go to the shelter on your own, stay alive." Their eyes met. "I don't think you should be helping me anymore. You've already done enough for which I'm grateful, but I wouldn't want them taking you on my account."

Now, it was Sam's turn to frown. "I didn't do all this to leave you behind. We will leave together. The issue is that the old tunnel isn't easily accessible. Over the years, the tunnel has collapsed in parts, but the army restored it. So we go together, we navigate together. I'm aware of the direction. Alone, you'd be lost down here."

Mujtaba thought about it, and after a few moments, he nodded. "Fine, but you're taking a huge risk remaining by my side."

"Mujtaba, there are risks even stepping outside my home right now. If by some chance you can end this nightmare through your visions, then I need to help you somehow." He paused, scratching his chin. "Speaking of risks, where's Nassir? Don't tell me something happened to him."

Mujtaba's face slackened as he twisted his body at an angle to lean against the cave wall. "He was knocking on the door of the Armenian Patriarchate when that black wind caught up to us. He now lies in a coma like everyone else."

"He was a good man." Sam got to his feet. "Before we leave, tell me more. Like how you're alive, and Nassir isn't. Were you inside the Patriarchate?"

Mujtaba shook his head. "I hid behind one of the large religious stones and lowered my face to the dirt, where I closed my eyes and pushed my face downward, leaving a small amount of space to breathe. I had this crazy notion that they couldn't take my soul out of my face if my face were closed off."

Sam raised a finger and waved it in the air with one side of his mouth quirked upward. "Oh, that's good. That makes sense." He lowered his hand. "Okay, now tell me about these visions of yours."

"What do you want to know?"

"The highlights, the important stuff. What are we looking for, and why are you convinced it's preordained?"

"An old man without eyes told me that I was supposed to save the world—"

"King Zedekiah?"

Mujtaba frowned, then shook his head. "No, some old man is sitting in my living room in my head. The wounds to his eyes were horrendous. There were times when I wondered if his blindness was symbolic, though. As if it meant I should follow Allah blindly, and the answers will come to me, and I will see again." Mujtaba coughed once, breathed slowly through the fist that now covered his mouth, and then felt like he could talk again. "I kept hearing the words 'Taboot Sakina,' which means Ark of the Covenant, and that I am a descendant of the Prophet Aaron so that only I could touch it. Then I saw the explosion in that factory, and here I am."

Sam stared at him for a long moment, his face blank. "How could you possibly be tasked to locate something scholars have searched for for millennia?" Sam snapped his fingers, his eyes widening. "That's why you were in the library when I met you, researching the Ark." He shook his head. "No, there must be another way to fix this mess. These visions must have some other meaning." He focused on Mujtaba's face, studying him. "Has the old man come again? Are the visions continuous, or have they stopped?"

"The visions ended weeks ago when I left my village for Saudi Arabia to start my search there. My dreams haven't stopped, though. Sometimes, I dream of the old man, but he just sits there like he is deaf and mute now."

"Why do you think that is?"

"Because I'm doing as instructed. I'm actively out looking for the Ark. The visions came, and I responded in kind. Hence, no more need for messages in the visions."

"Okay, suppose he didn't mean the *actual* Ark of the Covenant."

Mujtaba was taken aback. It had never crossed his mind. "What could he mean then?"

"According to the scriptures, the Ark was God's agreement with men. As far as I recall, it contained two plates with the Ten Commandments. What else was supposed to be inside?"

"According to the Holy Qur'an, it contained the holy relics of the prophets, too, like the Black Stone, which is in the Kaaba, Moses' stick, Solomon's ring, and Zulfiqar, the sword of the Prophet Muhammad, and later the original Torah was added."

"Could this old man in your vision simply want you to find these relics?"

"If so, there's the Black Stone in Mecca. I don't think that has anything to do with what's happening now, though. "

"The sword? What was its name?"

"Zulfiqar."

"I've heard something about that sword. It's been on Muslim flags, right?"

Mujtaba nodded. "One myth says that the Zulfiqar, a sword with two jagged forks, was sent by Allah to Muhammad while crossing the desert."

"And after?"

"Nobody knows."

"How about Solomon's ring?"

"It's said to have had supernatural powers, and whoever had it could talk to animals and subdue the elements of nature. They say it was found in a city in Turkey. Made of brass and iron, its claim to fame was that it could seal written commands to good and evil spirits."

"Now, that could be useful," Sam blurted out. "If we could find the ring, then maybe it would wield power over the evil spirits we all face at night."

Mujtaba stared off to the side for a moment. "There's also Moses' wand, or as some religions came to know it as, the Staff of Moses and the Staff of God. It was Moses' walking stick. He used it at the parting of the Red Sea. In the Book of Exodus, when God asked Moses about the stick, he claimed it was 'a staff.' At that point, it was turned into a snake and then back to a walking stick. It has been linked to his brother, known as Aaron's Rod—although that's a highly debated point. Some of it would appear to be science fiction through the multitude of translations throughout hundreds of years. Where could it ever be if it still existed?"

Sam shook his head, his face a mask of wonder. "It would seem impossible to find anything you're talking about. I wish there were a way to communicate with this old man again."

"Bear in mind, he spoke to me, not the other way around. Meaning, I couldn't just show up and ask questions like the sage at the top of a mountain."

Sam nodded his understanding.

They were at a dead-end, their knowledge limited, their direction stunted.

"Something interesting has come from this, though," Mujtaba said, contemplating where the visions had taken him.

"What's that?"

"I'm now in Zedekiah's Cave, the cave named after a man whose eyes were gouged out." He glanced over at Sam. "And my visions are of this old man in a chair whose eyes are also gouged out horrifically."

"And?"

"There's got to be something to that. Meeting you at the library was random, yet look how much you've helped me. Without you at that Jewish synagogue, I may have been killed. Before that, you helped me out of the police station. Nassir came to my aid after finding my way into his church." Mujtaba averted his gaze to where the rocks above were dripping. "And as I sit and breathe, Zedekiah's tears fall upon my person, proving to me that Allah is still with us, still guiding me. It isn't for us to assume or make connections where there aren't any, but there's got to be something to all of this. There just has to be. I won't give up hope."

Mujtaba rested his head back and closed his eyes to think. All those visions were meant to send him out into the world to save people, and all he had done so far was get injured and wound up hiding in a cave. But this cave proved he was on the right path—it had to. Or it was all for nothing, and he truly was delusional.

Where would they go from here? How could he fulfill his destiny?

A low noise interrupted his thoughts. A deep hum, as if coming from the depths of the Earth, rose to the surface.

They looked at each other.

"We aren't safe here," Sam whispered.

Without exchanging another word, Sam got up and collected two backpacks.

Mujtaba rose to his feet while holding onto the cave walls, suppressing the urge to cough as best as he could.

"Can you carry this?" Sam thrust out one of the backpacks. "I brought supplies in case we're on the run for several days."

Mujtaba nodded, and Sam gently placed the backpack onto his shoulders.

"Follow me." Sam pointed deeper into the cave. "I don't know if the religious symbols at the mouth of the cave will ward off what's coming, so we must move with haste."

Mujtaba nodded as Sam flicked on a flashlight and got moving.

That deep hum seemed closer like it was almost upon them.

Sam picked up his pace, and Mujtaba followed without complaining about his joint pain and soreness.

In the face of death, being uncomfortable didn't seem so important.

Chapter Thirty

LAUSANNE, SWITZERLAND

Cassandra woke up next to her mother. She was woken several times throughout the night by the screams and knocking on the doors to be let in, but they weren't opened.

Get to the church before the dark, or you're on your own. She didn't necessarily agree with that reasoning, but it wasn't her decision.

Even though she had a thousand questions for her father, she had avoided talking to him while her mother was with them.

She adjusted herself quietly so as not to bother her mother, then got up and stretched. Most occupants lay about the church's floor like a human mosaic.

This morning, there had to be a time that she could

corner her father and get some answers, but first, she wanted to go outside and breathe the morning air. Yet, she was afraid of the spectacle she would see. How many more soulless beings would be strewn about the cobblestones or stacked against a wall without care?

Cassandra stretched again, then tiptoed to the church doors. She lifted the wood out of the way that served as a lock bar, then opened the doors hesitantly. The sun flooded inside the dank church. She had to shut her eyes due to the sun's brightness, squinting at the scene before her.

Simon, the man who had been arguing with her father yesterday when she returned to the church, stood several meters away, surveying the soulless mass.

"I don't know how to stop it," she said, her tone sad.

Simon glanced over his shoulder at her. "None of us do."

"However, amid all this chaos, there's an upside."

"What do you mean?" Simon raised a hand over his eyes to shield the sun. "How can there be an upside to *this*?"

"I got to see my parents again. They've been dead for quite some time."

"I was dead, too." Simon looked away. "But I don't know if I came back for anything good."

"Sure you did. You said something about restoring the world to its previous glory. That was why you were so formal when we met each other."

Cassandra stared at him for a long moment, wondering how many were *alive* in the church and how many were the *dead*.

She stepped out of the doorway, moving closer to him. "Do you remember how you died?"

"Not exactly. I have scattered images of the past, but nothing specific."

"Were you sick?"

"No, I don't remember anything like that." He met her gaze. "Let's not waste time discussing a life I once lived. We need EpiPens or something that might help wake these people up."

"Let's go to the hospital, although finding a way in might prove difficult. The other day, people fought for a spot in line while others guarded the entrance."

Cassandra moved into the street and then stopped when she saw the clear expression of a woman who had died. She lowered to check the woman's pulse. There wasn't one. She surveyed the bodies scattered about, noticing many of them weren't breathing.

"Some of these people aren't just in comas anymore. They're dead."

"How long do you think people can lie around outside without food or water? Some need medicine. Some have heart problems, and without their pills, they'll die in the street like animals. This isn't right."

Cassandra wrinkled her nose at the foul stench oozing off the woman as she got to her feet and stepped back.

The wind had changed direction, and now the stench was pervasive, inviting all sorts of insects.

Cassandra wanted to close her nose, but breathing with her mouth would make her think she was eating the stench, so she covered her mouth.

On the way to the hospital, she chose empty pathways between buildings and tried to stay upwind as often as possible.

The queue was hundreds of meters long when they got to the hospital. People were willing to wait endless hours to have a chance at getting inside.

The shops and businesses in the surrounding area were all damaged by looters. Every window was broken, with doors missing and some hanging on a final hinge. Survivors of the black swarm had literally looted everything.

"It doesn't make sense to stand in this line," Simon said, staring at the front doors where several guards were posted. "Perhaps we can ask if they'll give us some basics."

As they strode to the main doors, walking along the length of the line, many of the people waiting to get in heckled them.

"We only want to ask them a question," Cassandra shouted back. "Nothing else."

At the hospital entrance, soldiers with weapons held back the crowd and tried to maintain a semblance of order.

Simon stepped past her and motioned for someone just inside the doors.

"Doctor Traves, Doctor Oliver Traves," he shouted.

The doctor looked over at them before stepping inside a door and disappearing.

Cassandra had heard the name and couldn't believe it.

Doctor Oliver Traves was the doctor who tried to save Leo. He was the one with the private clinic where she'd left Leo's body behind.

"How do you know that particular doctor?" she asked Simon.

"I was a trainee when we worked together in Geneva,"

Simon said. Then he turned to the armed soldiers. "We have to go inside. We belong to the medical staff. To verify that, speak with Dr. Oliver Traves. He was just here seconds ago."

One of the soldiers stared at them in disbelief, nodded, shrugged, and motioned for them to pass.

"You're a doctor?" Cassandra asked, baffled. "And you didn't say anything?"

"I didn't manage to become a full-fledged doctor before I died. But I know things like I said yesterday. I know the basics."

Cassandra stumbled through the doors behind Simon. The inside of the hospital was in chaos. Things were worse than the last time she was here.

"Follow me." She headed for the stairs with Simon in tow.

When they reached the second floor, they saw Doctor Traves again. He was just entering a room, the door closing behind him.

Simon called out to him, then headed for that door.

Cassandra followed him but then held back. What if Traves brought Leo to the hospital? If so, was he keeping that evil bastard alive here? She wasn't sure if she wanted to know what was happening to Leo's body now that she knew what kind of soul he had. Maybe she should've gone back to his body and killed it/him. Then maybe it would've put an end to all this madness.

Simon had run ahead and opened the door. He disappeared inside.

With Leo's death on her mind, she headed for the same door Doctor Traves and Simon had just entered.

"Doctor?" She knocked on the door. With the noise in the corridor so loud, she'd be surprised if anyone could hear her.

She placed an ear to the door but couldn't hear a thing. So she knocked again—this time harder—then opened the door and eased inside.

The room was empty.

How could that be?

She moved in farther, hearing the door close behind her, the sounds of the corridor now muffled.

Then, a large hand came around from behind and clamped over her mouth. An arm wrapped around her upper chest, lifting her off the ground as she kicked her legs and clawed at the arm.

The cloth in the hand covering her mouth stank of something terrible as she clawed at the man's flesh, her nails digging into his skin.

But then the room went dark, her eyes shut on their own, and unconsciousness left her slumped on the floor.

Chapter Thirty-One

INSIDE ZEDEKIAH'S CAVE

The passage through the cave was wide and easygoing. The area they were traversing felt like it had been abandoned years ago, the air dank, almost suffocating. Mujtaba thought the dust in the air was causing further congestion in his injured lungs—there just didn't seem to be much oxygen down there.

After slowing to cough several times, Sam offered him a piece of gauze to cover his mouth and nose so that they could keep moving without having to stop for more bouts of coughing.

Paranoia and claustrophobia enveloped him as they were surrounded by darkness at the front and rear. The darkness seemed to move in places, swirl, but the darkness stilled when he stared directly at it. Sam aimed the flashlight left and right, slicing through the pitch, but he was always meters ahead, so Mujtaba felt like he was suffocating in the dark cave.

He slowed again, bent over and panting to rest his legs and catch his breath. "Hey, Sam." The words came out as short squeaks, followed by more coughing.

He waited for Sam to stop and turn around before saying anything more.

"How sure are you that there's a way out of here?" They had been walking for hours now.

"There's a way out," Sam said, nodding in the flashlight's glow. "I've seen the maps. In case of a coup or a war, this was the route we would escort the political VIPs to safety."

"How long before we can exit this cave?" He lifted his head. "I can't endure much more down here."

"I've never done the walk myself, but I've been told it can be as long as seven hours before we're out of Jerusalem and closer to Jericho."

Mujtaba lowered to the rock floor, coughed, then controlled his breathing in slow spurts. "We've been on the move for over three hours. Let's rest a bit, then walk the other half after."

Sam moved closer, helped him get comfortable, and sat beside him.

Mujtaba closed his eyes and rested his head back, the bouts of coughing less and less as his heavier breathing decreased. "Let's just sit for a few minutes. Catch our breath."

Sam grunted assent beside him.

Mujtaba tried to conjure a vision of the old man in the chair with no eyes. He pictured his face, listened for his words, meditating on the messages he once conveyed. In trying to relive the visions mentally, he saw the eyeless old man sitting in the armchair of a house.

Then something broke, shattered, like glass.

The old man stared at him—well, *stared* may not be the right word—aimed his eyeless face at him.

"You have a mission to find what is eternally lost."

These words repeatedly played in Mujtaba's mind until the old man whispered, "Don't trust anyone."

Mujtaba opened his eyes—he wasn't in a cave anymore.

Glass broke again, startling him.

He glanced over and saw the eyeless old man in the armchair. This time, he wasn't old, though. This time, he was young and had eyes.

Mujtaba studied the man with eyes as he stared back at him intently until he felt his mouth fill with something eerily similar to salt. He spat it out when he couldn't hold it inside, coughing salt all over himself.

The vision ceased abruptly as he opened his eyes.

Sam was sleeping against the rock wall, propped up in a sitting position.

Should he leave him be and carry on without him?

Don't trust anyone resonated through his head.

Could Sam be trusted?

He glanced around and saw darkness, the flashlight beside Sam still on and offering a grim reminder of the comfort light offered.

What if Mujtaba got lost going alone? Perhaps he needed Sam for a short while longer.

"Get up." Mujtaba nudged Sam. "We must—" Cold air caressed his skin, cutting him off. That couldn't be a good sign. Where air could reach them, so could that black dust swarm.

Sam moaned and stirred against the rock wall.

Mujtaba leaned close to Sam's ear. "Tell me you know a way out of this place."

Sam blinked awake, then pushed himself to his feet, shouldering the backpack. "If we keep going that way," he pointed ahead, "we'll find the first station. Everything will be fine."

"What do you mean by 'station'?" Mujtaba stared at him, his face blank.

"I didn't want to tell you until we walked up to it."

"Why would that be?" *Trust has to be earned.*

"I didn't want to give you hope and then disappoint you."

"Seriously?" Mujtaba got up slowly and moved closer to Sam. "What sort of station?"

"Along this route to Jericho, somewhere near the middle of the journey, there's a box of supplies. Let's just keep moving."

Mujtaba nodded, and the men moved in tandem, keeping the flashlight aimed at the floor ahead of them. After another half-hour, with only slowing for two coughing bouts, they found a large wooden box on the ground on one side of the tunnel. It was about double the average size of a large suitcase and waist-high.

It took both of them pulling on the lid's edge to open it.

They tossed the cover aside and then peered inside. Knives, medical supplies, sealed water, flashlights, small shovels, pickaxes, and an envelope graced the interior.

Sam grabbed the envelope and opened it. He handed the flashlight to Mujtaba, who shone it on the contents. It appeared to be old government documents relating to granting power, emergency report forms, a list of all the supplies in the box, and an evacuation map.

"Mujtaba, let's take everything we can carry," Sam said, grabbing one of the shovels.

Mujtaba retrieved two knives, some of the water, and reached for more when Sam smashed the shovel against the rock wall about three meters away, startling him.

"What are you doing?" Mujtaba snapped in a harsh whisper.

Sam hit the wall again, causing dust particles to billow down.

Mujtaba moved to stand beside the crazy man, unsure if he should stop this insanity before there was a cave-in or wait to find out if there was a purpose.

A chunk of rock broke off on the next blow to the wall, revealing a wooden door. Mujtaba gasped, then immediately grabbed at the rock, impeding the door, and yanked it out of the way. The rock concealing the door was thin and easily broke off in their hands.

Sam flicked a latch, pulled the door open, then stepped inside it, the flashlight out in front of him. Mujtaba coughed from the dust but stepped inside behind Sam and closed the door. This made him feel more secure—somewhat. Perhaps when the evil darkness came, it would skip the door and continue to Jericho.

They followed this new path with caution.

"Soon," Sam whispered. "We should find stairs. Then we'll climb to the surface as the map says."

Mujtaba uncapped one of the bottles to drink some water.

Sam spun around and shoved the light in his face at the sound. Then, the water bottle was kicked from his hands.

"Hey, what're you doing?" Mujtaba didn't hide the irritation from his voice as the water gurgled out of the bottle on the rock floor somewhere to his right.

"I didn't protect you so far just to have you die of poisoning. Do you know how old that shit was? A little more patience, Mujtaba. We're almost there."

Mujtaba nodded, some of his anger dissipating. Sam was right. What had he been thinking?

They kept walking forward and found stairs ten minutes later. An iron hatch greeted them at the top. It resembled something commonly found on submarines. The hatch had a giant wheel, something akin to the size of a city bus's steering wheel.

Sam clutched it and tried to turn the wheel, but it only moved a few inches and then rattled to a stop. Sam pushed upward with his shoulder against the rock wall, but the hatch didn't move. So Mujtaba climbed up beside him and pushed, too.

The hatch lifted an inch, then another, and finally, they could shove it all the way open. It clanged loudly upon smacking down on the other side.

Sam climbed out of the cave first.

Mujtaba followed and looked up to see a swarm of

blackness envelope Sam.

"Sam, come back," Mujtaba shouted, but it was too late.

The blackness moved fast.

"No, Sam," Mujtaba shouted, emotion tinging his voice as he climbed upward and out of the hatch to grab at the man. "Close your eyes! Pray!"

Mujtaba stretched out his hand as Sam stared at him, a look of terror on his face.

Then, what looked like smoke bled from his ears and mouth. Before anything exited his eyes, Sam touched them and dropped to the ground.

Mujtaba couldn't bear to watch. He bent over, then dropped to the ground, half in and half out of the hole, his face pushed into the dirt.

Sam's body flopped beside him and didn't move.

Mujtaba remained where he was a moment longer, then lifted his head to look at Sam.

He mouthed the word, *no*, as the blackness gathered above Sam and turned toward Mujtaba. It appeared to be filled with hundreds—no, thousands—of tiny human faces watching him. Those faces grimaced like they were disturbed by something, then they flipped to an angry expression and charged him.

"You won't win," he muttered. "Whatever you do, you will not win. In Allah's name, I won't allow it." Mujtaba growled the last words as he closed his eyes and shoved his face into the dirt floor of the desert.

He whispered prayers while waiting for the inevitable.

His eyes closed; Satan's darkness hovered nearby but didn't enter him.

The first rays of the sun warmed the back of his head, then the tips of his ears, and finally his cheeks before he lifted his head from the dirt and glanced around.

Sam seemed to be unconscious beside him. Mujtaba was alive, though, and the blackness had dissipated for another day.

Surrounded by dirt and sand, like he was in the middle of the Sahara, how could he ever find what was eternally lost now?

Even though he was on the right path at times, it always felt that he was further and further from completing his mission.

Perhaps Allah had entrusted the wrong Muslim.

Mujtaba hung his head in prayer, unsure if he would ever rise to the challenge.

This was proof he wasn't the *guided one*, the Mahdi, the messianic figure who was to rise at the end of times—the second coming—and rid the world of evil and injustice.

Then Sam coughed beside him, restarting Mujtaba's heart.

Chapter Thirty-Two

WHEN CASSANDRA OPENED HER eyes, her ankles ached. A cloth had been stuck in her mouth. Her captors had tied her to a bed. On another bed to her right was Simon, also bound and gagged.

She moaned and glanced around the room. They were still in the hospital—in an operating room.

How long had she been unconscious? Minutes, hours? There were no windows, so she couldn't tell if it was day or night. Could she have been out most of the day? Or did they drug her to keep her sleeping this long?

She tried to sit up but couldn't move. Her wrists and ankles were too tight.

What the hell's going on?

Just as she opened her mouth to try to scream past the gag—if possible—the hospital room door opened, and

Doctor Traves entered, pulling another bed with him. The door closed, and he locked it behind him.

A body lay on the bed, covered in a white sheet.

The doctor touched something on the wall, and the room's brightness increased.

He approached her and touched her cheek. "I waited for you," he whispered. "We thought you loved Leo." Traves shook his head. "But you left him to die. You left him alone." He tsked once. "And then fate played a hand in returning you to me."

The doctor pulled back the sheet and exposed the face of the man on the bed.

"Leo?" Cassandra whispered past her gag, craning her neck.

"No," Traves said.

She angled her head as far as she could, straining to see who was on the other bed—it wasn't Leo.

It was Doctor Traves himself.

Cassandra gawked up at the man standing before her— the reanimated version of the body on the bed.

"What is this?" she asked, her voice dimmed behind the gag.

The doctor yanked it from her mouth and raised a finger in front of her face. "Don't scream."

"What's happening here?"

"I'm dying," he said.

"No shit," she whispered, her eyes darting to the body on the bed.

"No, you don't understand." Traves leaned back against the bed where his body now lay. "I've been on dialysis for my kidneys for years. The waitlist was too long for a new kidney. And when the world went to hell, I gave in and went outside at night."

"You did what—?" her voice caught in her throat.

"I figured, what the hell. I was going to die anyway. Might as well make it quick."

"So what's all this about then?" she asked, her mouth dry.

"Well, once I became this"—he looked down the length of his body, then back to Cassandra—"I realized that I could still perform the operation and get that kidney my body so needs without feeling an ounce of pain. And when this is all over, I'll merge with my carcass again and be as good as new."

She stared at him for a long moment, then whispered, "You're insane."

"Probably, but I also wield power and the knowledge to operate on you and me."

"*Me?* Why me?"

"Because you're a perfect match." He shrugged. "So, I'm going to need your kidneys." He shook his head again. "I waited for you at my clinic so I could do the operation there, but when you didn't show, I figured I'd lost you." He glanced at Simon, who was tied to a chair. "You made everything so easy, Simon. I never thought I'd get to kill you a second time."

Simon, awake now, struggled against his bonds, then glared red-faced at Traves. "When the sun sets, we'll see who's killing who. The darkness has increased its size and power these last few nights. They've been able to reanimate people to walk through the day and chase down the remaining souls. I'll join their side, give up my soul if only to make sure you are taken in their sweep of this farce you call a hospital."

Traves smiled, leaned back, and crossed his arms. "My kidney is malfunctioning, and Cassandra has a compatible one. How is that evil? How is that a farce?"

"You killed me, and you'll surely kill Cassandra by taking a piece of her she hasn't consented to have removed."

Traves scoffed. "There's no time to argue about this. The surgery will go as planned, but since I can't predict what will happen when it gets dark, we'll wait until tomorrow morning."

Cassandra listened to the men squabble, stunned at what she was hearing. How could Doctor Traves know she was compatible? How could any of this even be happening?

She wished she had a weapon. She wished she hadn't followed Simon this morning. She wished for many things, and lying in this hospital room wasn't one of them.

The doctor had moved to the side where he washed something in a small sink. The water turned off. Then he approached Simon to stand in front of him.

Then, the human form of Doctor Traves dematerialized like he'd been held together by gravity that was no more.

In its place was what looked like a mass of insects. That black mass moved closer to Simon as he struggled to free his hands.

Motionless in front of him for several seconds— appraising Simon, sizing him up, the insectile mass coalesced into random shapes, then formed a foot-long spear.

After holding that shape briefly, the darkness shot forward, entering through Simon's eyes, nose, mouth, and ears while he jerked and spasmed. He tried to scream, but his mouth had filled with those tiny insects before any sound escaped.

Then, when she thought she'd seen enough, Simon's essence blurred. He, too, became liquified in the air and disappeared into a swarm of insect-like particles, the black straps holding him flattening out, constraining nothing, useless.

The two masses were one, hovering off to Cassandra's right. She didn't want to breathe, move, or even blink.

The figure noticed her. It floated closer and stopped over her abdomen.

This was the end for her—she was sure of it. Yet something at the back of her mind told her that Traves needed her alive for the operation in the morning and that the blackness wouldn't take her yet.

So she screamed.

And screamed, her eyes closing as she didn't want to see that entity anymore.

Something smacked into the door, and she gasped for a breath, cutting off her scream.

Through eyes blurred with tears, she watched a man enter the room and rush over to her.

A quick scan of the room told her the Traves/Simon blackness was gone.

She recognized the man—Gerard.

"Everything'll be fine," he whispered as he untied her wrists and then worked on her legs.

Cassandra stared at the ceiling as if in a state of shock.

"Traves killed Simon," she muttered. "Then he took his soul." She let more tears run down her cheeks without rubbing them away now that her hands were free. "Simon couldn't do anything to defend himself. Those insects entered him. Then it was over. His soul is dead."

Gerard moved closer, and she leaned into his arm to cry on him. To have someone so close who wasn't trying to kill her was comfort enough.

"Cassandra," he said, his tone soft. "The sun is almost down. We must leave now and go to the church."

He placed an arm under her shoulders and lifted her off the bed. After so many hours of lying down, her body was stiff. She wanted to ask him how he knew she was here but didn't bother. What was important was that he came and they were leaving.

They approached the door slowly, then left the room and proceeded toward the elevator at the end of the corridor. When the elevator doors opened and no one got off, he ushered her on.

"We must move fast," he said as they entered the elevator.

Gerard stared at the buttons, then pushed the one for the basement.

"We'll use a stairwell exit from down there and get to the church before full dark."

Cassandra nodded as the elevator descended.

When it slowed at the basement level, she frowned at the sound of someone screaming.

The elevator stopped with a slight jerk, then the doors

opened.

Three people ran toward them, a blackness following close behind like a swarm of wasps.

"Close the door," Cassandra screamed, gesturing wildly.

"No," Gerard shouted, grabbing her wrist. "Come with me."

He pulled her to a side door at the right of the elevator.

Cassandra shouldered her way through it and looked back at the people not two meters away.

The blackness had just caught them, their bodies raised in the air, arms and legs pulled by gravity and dangling behind them. It was sucking what looked like their life from the bodies. Before the door closed, she saw all three bodies slump to the concrete floor, lifeless.

A staircase with a chain forbidding entry was on the other side of the door.

Gerard scrambled over the chain, and Cassandra followed with his help. They climbed the stairs quickly. At the next door, Gerard tore it open.

The lowering sun in the west revealed that they'd spilled out a side entrance of the hospital.

A man seemed to be waiting for them because he stood there, his arms crossed, watching them.

"You did it," he said.

For a second, her blood froze.

"Vincent?" Cassandra said, relief flooding her.

"Cassandra, this is the end, but there's one thing left to do."

"What?" she gasped, stumbling on her feet momentarily, Gerard helping her stay upright.

"You must find Leo's body."

"Why would I do that?" she snapped. "That's the last thing I want to do."

"Because you have to kill him this time. Kill his body."

She gawked at him, staring into his eyes, speechless.

Vincent continued. "He's so evil and dark on the inside that he's now leading these evil spirits that have been loosed upon the city. As long as there's a body, his connection with the living is even greater, and the power he acquires by taking new souls is making him even stronger. Soon, there'll be no going back. If you don't kill his body, the evil that rose from that explosion will be powerful enough to take the entire planet."

Cassandra took a few steps back from Vincent.

"How do you know he's their leader? What do you mean by connection with the living? How is any of this even possible?" Her hands clutched into fists at her side, her stomach clenching as she wondered how much more she could take.

"We don't have time for this," Gerard mumbled beside her. "The church, remember?"

Vincent stepped closer. "Many lives and souls depend on you, whether you like it or not, Cassandra. Do this, do your part, and a religiously devout Muslim man of holy descent will find a way to finish it all. Of this, I'm sure."

Cassandra pulled away from Vincent.

"Is it the same Muslim man you mentioned back at the cemetery that day?"

Vincent nodded. "The same man. Now, please, Cassandra, you must kill Leo's physical body."

She stared at him for a long moment, Gerard getting antsy beside her. "I didn't choose this, nor do I want to go around killing people's bodies without knowing what's happening. We've got less than an hour's light left. There's no time anyway."

"You must do what I'm telling you, Cassandra. Leo watched you follow your father yesterday. He knows what possessed your father to punch that body in the street. He's orchestrating everything now. Leo was the mastermind of your parents' deaths even before all this happened."

Cassandra glared at him. How the hell did he know something like that? Were those words meant to goad her into a decision she wanted nothing to do with? What else did he know?

She took a deep breath, watching them both, trying to piece it all together, then nodded briefly. Vincent hadn't done her wrong before. If Leo was some sort of evil source thing, she should be the one to end it.

Cassandra turned to Gerard. "Are you coming?"

"You're making a mistake." Gerard shook his head, staring at the ground. "We should be headed to the church."

Without replying, Cassandra walked away, Gerard following close behind, mumbling to himself.

Before they got two meters, Vincent tossed a flashlight at Gerard, and he caught it, then hurried to catch up to Cassandra.

"What's Leo got to do with all this?" Gerard asked.

"We'll find out soon enough," she said, picking up her pace.

What was all that about a religiously devout Muslim

man? It made her wonder how many people Vincent was working with to thwart the blackness from Hell.

Which led her to conclude that she'd do her part. She was intent on getting answers and likely committing a murder now.

If that was the only way to stop this madness, then so be it.

Chapter Thirty-Three

WHEN GERARD TURNED ON the flashlight, he kept his fingers over the lens to avoid unwanted attention.

"My father passed through here yesterday. He went up that tower"—Cassandra pointed at the tower she'd followed him to yesterday—"then left the area angry. I still haven't managed to find out why." Then she stopped walking, her eyes on the base of the tower. "Give me the flashlight. I want to go inside."

"Cassandra, that's dangerous, and we don't have much time. There's less than thirty minutes of light left."

"Really, Gerard? Are you kidding me? It's over. This'll likely be the last time I'm in this area before that swarm gets me or those demon daywalkers catch us. I need five minutes. Then we keep going. Now give me the flashlight."

She held out her hand and gripped the flashlight tight

when he gave it to her.

Gerard elected to remain outside as she stepped into the building. She shone the light around the pitch-dark area until she found the base of the stairs, then started climbing them, the flashlight in one hand, touching the wall with the other to keep orientated and balanced.

On the next level, a box with what looked like medical records strewn about was torn open.

She moved closer but then stopped and turned off the flashlight. Someone was coming up the stairs behind her.

The person on the stairs stopped moving.

"Cassandra," Gerard whispered.

She inhaled, the flashlight held tight to her chest.

"Yeah, up here," she said, turning the flashlight back on.

Beside the box on the floor was a large stone rolled across an opening in the wall.

A hiding place?

She grabbed some of the papers and scanned them. They were medical reports of patients with multiple stamps on the top corner. One stamp written in green letters said, "Approved for Transplant," and the second in red letters said, "Died."

Gerard sidled up next to her. "Give me the flashlight to help you so we can leave faster."

She handed it over and grabbed a few more documents, sifting through them alphabetically.

When she got to her name, she gasped.

Her own medical report was there. It had a current photo of her with a green stamp.

Her heart raced, and her hands trembled. She'd gone to

the hospital to remove her tonsils a year ago. Why were her medical records here in this box?

She turned to Gerard, staring at him.

"We need to leave. Now."

He nodded. "That's what I've been trying to say."

She started down the stairs.

"Where are we going?" he asked behind her.

"To the apartment where you found me yesterday, the one I followed my father to. He argued with a man there, and I need to know who that man is and why."

"Cassandra, there's no time left."

She stopped on the bottom stair and glanced back up at him. "That apartment is the key. Whoever lives there is connected in some way. Then we go find Leo." She shook her head. "I can't die without answers."

Outside, someone screamed in the distance. They were likely freaking out because the sun had dipped below the horizon. They would be taking risks, but this was the end anyway. How could they all come back from what was happening?

Gerard followed her silently until they reached the apartment building. The lobby door was still open. They raced up the stairs to the fourth floor, and Cassandra approached the apartment. She listened at the door for anyone talking but heard nothing.

She reared back to kick the door, but Gerard grabbed her arm, stopping her.

"I wasn't frank with you," he whispered, glancing at the floor. "Before all this happened, you need to know I had no intention of hiding things from you."

Nothing could surprise her anymore. "What are you talking about?"

Their eyes met.

"I was told that this was the only way to fix things and save thousands. I know what must happen and am prepared to do it. I'm so sorry I wasn't open with you before, but I was worried you wouldn't trust me."

"Gerard, you're scaring me. Tell me what you're talking about."

He took a deep breath and gestured with a nod toward the door. "Open it."

Her eyes widened. "Do you know who lives here?"

"Let's just go inside."

The door opened before she could touch it, and a man who appeared slightly older than her father stood there watching them.

"I told you she'd come to her senses," the man said as he stepped aside to let them pass.

Gerard entered first, and then Cassandra followed slowly.

What the hell is going on?

There was no electricity in the city yet, but a small battery-powered lamp lit up an area by the couch. That sword she held the day before wasn't on the couch where she'd thrown it. Perhaps it was back in its case.

"You're a lucky girl," the man said, gesturing at the couch.

Cassandra stared at him, her face slack. She chose to sit, weakened by lack of sustenance.

"Can I offer you anything?"

Cassandra shook her head, even though she was starving.

She didn't want anything from this man until she discovered what was going on.

"You're completely safe here. I made sure of that personally."

Cassandra nodded, even though she had no idea how he could *make sure of that.*

The man turned to Gerard. "What have you told her?"

"She knows it's over, that the swarm will eventually take everyone."

Cassandra snapped her head toward Gerard, trying hard to hide her anger. What the hell was he thinking? She was supposed to kill Leo to have a chance at stopping the swarm —if that would even work.

The man turned back to her. "I'm glad you see things that way."

Cassandra looked at Gerard, then back at the old man.

"Do you want to see Leo?" he asked. "We have him here. We've been taking care of him in your absence."

"He's here?" Cassandra said her first words since entering the apartment.

"We moved him from Traves's clinic." He waved for her to follow. "This way."

He led her to a large room with bookshelves. Once inside, he opened the closet door and stepped into another room. Leo's body, connected to an IV drip, was in that room.

The man turned back and signaled for Cassandra to come inside.

Gerard waited on the other side of the closet door.

Cassandra approached Leo and leaned against the bed next to his chest. Affectionately, she caressed his cheek while tears glazed her eyes. The love of her life lay there, barely alive and needing to die to save others.

"My love," she whispered while the older man watched her, a look of smug satisfaction on his face.

She detected movement in the room and shivered.

The man looked on reassuringly. "Don't be afraid. Nothing will hurt you in here."

Two dark figures floated by—one was Leo, and the other was Doctor Traves.

She watched Leo for a moment longer, her heart trembling, then stood.

The black entity entered Leo's body, and his eyes opened. He pulled the IV drip out of his arm and sat up.

Cassandra held her breath in fear of what was about to happen.

"Dad, get her out of there," Gerard shouted. "You didn't tell me she'd be in danger."

The man spun around and pushed Gerard back, then closed the door.

Dad? Is this man Gerard's father?

Was that what he meant when he said he hadn't been frank with her? Then, another thought crossed her mind. Did Gerard actually follow her yesterday when she was following her father? Or was he in this apartment and left behind for when she woke up—left behind with a plausible story?

Cassandra leaned away from Leo, remembering what his essence felt like when her skin brushed him back in the church tower. It was all darkness, lacking love or light.

"Don't be afraid of me," Leo whispered. "I've missed you so much." He pushed off the bed and approached her until she was up against the wall. Then he tugged at her pants, but she stopped him.

"Are you aware of the kind of power a child of ours would have?" he asked.

A tear slipped from her eye as her head pressed back against the wall. She was trapped. Leo was much stronger than her, and that old man guarded the exit.

"It will happen with or without your consent," Leo said, glancing over at the smiling old man.

Was this a show put on for his creepy amusement?

Cassandra found her voice. "I thought you wanted my kidney."

"Your body will be useful in many ways. We have the means to maintain you, to keep you alive, as long as we need. It's your soul that has no value to me."

Cassandra struggled to get out from under him, but it was no use—he held her firmly against the wall.

Gerard banged on the door, then shouted to be let inside.

When Leo tried to grab at her pants again, she slapped his face.

"Filthy bitch," he spat, then slapped her back, rocking her head sideways and into the wall, dazing her.

"Do you actually think I need you alive to do what I want?" he yelled, his tone filled with rage.

Then his body eased off her and collapsed to the floor, his soul freed from it and taking shape in front of her.

A black swarm of his essence rose before her.

This marked the end. She would die here tonight through a series of mistakes that led her to this place.

Cassandra closed her eyes and prayed. By the second line

of verse, she understood the power of prayer because she was still standing, and Leo's being hadn't stolen hers.

Then something smashed into the closet door, and she jumped, her eyes popping open.

Gerard was attacking the flimsy door with something big and heavy, like an ax.

Before Gerard's father—the old man—could do anything, Gerard rushed inside, holding an ax over his head —*where the hell did he get an ax?*—and shoved his father off balance. The man tumbled to the floor.

Gerard extended the ax across the gap to Cassandra, and she grabbed the handle without hesitation.

Before she could raise it and do any damage, Leo's figure rushed for her face.

Gerard jumped in front of the mass. It hit him instead, wrapped around his head until he glowed bright—luminescent—then disappeared. Soulless, Gerard's body slumped to the floor.

Leo's blackness returned to his body, but his physical form didn't wake. He seemed to be doing something with Gerard's essence.

Cassandra raised the ax over her head, watching in horror as light filled Leo's mouth.

Was he eating Gerard's soul? Turning it darker? Corrupting it?

Gerard's father watched Leo while moving closer to Cassandra.

Then Doctor Traves stepped into the room through the closet.

She was out of time—too many men in the room. Any

one of them could overpower her.

So she ran to Leo's body beside the bed.

"Crazy bitch," Traves shouted as he dove for her.

Instead of striking Leo with the ax, she swung sideways, the blade slashing through Doctor Traves's animated being.

His head came clean off, and his body lost its human form, scattering into particles in the air like smoke.

Gerard's father saw something in her eyes—madness? psychosis?—panicked and ran from the room.

Cassandra spun around and stared at Leo's body, her breath coming in fits and starts.

Before any moments of doubt could arise, she raised the ax, then yanked it down into the center of Leo's chest plate. The blade disappeared through his ribs and entered the vital organs.

She exhaled a heavy scream/cry and yanked it out of Leo's chest. Then she struck him again, blood squirting to all parts of the room.

On the fourth hack, his chest caved in, and the black being rushed her face and entered through her mouth, which was still wide open and screaming with each blow.

Cassandra struggled to breathe, her head tilted backward, the ax falling from her hands.

When the blackness exited her face, her unconscious body collapsed to the floor.

Chapter Thirty-Four

SOMEWHERE IN THE DESERT Near Jericho

"Allah Akbar," Mujtaba said, staring at Sam.

He slapped Sam to wake him up even though he appeared to be awake.

But nothing happened.

After staring at Sam momentarily, he retrieved water from the backpack and wet the man's face.

Sam's eyes fluttered, then focused on Mujtaba.

Mujtaba jumped back, astounded. "Sam? Are you … okay?"

"What happened?" Sam mumbled, trying to get up.

"We almost lost you. Something had seized you, but the sun must've been just high enough that it didn't get a full hold."

Sam pushed up to his feet and glanced around. "Where are we? Did you check the map?"

Mujtaba shook his head. "We must have lost it along the way."

Sam stared off into the distance. "There's a military camp nearby." He picked up his backpack, jerked his head toward the south, and strolled away.

Mujtaba scrambled to his feet—amazed that Sam was up and walking and talking—and followed the man without delay. He was exhausted and sore, but this journey didn't seem to be ending anytime soon. As much as he believed in the mission, he was losing faith in its success.

He slugged along behind Sam without saying a word, and after two hours of grueling walking over the sand, they saw a camp from afar.

Sam slowed, then stopped, staring at the camp. "What are we planning to tell them?" He turned to face Mujtaba. "What's the next stop?"

Mujtaba moved in beside him, then lowered to his knees to catch his breath. "We need to go to the Khirbet Qumran."

Sam spun sideways to look at him. "Khirbet Qumran? Do you mean Qumran National Park on the northwestern shore of the Dead Sea? You didn't tell me that."

Mujtaba shrugged. "I didn't think about it." He met Sam's gaze, a hand over his eyes to block the sun. "I was injured and barely conscious in that cave when we started."

"Why is that our destination?"

"I had another vision while resting in the cave."

Sam placed his hands on his hips, eyebrows raised. "Oh yeah? Tell me about this vision of yours."

"In my vision, my mouth was full of salt, so I figure it had to do with the Dead Sea or Lot's wife."

"Lot's wife?" Sam's voice rose a notch.

Mujtaba nodded, raising two fingers. "There are two places that would be of interest. The Qumran Park with the ancient manuscripts is one, and the other is the salt remnant of Lot's wife when she turned and looked at the burning Sodom. Since no one would hide a relic where Lot's wife once stood, it has to be in the caves."

"What do you know about the Dead Sea Scrolls? Do you even know where to look?" Sam dropped his hands and turned to face the camp again, disbelief evident in his tone.

"I've read they found a thousand manuscripts with thousands of excerpts from manuscripts relating to the Old Testament, the Book of Isaiah, and other things that I don't remember." He paused to stare at the camp from his knees. "I know in my heart that I must go there. This is my mission."

Sam shook his head, muttered something, and then started walking again.

Mujtaba pushed up off the sand and followed him.

As they neared the camp entrance, two soldiers guarded the front access. When the soldiers spotted them, they raised their weapons, and Sam lifted one arm to salute them.

"We are unarmed," Sam shouted.

"What do you want?" one of them shouted back.

"Shelter," Sam replied in his language, now both hands raised above his head.

Mujtaba raised his hands as well.

The guards exchanged a glance, and then one of them lowered his weapon and moved closer.

"I need to search you."

Sam consented with a nod and was searched. The soldier moved on to Mujtaba, who also consented with a subtle nod.

"I've got two knives in my beltline," Mujtaba warned before the man's hands touched him.

The guard eased the knives out and continued his search. Once it was determined that they were unarmed, the other man lowered his weapon.

"Follow me," the guard said, moving toward the gate.

Sam and Mujtaba followed the guard inside the camp, which seemed to have half as many soldiers as one would expect.

The soldier led them into an office-like structure where they entered through the main doors, were greeted by another soldier, then moved down a corridor to stop outside a large brown door. The soldier knocked, and when he heard "Enter," he opened the door.

He greeted the man inside, then said, "Sergeant, two men approached from the desert. They're unarmed and asked for shelter."

Mujtaba could see over the soldier's shoulder. The sergeant sat behind a desk with papers scattered across it.

"What is your business here?" The sergeant looked directly at him.

"That black swarm thing chased us into the cave of Zedekiah," Mujtaba said before Sam could answer. "We found a passage that led us into the desert, and now here we are. We'd love some water and a means to travel farther."

"Why should I help you?"

Sam pointed at Mujtaba. "Because he thinks he can stop

this new reality we're living."

The sergeant eyed the men briefly, then lowered his head. "I can send you to Jerusalem or Jericho on the first ride out. That is all."

Sam stepped forward. "Sir, it's important that we go to the Khirbet Qumran."

The sergeant looked up again, a look of annoyance on his face. "What is your proof?"

"Proof of what?"

"That you're army. What's your rank?"

"I don't have proof with me, but to verify my name and rank, you can call—"

"I can't call anyone. The lines are dead. Why do you need to go to Qumran? What's there?"

"I'm on a mission to stop the black swarm from taking everyone," Mujtaba said in his most firm voice. "I've dealt with it already, and it lost."

The sergeant stared at him a moment longer, then burst out laughing.

"Are you serious? You think you can *fight* the legion of black mass?" His laughing died down slightly. "Let me ask you something. Are you aware of what's happening out there in the world?"

Undeterred, Mujtaba stood tall. "I hadn't considered the rest of the world—I've been fighting to stay alive. The blackness, the Satan-like entity that takes people's souls and leaves them unconscious, *can* be stopped, and I'm the one who can stop it. That's been my focus."

The sergeant laughed again, his shoulders jerking up and down. When he gathered himself, he stared at Mujtaba. "All the dangerous criminals have risen from the dead. We don't know who's dead or alive anymore, and you tell me you can stop this global catastrophe. Just one man?" He shook his head and leaned back in his chair. "Okay, go ahead. Tell me your plan. I'm listening."

Being put on the spot made Mujtaba feel ridiculous. He had no actionable plan. He didn't know if he'd find the Ark of the Covenant, more Dead Sea Scrolls, or if he'd have some other vision and solve it then. All he knew was that he needed to get there.

"I can't speak openly about my plans." Mujtaba glanced back over his shoulder. "We can't trust anyone. That includes you, sir. However, we must go to that location."

The sergeant eyed them without saying a word for at least a full minute.

"Gentlemen," he finally said. "We have lost so many men, women, and children. Dozens more were taken yesterday and hundreds last night." He rose from behind his desk. "The situation is bleak. Unlike any war I've ever fought." The sergeant stepped around from behind his desk and moved to stand in front of Sam. "I suspect that this camp will be empty within a few days. All my men will be dead or dying as lifeless husks of their former selves."

Sam nodded but didn't speak.

"If you think you know how to end this, I'll go along with it. At least you won't be my responsibility if you're wrong." The sergeant moved toward the door. "I'll have a car take you to where you want to go, but on one condition."

"Sir?"

"I come with you to watch this miracle happen."

Sam peered at Mujtaba with an expression that Mujtaba read as *I hope you know what you're doing.*

Within half an hour, they were settled in a car. The sergeant sat beside a driver in the front, with Mujtaba and Sam in the back.

The sergeant turned around in his seat to look at Mujtaba. "I don't know what you think you'll find there. The place is closed, and some of the Dead Sea Scrolls were discovered to have been fake."

Flustered, Mujtaba chose to remain silent.

The sergeant continued. "When the explosion happened, we used as many soldiers as we could to gather people from the middle of the streets. They were collected and placed in large halls, stadiums, and schools until they wake up or pass away." The sergeant shrugged. "There wasn't much more we could do. The abandoned cars along all the roads proved difficult."

Mujtaba's body ached from fatigue and exertion as he listened to the sergeant drone on with his tale of sadness. He leaned back in his seat, rested his head, and nodded at the appropriate times. He'd give anything for a bed and a good meal.

When they arrived, the door to the park entrance was ajar. The soldier behind the wheel drove them to the side and eased to a stop by the visitors' information booth. They all got out and stretched, then stared at Mujtaba.

"I'll go alone," Mujtaba said. "Wait for me here."

The sergeant watched him with something of an amused expression on his face. Sam was about to respond, but Mujtaba shook his head and then stumbled off toward the main entrance of the archeological site.

Passing among soulless bodies scattered near the opening, he passed a large excavation site involving thousands of year-old buildings and found a sign showing the route to the caves.

He entered the first, second, and finally, the third cave but found nothing. Only dirt and signs of what was there. He was so tired and exhausted that he sat on a rock and wept. Maybe he wasn't the one who would make a difference. Could his visions merely be the delusions of a mentally ill person? What intelligent man with logic and reason would believe a dream and call it a vision?

He wiped his eyes and got to his feet. Determined to put an end to this, he continued his search. Not a minute later, he slipped on the dry, rocky ground and collapsed.

Spread out on the dirt now, he rolled his head to the side and blinked away the tears of failure.

And then he saw it.

A fire of some sort.

It came from another corridor.

As if hypnotized, he pushed himself up and walked toward it. After a few meters, he saw that it was a giant tree whose branches were on fire but not literally burning—there was no heat. The trunk of the tree was big enough to fit a human inside. This tree had to be thousands of years old.

At the base of the burning tree sat a clay jar. He tried to look to see what was inside, but it was too dark—even with the light of the fire above—so he took a deep breath and plunged his hand in, hoping there wasn't a snake curled up at the base.

When he touched an object, he pulled it out. Something was rolled up in a piece of cloth. Gently, he unwrapped the fabric, took out a piece of papyrus, and then unfolded it. He had no idea what it said, but he could see there were ten items.

Had he just found an ancient papyrus with the Ten Commandments scrolled out on it? Perhaps it was another delusion, and this was nothing more than a cheap souvenir tossed in a clay jar as an afterthought.

Maybe that was what he was supposed to find, but his search for the Ark of the Covenant was meant to lead him here. A papyrus scroll with religious text, commonly accepted by several religions, now resided in his hands. He was so excited he couldn't articulate a word if he tried.

"Look," he heard the blind old man talking to him in his head.

He closed his eyes and saw a large sign with four letters: CERN.

"The God particle," he whispered to himself as the blind man told him everything. "How the world was created. The evil in the dark matter. That's it. This ends in Cern."

Mujtaba collapsed to the floor again, exhaustion winning this time.

Chapter Thirty-Five

"Wet his face, his lips. He looks dehydrated."

"What's he holding?"

"Give him a moment to collect himself."

Mujtaba listened to them, his eyes closed. Even though he yearned to sleep, even just for an hour, he opened his eyes with great effort and saw them gathered around him, staring down. He tried to get up but was too weak.

"How did I get here?" he asked as Sam helped him stand.

The sergeant stared expressionless while the driver stood beside them, arms crossed.

"You were missing for a while," Sam said. "So we came in looking for you. We entered several caves without success until we stumbled upon you."

Mujtaba held the cylinder tighter, clutching it against his chest. *The commandments on papyrus.* Yet another sign he was on the right path.

The sergeant nodded toward Mujtaba's hands. "What do you have there?"

Mujtaba glanced down, then looked up at everyone as they expectantly waited for an answer. "It's The Ten Commandments on brittle papyrus." Mujtaba remained calm, unsure if they'd ridicule him or have him committed—or worse, shot as a charlatan.

They all eyed him suspiciously. Were they wondering if he still had his mental faculty? Was he still a functioning human being?

"Where did you find this … relic?" the sergeant asked, a dazed look of disbelief crossing his features.

"In a burning tree." Even after he spoke the words, he knew how they sounded.

He surveyed the area. There was no tree. And even if there was a tree—or a burning bush—as a replica of the one where God spoke to Moses, there was no electricity to power it. If they claimed he'd lost his mind, they'd likely be correct now more than ever.

"Under any other circumstances, I'd be convinced you were high on something, but I'll let it go as delirium—"

"Where's Cern?" Mujtaba asked.

"Cern?" Sam asked, eyebrows touching above the bridge of his nose as he scrunched up his face. "Why Cern?"

"It all started there."

The sergeant nodded. "That's the intel we received." He moved closer to Mujtaba and then placed a hand on his shoulder. "But how would you know that, son?"

Mujtaba gazed up into the sergeant's eyes. "They were

looking for the God particle in something that accelerates. An explosion upset the balance between the living and dead, good and evil. Some sort of gate opened, and it must be closed. For that to happen, I must go there. I know how to close it, which may reverse everything that's happened."

"Reverse it?" Sam stepped back, frowning. "What, go back in time?"

Mujtaba shook his head, then regretted that movement as a dizzy spell overcame him, and he stumbled into the wall.

Sam clutched at him, keeping him on his feet.

"Not time travel." He took a breath. "All the souls that have been separated from their bodies will be freed to return to them unbidden. The dark entities that have been fueling this twisted Judgment Day will expire. Unfortunately, the bodies in the streets that are already dead will remain so."

"But how will you get to Cern?" the driver asked, stepping closer. "It's in Switzerland, which is quite far from here."

The sergeant's gaze didn't falter. He stared at Mujtaba like he was the prophet resurrected. "If it is as you say, I'll take you myself, but we must go by helicopter."

"How would we acquire a helicopter?"

"At the nearest military airport." He shrugged. "Providing they're upright and able to help us." The sergeant did an about-face and headed for the exit.

On the way back toward the car, Sam ran into the visitors' booth. After a minute, he exited with a food package and a water jug.

Once they were in the vehicle, the driver headed toward the military airport under the sergeant's direction. Sam and

Mujtaba ate well from the nuts and berries Sam found while the sergeant mumbled something to himself.

"What was that?" Sam asked.

"It doesn't make sense." The sergeant turned around in his seat and studied them both. "Why are we trying to play God? Why attempt to find His particle? Just leave it all alone."

Mujtaba nodded. "I agree, but what's done is done, and we must be on Swiss soil before dark."

Sam and Mujtaba exchanged a look. Neither of them wanted to know what would happen if they were in a helicopter when the dark swarm arrived—could they outrun it?

It took hours, but they reached the military airport just outside Jerusalem.

The gates were closed, and no one showed up to open them when the driver honked the horn.

"What should we do, sir?" the driver asked.

The gates clicked and shook before the sergeant could answer, then rolled aside far enough for their vehicle to enter.

The driver pulled ahead until a heavily armed soldier stepped out in front of them. Once the vehicle was stopped, the soldier went to the driver's side window.

The sergeant lowered his head to look out at the soldier from the passenger side.

"How did you get here, Gabriel?" the sergeant said.

The soldier broke into a wide grin.

"The last time I saw you," the sergeant continued, "You had gone to Syria."

"Move on ahead, sir. We'll talk in a moment."

The driver eased forward, and Gabriel moved behind the vehicle to lock the gates.

Gabriel came up to the passenger side window. "Come on inside. We can talk in there."

Everyone got out, and Mujtaba stretched his weary legs and back beside the car before following the group.

"There's only a few of us left here," Gabriel said over his shoulder. "The rest headed into the city."

Gabriel led them inside what looked like his office. Without delay, the sergeant instructed Mujtaba to explain why they were there.

Gabriel listened but remained skeptical—which was evident by his expression. Then he stared at them as if they'd all gone mad.

"I can't be involved in any of this, sir."

The sergeant went to say something, but Gabriel held up a hand.

"But, I know a pilot." Gabriel stared at the four of them for a long moment. "If you can persuade him to cooperate … that's another story."

"Can you introduce this pilot to Mujtaba and Sam?"

Mujtaba turned to the sergeant. "Aren't you coming, too?"

The sergeant shook his head. "We left our base and need to return before dark. With several hours' drive back ahead of us, we must leave soon." He looked at Mujtaba and Sam. "Good luck, guys." Then he waved for the driver to follow him.

"I'll come and open the gate for you to leave," Gabriel said, following them back outside.

"This is all too easy," Sam muttered.

"Too easy? How's that?"

"I don't like it. The sergeant drove us here, then walked away so fast. Is there really a helicopter? A pilot? Or are we being detained?" Sam surveyed the office, looking for something. "Just watch your back and follow my lead if something happens."

"If they're *not* working with us, what would you suggest we do?"

Sam faced him and met his gaze. "Kill as many as we have to and find our own pilot. If what you're saying is true, getting you to Cern is more important than any of this."

Feeling validated for the first time in a week, Mujtaba followed Sam to the door, where the man placed an ear to listen to the outside.

"All clear," Sam whispered.

He eased the door open, then popped his head out. A second later, he exited the office with Mujtaba close behind.

Sam opened several more doors, but they found nothing in any of the rooms.

Moving deeper onto the airport's grounds, they heard Gabriel shouting for them to come back, his footsteps coming fast and heavy as he ran toward them.

Sam stopped before a door with a red exit sign above it, and Mujtaba almost bumped into him.

Mujtaba tried to open it, but it was locked.

Sam kicked at the door, but it didn't budge.

Then Gabriel rounded a corner twenty meters behind them.

"Guys, what happened? Why so much haste? I offered to

help, and then you're running off in a panic?"

Sam glared at the man. "It's imperative that we leave immediately. Mujtaba had a vision." He pointed at the door. "Can you open this?"

"Of course," Gabriel said, moving toward them. He patted his pocket. "Key's right here."

Mujtaba watched all this, wondering what could be bothering the man.

Gabriel slipped a hand in his pocket for the key. When his hand withdrew, it held a knife.

Mujtaba's eyes widened, and he jumped back as Gabriel took a swing at him.

There was a blur of motion to Mujtaba's left as Sam dove toward Gabriel. It all happened so fast. Mujtaba was jumping back, and Sam was landing on the guard.

Then the knife was airborne, and Sam was mashing his fist into Gabriel's face, with Gabriel trying to dodge the fists like a pro boxer, forearms framing his face.

In some sort of stuntman jump, Sam launched away from Gabriel, landed on the ground beside the knife, snatched it up, and pushed off the wall to hurtle back toward Gabriel before the man could get his bearings.

The knife plunged into Gabriel's chest, the man's head jerking back in shock, eyes so wide they looked like they were about to pop out of his face.

Sam twisted the knife as Gabriel's hands came up to push him away, then he yanked it out—a thick squirt of blood came with it—and stabbed it back into Gabriel slightly to the left.

Gabriel's head lulled to the side as he struggled for a

breath.

Sam leaned close to the guard's face. "You were going to kill us," Sam shouted at the man. "Why the fuck would you do that? Why take a swing at Mujtaba?"

He rifled through Gabriel's pockets and came up with a set of keys. Sam yanked the knife out again, got to his feet, and ran to open the door.

"You won't succeed," Gabriel muttered, blood spitting from the corner of his mouth.

Mujtaba watched the man as even more blood pumped out of the wound in his chest.

"You won't win," he added, his voice catching on the liquid filling his airways. "We are hundreds of thousands strong now. We're increasing tenfold every day." Gabriel blinked, staring up at nothing. "You will die. You will ..." Gabriel's shoulders hitched, and then his eyes found Mujtaba. "... fail."

The man's last breath left him.

The entire scene shocked Mujtaba into paralysis. He had never witnessed that level of violence up close. A violent stabbing, a man's last breath.

No one had ever tried to kill him before, either, though.

A door clicked behind him, then swung open.

"Hey," Sam called. "We didn't kill the guy for nothing. Let's go."

Mujtaba stared at Gabriel a moment longer, then turned to the open door.

Allah had called upon him to step up and do the right thing. Allah had trusted him. He could do this and would certainly try to do this.

When he stepped out onto the tarmac and the sun hit him, he couldn't believe what he saw.

Three soldiers were shouting at two men on their knees beside a helicopter. They all glanced toward Mujtaba and Sam.

Two of the soldiers started their way.

"You have to get out of here, Mujtaba," Sam said. "Get on the chopper and get to Cern."

One of the men on their knees slipped a hand down the side of his leg. He seemed to be waiting for something.

The two soldiers heading toward Mujtaba were twenty meters away, then fifteen, then ten.

And it all came to Mujtaba about what the pilot would do.

"They'll take out that single soldier on their own," Mujtaba whispered to Sam.

"I've got these two." Sam nudged Mujtaba. "Run around them and make sure you get on that helicopter."

Mujtaba hesitated until the last second, then bolted to the left.

Sam shouted like a wild man and dove at the man closest to Mujtaba.

In that same moment of madness, one of the men on his knees jerked upward, a knife in his hand, slashing at the soldier's neck before the soldier could aim his weapon.

The soldier dropped to his knees, blood spurting through the hand that clutched at the wound.

Mujtaba looked back over his shoulder as he ran. One of the soldiers Sam was fighting was on the ground, writhing in pain, while the other rolled on the tarmac with Sam, arms flailing.

When he turned back around, the man who had used the knife on the guard was inside the helicopter and had already gotten the rotors moving, headphones over his ears.

The soldier he'd slashed in the neck was on the ground, an odd-shaped pool of blood framing his upper torso as Mujtaba sprinted past him.

Then Mujtaba saw something that made him almost stop in his tracks.

At least a hundred soldiers came from either side of the hangar, several armed with automatic weapons. They lowered their weapons with the intent of using them.

They were all dead.

No one could survive such a barrage of weaponry. Sam would never make it now. He'd given his life so that Mujtaba could get to the helicopter and ultimately to Cern. Although, Mujtaba wouldn't make it if he didn't keep running.

The helicopter's rotors were spinning so fast now that he couldn't see where one stopped and the other began.

Unwilling to have Sam's sacrifice be for nothing, Mujtaba found the inner strength from somewhere to run at that helicopter as if his life depended on it—because it quite literally did.

He dove in the side door a mere second before the loud beast lifted off the ground.

Metallic tings echoed from the side as soldiers fired their weapons at the rising machine, but the pilot was adept at the controls and soon had them turned away and racing over the ground at a high rate of speed.

Mujtaba held onto a strap, shouting at nothing, the fear

making him hoarse. He was too afraid to sit up lest he fall out the still-open side door.

The wind was intense in the back, but he managed to get his foot on the door latch and kick it mostly closed as soon as the tinging sound of bullets ended.

After taking a deep breath and asking Allah to spare his life a little longer, he released the strap and rolled to the door, where he slammed it closed. The cyclone-like wind inside the helicopter died off, and his hair fell back to rest on his forehead.

He grabbed headphones from a hook in front of the seat and placed them on his head.

"Where did you guys come from?" the pilot asked. "What's going on?"

"We were brought here by a sergeant in the Israeli Army so I could be flown to Cern," Mujtaba said as he glanced out the window.

The pilot had taken them higher. Mujtaba glanced out the windows but didn't like what he saw, so he averted his eyes. Heights weren't his thing.

"Seriously?" the pilot asked.

"Yes. When those soldiers found out that I knew how to end this nightmare, they tried to stop us."

"You know how to end all this?" the pilot asked, his voice frantic as he tried to look at Mujtaba over his shoulder.

"I do. I just need to get to Cern to do it." Mujtaba shook out his arms, the adrenaline playing tricks on his body. "What were you guys doing there?"

"We fueled these birds to fly as far as we could to see how widespread the damage was. Maybe there's a circumference of damage, and after that, people are fine. We just didn't know. But on the last two flight missions, we only saw bodies in the streets of cities in a two-hundred-mile radius."

If it were possible, Mujtaba's stomach dropped even further.

"Well, I can stop it all," he said. "I can stop it all."

The pilot tapped buttons on the dash of the helicopter, adjusted some things, and then sat back in his seat, angling the chopper slightly to the left.

"What are you doing?"

"I entered the coordinates for Cern. We'll have to refuel along the way, but I know a few spots where there won't be soldiers with guns. Put your head back. Rest easy now. We should be there sometime after midnight."

Midnight? Could that work? Or would he be too late?

Chapter Thirty-Six

Cassandra snapped awake and jerked upward, forgetting where she was and what had happened.

Why am I awake—alive?

Leo's body, no longer unconscious, lay beside her.

She looked at her hands and clothes—covered in blood—and it all came back to her.

Her stomach clenched, and she averted her gaze from the blood so she wouldn't vomit.

On her feet, she grabbed the ax she'd killed Leo with and searched for running water to wash off the blood. She'd need a flashlight and a safe way to get to the church to tell her father what happened. Then she'd tell Vincent—unless it was all over because she'd killed Leo.

Once through the closet door, she stopped in the middle of the apartment's living room as a thought hit her. Killing Leo was supposed to end everything. If that were true, would she find her parents at the church? Would Vincent still be preaching his knowledge in the cemetery?

She'd find out soon enough.

A flashlight sat on the dining room table. She set the ax beside it, ran to the bathroom, rinsed her hands off in the sink, dried them, and then ran back out to grab her supplies.

Feeling better after removing Leo's blood from her skin, she held the ax in one hand—the blood on the ax didn't bother her. If anyone got in her way, it would serve as a warning—and the flashlight in the other hand and then headed for the stairs.

Cassandra stared out into the darkness on the main level, not seeing a thing.

Could Vincent be right? By killing Leo's body—his unconscious body—did it end the plague of the swarm?

The actual question on her mind was, could she, or *should* she, risk walking to the church at this hour *if* it wasn't over?

After waiting another few minutes and seeing no activity in the street whatsoever, she banged on the door to draw the attention of something—anything—but there was no response. A few crickets stopped their mating call and waited a moment, and they started up once more when she didn't make any more noise.

Cassandra opened the door and moved outside, her nerves all firing one message: go back inside!

The cool night air felt refreshing and invigorating. There

was enough light from the moon to make her way safely, and when needed, she could use the flashlight. But she'd only use the flashlight when needed to keep as much in the shadows as possible.

One block from the building felt like walking in a haunted house. Screams rent the air far off in the distance, shooting spikes of fear into her stomach. Was that the swarm? Or people coming outside now that it was over and screaming at the sight of their dead loved ones?

Whatever was happening on the streets around her, those screams didn't offer comfort as she ran for the church with the feeling that she was being chased.

Twenty minutes later, when the church came into view, she gasped a sigh of relief.

Maybe it was over. Maybe Leo's army of blackness shit had died with him.

After one more glance over her shoulder, she sprinted for the church's front door as if the Devil himself was nipping at her ankles.

When she reached the door, she tapped on it loud enough for someone inside to hear.

"Open up," she whispered near the crack between the wooden doors. "It's me, Cassandra. My mom and dad are inside."

She knocked again, then studied the street behind her.

"Open up. You have nothing to fear now. It's over."

Even as she said those words, she remembered that likely meant her parents were dead—again.

Voices emanated from inside the church. It sounded like people were arguing. Then, there was a thumping noise and a scream.

They probably didn't want to risk opening the door, and her parents were making a fuss.

A lock clicked, and she detected the sound of the wooden bar lifting. The door opened wide enough to see her mother smiling at her.

"I can't leave my child outside," her mother said. "No matter how much they shout at me."

Cassandra took a step inside, but something clenched in her abdomen. She grabbed at her stomach with the flashlight hand and stepped back. Astonished at the spike in pain, she took a deep breath, tightened her fist on the ax's handle, and tried to enter the church again but dropped to her knees in pain, the ax falling to the concrete beside her.

"What happened?" her mother asked, clutching Cassandra's arm. "Baby, are you okay?"

"I don't know. Call Dad over. I have to talk to him."

What the hell had happened to her in that apartment? She fought them off. She killed Leo's body. Then his essence entered—

"He entered me ..." she whispered to herself.

"Cassandra?" Her father moved into the doorway.

Angry voices inside the church called for the door to be shut.

She looked up at her father. "Dad, tell me about yesterday. The apartment? The medical files, the man you fought with. Why did he say he spared my life?"

Her father, a stranger to her since he'd been dead, stared down at her and then focused on his wife.

"Close the damn door," someone yelled.

Ignoring them, her father said, "When you went to the hospital for your tonsils, I asked about all the tests they did on you. They told me it was routine. However, I felt something wasn't adding up."

He stepped outside and whispered that he'd only be a moment to his wife. She nodded and eased the door closed.

Now, it was just the two of them.

"The day after the operation," he continued, "one of the doctors came to see me. He said that everything looked good to go ahead with the transplant and that I didn't need to worry. Naturally, I was surprised. Transplant? So I asked him what he meant. He claimed not to be privy to all the details and that he'd find the doctor in charge for me. When he left, I opened your file. He'd set it on the desk in front of me. It said you were approved for a transplant. Infuriated, since you were only in for tonsil removal, I went looking for that *nurse* and was told he was on another floor. I ran for the staircase and stopped when I overheard two men talking in hushed whispers one floor below me. They discussed a patient's death and how their organs were ideal for some wealthy clients. I couldn't hear the name properly, but it sounded like Mr. Rohner, a well-known businessman in Lausanne and a great benefactor to the hospital. I was pissed, couldn't keep my composure, and stumbled. I think it was the railing I bumped into. They heard me and stopped talking, then entered the door to their floor and disappeared inside.

"I jumped down the stairs to their level, ripped open that door, and ran onto the maternity ward. Under another exit sign, I saw Leo look back before the door closed at the end of the corridor. Behind him was a man I knew. A Doctor

Mueller."

Cassandra lowered her head and stared at the blood on the blade of the ax—Leo's blood. She felt dizzy thinking about how she met Leo in a bar after the death of her parents in that car accident. What if she was their target to harvest some part of her body for Rohner? Did Leo ever love her, ever feel anything for her? Or was he always on the clock when he was with her, ensuring she remained safe until Rohner needed some harvested piece of her?

Something Leo once said popped into her mind. *Stay safe. I can't have anything happen to you. You're too valuable.*

All of that made sense now—from the moment she touched his essence in the church tower. It all made sense, and yet, none of it mattered anymore.

Leo was dead, her parents were dead, and she was empty.

The church door opened a crack, and her mother stepped outside. She stared at her husband.

"What did you do next?" her mother asked him, obviously having listened in from the other side of the door.

Her father glanced between the women, then said, "I left, taking all the files with me. I went to your room"—he nodded at Cassandra—"where you were sleeping. I couldn't risk you being their next victim. I got you settled into a wheelchair, and we left the hospital. I left some of the case files on the main triage desk, right beside the security booth. The rest I took with me for the police.

"Before deciding when I would go to the police—you have to understand that I had stolen confidential hospital records on me—I received a threatening phone call. A man disguising his voice said that you would be killed if I didn't return the files to the hospital. But I'd have nothing to prove their malfeasance if I did that. So, I went to find Rohner to make a deal. We agreed that he wouldn't bother you, and I wouldn't say anything to the authorities. He told me he'd find another suitable donor. I placed my originals in a safety deposit box at the bank if I ever needed to go after them, then went home. The next morning, your mother and I were in that car accident."

Cassandra turned away to stare up at the dark sky. "The safety deposit box at the bank." She looked back at her dad. "Is that why you went there yesterday? To see if the originals were still there?"

He nodded. "They weren't. Nothing was there. They must've had someone follow me to the bank that day. With his influence and power, that box was opened, and the contents were destroyed. Then we could have our *accident*, and you'd remain a viable match."

"So they let me live in case Rohner needed some organ or whatever and sent Leo out to watch over me to take care of Rohner's future organ farm." She glanced at him over her shoulder. "Why didn't you tell me any of this when we got home from the hospital? Or now, since you're alive again, reanimated."

"Well, we didn't remember much of our past when we arrived here a few days ago. Vincent helped with some gray areas but then instructed me to remain silent on the past. He claimed to know from the beginning what would happen, and he told us that you would help stop this mess, but you needed a clear head to do it."

Cassandra was silent for a moment, thinking it all over. "Who was that man you punched yesterday in the street? You searched other bodies for ID, too. What was that about?"

He tsked once. "That was juvenile. I recognized one of the doctors who worked on your file. Then I wondered if the bodies near him were hospital employees." He shrugged. "I wanted to step on their throats for what they did to our family. End their unconscious existences."

Something caught Cassandra's eye. It moved at the end of the street, merging into random shapes.

The swarm was still out there.

Killing Leo hadn't ended the evil blackness.

Her parents were still here, so that made sense.

But if the black entities were still out there, why didn't they attack her on her way to the church?

"You have to get inside," she said as the swarm rushed along the street toward them.

Her parents knocked on the church door, but it didn't open.

Cassandra stepped out into the street, hoping to keep the swarm from her parents as long as she could.

Even if the door opened, she couldn't cross that threshold with whatever was wrong with her abdomen.

Her parents, long dead, now stood on the church steps and stared at their daughter, their eyes watering.

"Vincent told us our time would be short," her mother said. "My lovely daughter, I'm so proud of you."

The swarm became one entity and hovered to the side of her parents' heads while Cassandra watched on in horror.

"What are you doing?" she asked, raising the ax over her

head. "No. Mom, Dad. No. Get inside!"

The entities rushed around her mother's head, entered her eyes and mouth, and lifted her off the ground as Cassandra screamed.

Then, her mother dropped to the ground at her father's feet.

A gush of air expelled from Cassandra's mouth as the swarm raced up to hover over her father's head. There wasn't the slightest hint of fear on his face.

"Cassandra. You are the best daughter a father could ever have. I'll miss you, my little rose—"

The swarm moved in, taking her father from her a second time.

"I love you, Daddy," she whispered as her father's body dropped beside his wife's inert form.

Then, as if someone had performed a magic trick, their reanimated bodies disappeared before her.

"Nothing matters anymore." She dropped the ax, knowing it was a useless tool against something like the black swarm. Her will to live diminished to a mere blip on the radar of self-preservation. Leo betrayed her. Someone murdered her parents to keep them quiet, and all because she was an unwilling organ donor for some rich guy. Why didn't he just offer to buy one of her kidneys? She could live with the other one? None of this made sense.

"Let it be done then." She splayed her hands out at the sides, tilted her head back, and stared at the night sky. "Take me. I won't fight anymore. I'm done."

She wasn't afraid to die now. Maybe she'd be reunited with her parents in the hereafter.

But nothing happened.

With tears in her eyes, she opened them and shouted, "Come on, what are you waiting for? Finish it."

The swarm only circled her, staying back at least a meter.

She couldn't understand why it wasn't taking her. After it circled her a few more times, it floated off down the street to leave her alone on the church's front steps.

A man cleared his throat behind her.

Cassandra spun around to stare at Vincent.

"What are you doing here?" she asked, wiping her eyes.

"Allow me to show you something before I leave."

He lunged forward and grabbed her arm.

A vision filled her mind instantly like someone flicked on an eighty-inch screen in her mind's eye.

Images of an explosion filled the screen, with Gerard running toward the building. A crater with a huge concentration of black matter swirled up from the hole created after the explosion, energized by some sort of blackness that swirled in a circle. She saw bodies lying everywhere, people running, the blackness taking soul after soul. Finally, a vision of herself filled the screen—herself with a distended belly—she was pregnant?

Then, an image of her holding a long knife near her abdomen.

The vision ended when the swarm hit Vincent, taking him off his feet and yanking his hand off Cassandra's arm.

She screamed at its suddenness, her hands clutching at her belly.

Am I pregnant?

"You bastard," she whispered to Leo.

Vincent dropped to the ground and then was whisked away like her parents as if his entity had never existed.

"How did you do it?" she asked Leo, spinning in a circle to locate the swarm. "Through my mouth, my face? Or did you enter me elsewhere before you took your last breath?"

Now she knew who Gerard was—the man who tried to stop the experiment before it went wrong. But he had been too late.

Then, she understood why the swarm was leaving her alone at that moment. Something of Leo's essence had been planted in her womb, and the swarm knew that.

She had been marked to survive the gestation period.

But she couldn't let it live. So she would die, after all.

She glanced up at the moon as she put one foot in front of the other.

Within an hour, she found a bicycle. It wasn't the best means of transportation to get to Cern, but it was her only choice.

She would go back to where it all began, and she would bury the blackness in her womb before it ever had a chance to see the light of day.

Or she'd die trying.

Chapter Thirty-Seven

CERN, SWITZERLAND.
After Midnight

"I don't know where to land," the pilot shouted from the front. "Wait, I see something." The helicopter dipped nose first, making Mujtaba's stomach rise to his throat like he'd gone over the peak of a roller coaster.

After refueling only once at a civilian airport filled with bodies and no soldiers, the helicopter pilot got them to Cern without much delay. The skies were vast and empty of air traffic, so they flew on a direct route without interruption.

"This is it." The pilot continued to lower the chopper to a clearing on the left of the large crater where the explosion had opened the earth. "Ride's over," the pilot added. "You're on your own. Have you got the flashlight?"

Mujtaba tapped the pocket that held it, then placed a hand on the shoulder of the pilot from behind. "Thank you. You've been a huge help."

He pulled the lever to open the door, stepped onto the bar below the door, the wind from the rotors buffeting his hair into his face, and then hopped about a meter to the ground.

He fell awkwardly, his right knee buckling, then rolled onto his back. By the time he righted himself and withdrew the small flashlight from his pocket, the helicopter was gaining altitude and leaving the area.

He turned on the little light and got to his feet. It was dark, and that blackness would find him soon, so he headed off in a run, even though his knee hurt from the jump.

Every step he took toward the crater in the earth was a blessing—the blackness hadn't taken him yet.

He marveled at all he had done to get here, all the people who had helped him and sacrificed for him to have this moment.

Up ahead, there was a strange light emitting from the crater's center. He ran harder, glancing over his shoulder several times.

In the distance, a mass of blackness rushed toward him.

"Run harder," a woman shouted.

Mujtaba stumbled and almost tripped when he spun to his left and saw a woman pulling up on a bicycle not four meters from him.

"You are the religiously devout Muslim man of holy descent that Vincent told me about," she shouted, her face a mask of awe at the sight of him. "Even though Vincent had no eyes, he could see better than all of us. Do what you came here to do. Finish it off." The woman gestured wildly with her hands toward the hole in the ground.

Mujtaba couldn't believe his eyes or ears. He was filled with euphoric glory at the sight and sound of that woman as he ran. Allah had truly chosen him. And Vincent had come to her as he'd come to him.

That woman was here to distract the swarm. He now understood everything.

This was his chance.

My life for Allah. My life for my fellow man.

Praise be to Allah.

He glanced over his shoulder to prove she wasn't a vision like the burning tree.

There was a woman there, pumping the pedals of her bike along the access road, a small light in her right hand.

Why wasn't the darkness taking her?

"Just keep running," she said as she neared him on her bike.

He stared forward at the eerie glow rising from the center of the hole in the ground.

Then, through the haze still emanating from the crater, the figure of a man appeared in front of Mujtaba.

"No, Leo," the woman shouted from behind him. "Do not touch this man."

"Leave this area," the entity—Leo—said, "and I won't hurt you. You will be spared."

Mujtaba slowed and peered over the edge of the crater. It wasn't the shape of a large bowl as he had suspected. It was more of a cone shape, like a funnel wedged in the ground by God's hand alone. At the lowest section in the funnel's center was a small circular hole that didn't look wide enough for a man's shoulders to fit through.

That was the spot where the eerie light rose from. Mujtaba suspected it was where all the evil souls had risen from, too—Hell.

Leo's form moved to look at the woman.

When that happened, Mujtaba took his one chance to end it all. He retrieved the small container that held the commandments on papyrus—a religious artifact offered to him by a burning tree—and tossed it over the crater's edge.

Seconds later, it disappeared inside the hole at the bottom.

He readied himself for something to happen. An explosion. The earth to shake. God to appear.

But nothing happened.

"Cassandra, you must give up," the Leo thing said. "Please, have our child, then be a queen next to me. Everyone will worship us. Everyone who spat on us and underestimated us will now please us. Our kingdom will reign on Earth as it is in Hell, hallowed be thy name, this kingdom will come, here as it is in Hell it shall be on Earth."

Leo moved closer to Mujtaba, likely preparing to relieve him of his soul.

Mujtaba jerked back, not because of how close the blackness was but because of Cassandra's piercing scream.

That woman had the lungs of a jackal and the screech of a wild boar being stabbed.

Leo and Mujtaba both turned to stare at her as she held a knife in her hand, the tip pressed on her belly.

"Leave that man alone, or I'll do it," the woman yelled

from several meters away. "I'll rip this entity from my belly before my heart takes its final beat. I swear I will."

The madness in the woman's eyes convinced Mujtaba of her intentions. Goosebumps rose on his arms and legs at her ferocity.

"Cassandra," Leo said, his voice firm, hard. "Do not do that. Do not ruin your chance at everlasting life with such a senseless act."

Leo's form floated away from Mujtaba, oozing closer to Cassandra.

Whatever history they had, they would have to work it out on their own.

Mujtaba still had a job to do. For Allah, he was prepared to do it as he had been called upon. There was no greater glory.

When offered that artifact by the burning tree, he'd become convinced it was needed to end this. And now, as it hadn't ended, Mujtaba knew that it wasn't a false idol, something humanity worshipped, that would end this. Religiosity was inside us all. We are *of* the divine, a divine spark made from the hand of God.

No artifact would stop this madness. Only a descendant of Aaron, a religiously devout man of holy descent, could enter that hole to Hell and end this.

The commandments and all that is holy are inside us all.

God doesn't live within the walls of churches, as the Dead Sea Scrolls proclaimed.

He lives in our hearts.

So Mujtaba stepped closer to the edge and found a spot where, once he jumped, he would slide about a hundred meters downward before coming in contact with that small hole at the bottom.

He took one more look over his shoulder as the entity she'd called Leo rushed at Cassandra and bumped her arm to knock the knife from her hand.

A movement to his left made him jerk his head that way.

A giant mass of black souls had formed there, but he didn't care anymore. He'd gotten where he needed to go. He made it to the lip of the crater, to his destiny, and he knew they couldn't touch him if he closed his eyes and prayed to Allah.

At that moment, several things happened all at once.

As the blackness rushed toward him, Mujtaba leaped from the crater's edge like a cliff diver.

Leo screamed behind him—an altogether horrid scream. One that penetrated the terror Mujtaba felt as something deep inside him was yanked from within, like a rope he was once tethered to had snapped.

He hit the inside edge of the crater with a heavy thump and continued to descend toward the hole.

Eyes closed, he whispered Allah's name repeatedly, forgoing any fear of heights he may have once had.

There was a sudden stop at the bottom, where the lights went out, and the screaming ceased.

Mujtaba didn't feel the impact as he slipped into the hole, plugging it with faith heretofore rarely seen.

***

Cassandra had seen the man throw something over the

edge. When nothing happened, she read the confusion on his face. But then she had to tangle with Leo as he bumped her arm, dislodging the knife.

Leo spun away from her in a rush, and Cassandra caught what grabbed Leo's attention.

The religiously devout Muslim man Vincent told her about had jumped over the edge.

As Leo came at her, he must've realized his mistake and rushed over the edge after the man, screaming something unintelligible.

For a few seconds, nothing happened.

Then, the light emanating from the center of the crater dimmed. Could her eyes be playing a trick on her?

She closed them and shook her head.

When she opened them, the light had dimmed more.

Cassandra froze as she watched it slowly disappear. The blackness hovering to the side dispersed into a thin wave of tiny dots, then disappeared as if evaporated.

It reminded her of what happened to her parents and Vincent after their new bodies were killed.

Leo, such a strong leader of the blackness, hovered over the top of the crater for a moment longer, eyeing her as his essence oozed apart.

At that moment, all the light from below finally winked out of existence, and so did Leo's entity—he literally dematerialized in front of her.

Could it be over? Could it be over?

Cassandra moved toward the crater's edge until she could see the bottom.

The man who had jumped was gone.

The source of the light was gone.

Nothing remained but a small black hole near the center of the bottom of the cone-like crater, about a hundred meters down.

Would they ever know what happened here or how it ended?

Could she hope that it was over?

Exhausted after pedaling that bike for hours, Cassandra lowered to her knees, then laid on a flat rock and stared at the starlit sky.

She would wait until the sun rose, then decide if it was over. Hoping too soon would break her if it hadn't ended.

Maybe tomorrow night, the black swarm would come again.

Maybe not.

She closed her eyes and breathed.

And breathed … a hand on her belly.

Whether it was over or not, it wouldn't end for her.

A decision had to be made.

And only she could make it.

Chapter Thirty-Eight

Cern, Switzerland
Three months later ...

Cassandra sat on a park bench as she watched the construction workers rebuild multiple buildings—on the same road she used to walk hand in hand with Leo.

It had been a few months since the world took back its soul. Every single person on every street and in every building that had become soulless received their soul back once the evil lost its grip on them. Like tethered to their bodies, they flew back into them and woke from their coma state. No one remembered a thing other than to say they were in a dark place.

That man, that one Muslim man, had given everything for humanity. How many would know his name? She spoke to several people about his sacrifice when they found her curled up by the crater the next morning. She explained what had happened in detail, but most of the people who listened just wanted to believe it was over, and that was it.

They excavated the crater, dug deep, and eventually sealed it with mammoth concrete slabs.

Mujtaba's body was never recovered.

In the official statement given to the media, not a single body was recovered within a twenty-mile radius of the blast site as all bodies inside that zone were vaporized in seconds when the Hadron Collider exploded.

If only she could be as brave as Mujtaba. Then perhaps the baby in her belly wouldn't still be alive.

Whatever Leo did to impregnate her, it couldn't—literally—see the light of day.

But she had not taken the abortion route because of one question: could a baby be born inherently evil?

What if she could teach the baby goodness? A healthy introduction to religion and a comfortable relationship with faith might be all the baby needed. What mother could abort such a chance to turn what was once evil into something worth saving?

Yet, it came from Leo; it came from evil incarnate. The chances of her baby leading a life of faith were remote to non-existent.

After months of internal debate, there was only one way to end this, and only she could do it—her dreams told her so.

It was only yesterday that she dreamed of Vincent again. He came several times a week. By now, she knew the message by heart as it never varied.

His words were, "To right this upset, we need a truly holy act. Think of Jesus and how he died on the cross for our sins. We needed someone to perform some act that would be wholesome in every way. Someone without moral blemish, someone noble and religious, someone willing to be crucified for the rest of us. And this man, this *Mahdi*, gave his life for us." Vincent shook his head and stared at the floor in her dream, as he had done dozens of times. "But I fear that it'll never happen again in this world. This was our last chance, our last forgiveness."

Was he referring to her? That she wouldn't be strong enough to kill herself for the monster in her womb to perish?

"The baby must die," Cassandra whispered to no one. "I can't bring it into this world."

Cars drove by on cleared streets now. The windows of looted stores had been replaced, and people were shopping again. The world around her had found itself wounded and now yearned to heal. They'd all moved on, buried their dead, and left her behind to carry the weight of the vileness in her womb.

When the darkness fell at night, the streets were still empty, though. Nightclubs hadn't started up yet. Stores closed by five in the afternoon so employees could return to their loved ones. Virtually no one was out after dark except for a few brave souls.

But that would change soon. Eventually, this nightmare would become a memory, a fable, a story once told or written about.

Like Sodom and Gomorrah, the two biblical cities were destroyed by God for their wickedness. Or, like when the world-engulfing flood was coming, God instructed Noah to build the Ark to spare his family and two of the world's animals.

God was all-loving, but Cassandra felt his patience was running thin. He'd warned us in the past repeatedly, and we didn't listen. He allowed his son to walk the Earth and offer His teachings, and not only did we not listen, but we crucified the son of God.

And now, while searching for the God particle, our Heavenly Father has warned us once more.

Will we listen? Cassandra didn't think so. Perhaps for a time, we might, though. Most of the unconscious people—now conscious—who roamed the streets felt like the lottery of life gave them a win. They'd learned that millions worldwide had died. People in need of heart medication died. Patients in hospitals on life support when generators ran out of juice didn't make it. Others died after many sick men did terrible things to unconscious female bodies.

The world was coated in evil, and Cassandra wondered why God even cared about us anymore.

The world hadn't been saved; it had only been given a reprieve—for now.

But the world would know evil again when Cassandra's baby was born. Of this, she was sure.

Cassandra closed her eyes and slipped her hand into her pocket.

She gripped the knife's hilt, slid it out, and opened her eyes.

Vincent had said that the sacrifice Mujtaba made for humanity was something the world wouldn't ever see again.

"You're wrong, Vincent." She clenched her jaw as tears threatened to flow over her eyelids. "I will not let this demonic baby inside me come to term." She placed the tip of the blade slightly below her belly button. "I will kill it in the womb, opening myself up on this the brightest day of the week, so the light will kill it if it miraculously survives the blade."

The sun was high and warm, sitting in the exact position and at the right angle to gleam into her torn womb if the knife got that far before she passed out. She edged her butt forward, her shoulder blades on the back of the bench near the nape of her neck. Then she raised her shirt over her belly to expose it to the sunshine.

She once heard someone say that evil may win but never conquer.

That is precisely what happened here, on planet Earth.

When a door opens in a lighted room, the darkness in the hallway doesn't spill into the room. No, the light in the room spills out into the dark hall, making it brighter.

The darkness in her womb cannot be allowed to spread into the light of this world.

God's will, His radiance, will enter her womb and end the evil there for good.

Cassandra gripped the knife tighter, stomped the ground a couple of times with her feet to see if Leo could hear her down there, then said, "I'll see you in Hell, Leo," and raised her knife hand to make the first strike of many.

Afterword

DEAR READER,

Rania and I wanted to write this novel for two main reasons. One, because the Large Hadron Collider (LHC) seems like a scary venture, one fraught with obstacles, and two, our mutual respect for all religions and faiths.

The Large Hadron Collider (LHC) is back online as of March 2022. It's made up of a twenty-seven-kilometer ring of superconducting magnets, along with accelerating devices that boost the energy of particles. While searching for the God particle, some scientists warn that the (LHC) will generate small black holes on Earth. Several theories posit that these tiny quantum black holes are entirely possible— and safe, while others disagree.

According to a warning from famed British physicist

Stephen Hawking, the elusive God particle, discovered in 2012, can become unstable and potentially destroy our universe when mishandled. According to Hawking, the God particle that created the world could end it, too.

None of this is fiction.

The novel Rania and I wrote is entirely a work of fiction.

But the LHC is real, their experiments are real, and the potential danger is real.

That said, hundreds, if not thousands, of scientists claim there's no danger. They've taken all the necessary precautions to avert any sort of breakdown.

However, some estimates claim if the LHC exploded, the resulting earthquake would be severe. Dust and debris created by such an event would encircle the Earth, potentially triggering a nuclear winter event, which could cool the Earth's temperature for some time to come. Vegetation would struggle to survive. Animals would perish. Humans would suffer and die.

Recently, the LHC was shut down for three years for maintenance to enable upgrades and renovations. The shutdown was initially set for two years, but COVID delays made it a three-year shutdown.

As mentioned above, the LHC in Cern was restarted in early March 2022 for a three-year run.

Regarding religion, Rania wanted Mujtaba to have a leading role. The Islamic faith is often negatively targeted in thrillers. Because of that, we discussed having an Islamic man save the day.

I thought it was brilliant.

We respect and want to honor all religions. Whatever

denomination or dogma you believe in, the one that gets you through the day can be wonderful.

If you felt we displayed religion in a negative light during the reading of this novel, that wasn't our intention. Throughout the development of this book, we both focused on being positive when mentioning belief and faith. An example would be when Mujtaba speaks to Nassir about converting to Christianity and how he betrayed the Islamic religion. Upon discovering Nassir dead at the door to the Armenian Patriarchate, Mujtaba prays to Allah to forgive Nassir.

Islam and Christianity have many similarities, which we found difficult to navigate. Some of that came up in the library scene with Sam speaking to Mujtaba about the Ark of the Covenant, and more of it rose to the surface as Mujtaba navigated the old city of Jerusalem.

Ultimately, the goal was to shed light on the darkness in our souls and how it can't survive God's light while positively writing about religion.

We hope you enjoyed the read and will return for more collaborations as Jonas Saul and Rania Stone release more novels later this year.

Take care of yourself and each other.

Until next time,

Jonas Saul

Rania Stone

Also by Jonas Saul

The Sarah Roberts Series

Dark Visions (One)
The Warning (Two)
The Crypt (Three)
The Hostage (Four)
The Victim (Five)
The Enigma (Six)
The Vigilante (Seven)
The Rogue (Eight)
Killing Sarah (Nine)
The Antagonist (Ten)
The Redeemed (Eleven)
The Haunted (Twelve)
The Unlucky (Thirteen)
The Abandoned (Fourteen)
The Cartel (Fifteen)
Losing Sarah (Sixteen)
The Pact (Seventeen)
The Terror (Eighteen)
The Chase (Nineteen)
The Betrayal (Twenty)
Sarah's Return (Twenty-One)
The Hunt (Twenty-Two)
The Delivery (Twenty-Three)
The Trap (Twenty-Four)
The Ultimatum (Twenty-Five)
The Depraved (Twenty-Six)
The Condemned (Twenty-Seven)
Payback (Twenty-Eight)
The Unknown (Twenty-Nine)

Wrath (Thirty)
The Damned (Thirty-One)
The Game (Thirty-Two)
The Decoy (Thirty-Three)
The Disappearance (Thirty-Four)
The Whole Truth (Thirty-Five)
Alex (Thirty-Six)
Parkman (Thirty-Seven)
Darwin (Thirty-Eight)
Aaron (Thirty-Nine)
Remains To Be Seen (Forty)

The Jake Wood Novels

The Immortal Gene (Book One)
The Immortal Target (Book Two)

Standalone Novels

'Til Death Do Us Part
The Drowning
The Woman in the Woods
The Threat
The Specter
The Mafia Trilogy
A Murder in Time
Frequency of the Dead

Co-Authored Novels

Collision Course (Written with Gary Ponzo)
There Will Be Blood (Written with Rania Stone)
The Soulless (Written with Rania Stone)

Jonas Saul

Short Story Collections

Twisted Fate (Tales of Horror)
Twists of Fate (Tales of Hope)

About Jonas Saul

Jonas Saul is the bestselling author of the Sarah Roberts Series—more than two million sold!—and has written and published over sixty thrillers. After acquiring an agent, he signed several deals in Los Angeles, with MadRiver Pictures optioning his Sarah Roberts Series— over forty books!—(currently in development).

Jonas has often outranked Stephen King and Dean

Koontz on Amazon over the past decade. He's regularly invited to be a guest speaker, teacher, or workshop presenter at international writing conferences and film festivals worldwide. He hosts an annual writer's retreat in Greece, where he currently lives. He focuses his teaching on how to get tension and emotion in every scene, on every page, how he made it as a creator/writer, the path to success in this business, and the pitfalls to avoid. He also hosts a reading retreat in Greece with guest authors, yoga retreats, and hiking retreats. Visit the Imagine Greece Retreats website at www.imaginegreeceretreats.com, or email him directly to discuss an opportunity to join one of the retreats at jonas@imaginegreeceretreats.com.

Jonas is also a professional freelance editor. He works for several publishers and does private editing for clients, with many testimonials on his website at www.imaginepress.org, which details each author's response to Jonas's editing skills. Email Jonas directly for an editing quote at editor@imaginepress.org.

To book Jonas for a speaking engagement at a writer's conference/festival, to have him on your jury at a film festival, or even to say hello, email Jonas directly at jonassaul@icloud.com.

For updates on releases, hit the "Follow" button on Amazon or Bookbub, and join Jonas on Facebook, where he's most active.

Contact Jonas Saul

Linktree: Find me here

Email: jonassaul@icloud.com

Rania Stone Titles

Novels

What He Didn't Know (Translated to English)
The Lives Between Us (Translated to English)
There Will Be Blood (Co-written with Jonas Saul)
The Soulless (Co-written with Jonas Saul)

Children's Books (All in Greek)

A Walk In The Garbage City
The Magic Ring
The War Of Fire And Water Drops
The Well Of Colors
Adventures In Bunny Land
Adventures In Bunny Land 2
Melinda And The 100 Princesses
The Cursed Chest
The Christmas Reindeer
Melinda And The Magical Crystal Ball
Cat-Tales

About Rania Stone

Rania Stone is the author of five adult novels and eleven children's stories. She's a well-known author in Greece and has recently had several novels translated into English. Her first English release, *What He Didn't Know*, came out in late 2020.

She's been writing for two decades and calls Greece her home.

Contact Rania Stone

Website: www.raniastone.com

Facebook: RaniaStone/Facebook

Bookbub: Rania Stone

Email: contact@raniastone.com

Instagram: Rania/Instagram

www.ingramcontent.com/pod-product-compliance
Lightning Source LLC
Chambersburg PA
CBHW031305210726
48287CB00005B/1428